By Any Means Necessary

Zach Adams

Milligan Books   **California**

Published and Distributed by:
Milligan Books, Inc.

Cover Design by
Gary Scott: A3Arts

Formatting by
Alpha Desktop Publishing

First Printing, April 2005
10987654321

ISBN 0-9759654-6-8

Publisher's note
This is a work of fiction. Names, characters, places and incidents either are product of the author's imagination or are used fictitiously, and any resemblance to actual persons, living or dead, events, or locales is entirely coincidental.

Milligan Books, Inc.
1425 W. Manchester Ave., Suite C
Los Angeles, California 90047
www.milliganbooks.com
(323) 750-3592

Dedication

This book is dedicated to my mother, Elizabeth Bungert. Thank you for enduring so many burdens so your children could succeed.

Acknowledgments

I would like to thank my sister, Helen Bungert, for her invaluable assistance, encouragement and expertise.

I would also like to acknowledge the treasure trove of talent and intellect I have had at my disposal with my wonderful writing group: Adam-Troy Castro, Ed Gaillard, Elena Gaillard, Susan Solan, Madeline Robbins, Ken Houghton, and Shira Daemon.

About The Author

Zach Adams lives in Fair Lawn, N.J. with his wife and two teenage sons. "By Any Means Necessary" is his fourth novel.

1

Elijah would shiver every night, with nothing but a piece of rough burlap to wrap around his almost-naked body. A body with none of the natural insulation of fat that seemed to cling abundantly to the stomachs and chins of his cruel owners. His back and shoulders bled from wounds that were never allowed to heal. His feet were covered with infected, blistering sores—the result of being forced to work shoeless clearing rocks and trees from the rough terrain on the north side of the Moore plantation. Bentley and Elizabeth Moore were expecting their first child, and Master Moore wanted the view outside the nursery window to be the finest in Georgia. The trees would be thinned, gardens planted, and a stone path inlaid that would stretch all the way to the back porch.

Elijah lay on his side, unable to find a position free from pain. The damp and musty smell from the cold floorboards was a welcome distraction. Master Moore had been particularly vicious to the slaves that day.

"If my child arrives 'fore you clear that hillside, I'll beat you lazy niggers sillier than cow dung," he had said, driving his walking stick into Elijah's ribs with every other word.

"Belinda!" Elijah sobbed into his forearm, shifting his position once again.

"Hush up, Elijah," mumbled one of the other slaves. "Hush up and sleep."

Elijah curled up and hugged his knees tightly into his chest. The anguish he felt at being separated from his darling Belinda for almost two months was as real as the agony from his injuries. Elijah was thankful that Mr. Shannon owned her since he was a kinder master than Mr. Moore. Mr. Shannon knew that the slaves would, on occasion, hold wedding ceremonies on Friday afternoons when they had their idle hour— something unheard of on the Moore plantation.

Elijah prayed to sweet Jesus that his master would never learn of their marriage. He would probably buy Belinda from Mr. Shannon and force Elijah to whip her for some minor or imagined offence. Elijah had seen it before. Poor old Henry was made to beat his wife half to death while Master Moore and his two teenage nephews leaned against the horse gate— laughing and smoking cigars like they were at a church picnic.

Belinda. He repeated the name over and over again until his mind followed the rhythm of his beloved's name into the peace and freedom of sleep.

The next morning, because Elijah didn't move quickly enough to satisfy Bentley Moore, he was beaten to death with an axe handle. Eight months later Belinda gave birth to a son.

*   *   *

Edwin Moore placed the tattered diary on top of the dressing table. The delicate pages, browned with age, no longer adhered to their bindings. He turned the pages, holding his

8

breath each time as he gently separated each one. His great-great-grandmother's words were barely discernable, but he had memorized every word when Grandpa Moore used to read to him at his bedside when he was a boy. Edwin Moore would often close his eyes and imagine what it must have been like for his family to live confined by the chains of slavery and prejudice. As his grandfather spoke, he could feel the pain and sorrow that Anne Moore expressed in her writings when her husband was murdered by Klansmen in 1881. He often cried as her writing described how her husband was ripped from his mother's arms when he was just an infant and sold to his father's murderer for six hundred dollars. Edwin promised himself that he would avenge the way his family had been treated. The way his race had been treated.

A knock at the dressing-room door caused him to close the diary. "Yes?"

"It's time, Mr. Moore," came a muffled voice from behind the door.

"Thank you." Moore stood in front of the mirror and adjusted his tie. He couldn't help but smile as he studied his image. He had dedicated his life to instilling pride in his race. He wanted everyone to be proud of who they were. Even though many blacks carried the blood of the slave owners who had forced themselves on the female slaves, his lectures always contained some reference to the scientist's discovery of ancient remains in what he called the birthplace of human life—Africa.

Yet he couldn't help but feel some guilty pride that his skin was dark brown, his cheekbones high and sharp, his eyes set deep. *Pure Burundi—no white blood.* He raised his square jaw a little higher to tighten up the flab that was developing under his chin. Forty-something was taking its toll.

A second knock, and the muffled voice again reminded him that it was time. Time to speak to six thousand people—members of Moore's United African-American Coalition, students, teachers, reporters, and maybe even a federal agent or two who would report to the President's security council the word-for-word content of the possibly subversive speech.

He carefully placed his grandmother's writings in his leather attaché and spun the combination dials. He would carry the case to the podium as he always did—never letting the family heirloom out of his sight.

Outside the door, four bodyguards greeted him for the trip to the stage. Edwin Moore didn't use members of the coalition for this important job. Instead he had spent months interviewing, and then handpicked four men for the job. Moore was convinced that these men were not only capable of providing security, but that they also knew him as a person and understood the importance of his work for the coalition. Two of them were black, ex-football players with advanced degrees in karate and jujitsu. The third man, the tallest and burliest of the bunch, was a white man who had fallen into professional wrestling, having been cut from training with the Secret Service. The fourth was Asian, slighter than the rest, but an expert marksman who, whenever Moore made public appearances, carried two nine-millimeter pistols in quick-release holsters under each armpit. The yearly cost to the coalition—$580,000.

The wrestler, whom everyone called by his old wrestling handle, Huck, led the way down the corridor to the stage entrance. Max Smith, who had once played guard for the Vikings, walked on Moore's right. Lucas Green, a former defensive end from New England, walked on the opposite side. Danny Park completed the diamond of protection, his trained eyes scanning the corridor for any suspicious movement.

The mini-entourage stopped short outside the stage door. Perkins slowly opened it and looked in. He turned and nodded, then ducked his six-foot-three frame and walked through. Moore could hear the UAAC's master of ceremonies introduce him, as Max and Green escorted him through the door.

10

"My brothers and sisters of the United African-American Coalition—I give you Mr. Edwin Moore."

Every cell in his body reacted to the crowd's applause. His eyes misted and his throat dried as he approached the podium. Max and Lucas took their places on either side of him. Huck stood to the far left, next to Lucas. Park stood to the far right.

Moore took a deep, almost intoxicating breath.

*　　*　　*

Raymond Hill had spent the night suspended between two stage curtains in a special harness that let him rest undetected by the night security, as well as the UAAC's early sweep of the old theater. Covered by a red velvet blanket with an M24 Super Sniper rifle strapped firmly to his chest, Hill was the perfect chameleon—the perfect soldier. It didn't matter that he could possibly be caught, even killed, as long as his mission was successful—as long as the enemy was killed.

Hill stretched his muscles like a cat just awaking from a nap. He removed the blanket and clipped it onto the rear of the harness. He then took a firm hold of the cable above his head and released himself from the straps. His powerful arms carried him up to the ceiling where a suspended platform, used by the lighting technicians during concerts, would provide him a clear shot at the stage below.

People quickly filtered into the theater, filling every seat. There were reporters and photographers cramming the aisles on either side. There must be a million niggers down there, thought Hill. Easier just to blow the whole stinking place. But then, any idiot could blow up a building. The actual target might even survive it. This way is surer. One bullet. One dead troublemaker who should have learned to keep his place. One great beginning to the race war.

11

A black figure approached the podium. Hill quickly removed his rifle from its chest strap, and his heart felt like a dragster going from zero to one-fifty.

False alarm.

The man thanked the audience for coming and talked about how there was a new day about to dawn in American race relations through the UAAC under the leadership of Edwin Moore. *Bull!* thought Hill. *It would be this country's downfall.*

"My brothers and sisters of the United African-American Coalition—I give you Mr. Edwin Moore."

Hill readied his rifle. The first person to come into view was the huge white guy. *Traitor!* thought Hill. Then came two black men with Moore between them. At the rear of the diamond was a skinny Asian guy who seemed more active than the rest in the way he kept moving his head from side to side, surveying up and down the large hall. *Got to take the shot before that slant-eyed mother scopes me out. The second bullet will be his.*

Moore placed his hands on the podium. Danny Park turned to look up and around. Raymond Hill squeezed the trigger and the crowd seemed to gasp in unison before screams and panic ensued as they bulldozed toward the exits. Hill strapped the rifle to his chest and jumped, grabbing the supporting harness and clicking open the release cable that he had rigged to a steel crossbeam the night before. He slid faster than anticipated to the hardwood floor, spraining his ankle. A flash of pain shot up his leg as he tried to run. He then realized he had been shot.

Hill clutched his wounded leg, and through blurred vision, could just about make out the image of the young Asian pointing a gun at his head.

*　　*　　*

Martin Walsh pressed his son's head down below the tops of the shrubs.

"Stay down, Alex," he commanded. "And point that away."

Walsh looked over the top of the bush, then collapsed to a prone position. "Someone's coming."

"Who, Dad?" the boy whispered.

"Can't tell. You remember what I told you?" The boy nodded. "Good, just shoot for the middle of the chest. You're bound to hit something." Alex's hands were shaking and he almost dropped the pistol. Walsh placed his hands over his son's. "There's nothing to be nervous about, okay?" Another nod, although uncertain. Walsh peeked slowly over the top of the bush. Nobody.

"Where the heck ...?"

"Daddy!" Alex screamed.

"Freeze!" someone barked from behind them. Walsh spun around fast and gently pushed Alex away with his foot. Walsh rolled over twice and fired two shots at their would-be-assailants.

"Damn!" shouted one of the men, his hand on his blue-covered chest. "No freaking way."

Walsh helped his son to his feet and approached the men. "Easy on the language, fella. There's a ten-year-old present," he said to the burlier of the two.

"I had you. You should have given up." The man was a little taller than Walsh and his camouflage fatigues fit him too tightly. He wore mirrored sunglasses and a black beret. Both men wore blue armbands. Walsh and Alex wore red.

"We could have shot you," said the other man, a short but stocky sort in his late twenties—at least ten years Walsh's junior.

Walsh sighed and reached into the pocket of his jump suit. He yanked out a piece of paper and held it out in front of him. "Did you happen to *read* the rules?"

Both men looked at each other and shrugged.

Walsh handed the paper to his son. Alex read, "Paint Wars rule number six; no player shall shoot another in the back."

"We had the right to resist capture," said Walsh, removing his safety goggles. His vibrating pager activated, shaking the keys in his breast pocket. The dejected players walked off, grumbling something about being greedy for capture points, and how they should have just shot the guy and his brat, and taken two kills.

"Come on, Alex," said Walsh. "Daddy's got to get to a phone." Walsh tied a white headband around his son's head, then his own, so they could walk back to the reception building unmolested.

"Why, Dad? I'm having fun." Alex rolled on the ground, imitating his father's maneuver and pointing his paint gun at a boulder. "Pow, pow, pow."

"Sorry, little man. Duty calls." Walsh turned to walk away, Alex reluctantly at his heels.

"Freaking FBI," said Alex under his breath. Walsh stopped short.

"What did you say? No. Don't say it again." Walsh took a deep breath, fighting back laughter. *Got to do the parent thing.* He knelt on one knee and grabbed his son by the shoulders. "I don't want you talking like that." Alex looked like he was about to cry.

"I'm sorry." The little boy looked down at the ground. "I hate it when they call you away."

"I mean using the curse word. I don't blame you for being mad at the FBI. Sometimes I get mad at them too." Walsh stood up and patted his son gently on the back. "Let's go."

Two blue-armed players, another father-and-son team, sprang from behind a rock, then retreated after noticing Walsh's and Alex's neutral headbands. Walsh waved them off.

"Why can't I use the curse word, Dad?" Alex asked, pointing his paint pistol at a grouping of pine trees.

"It's just not nice," said Walsh. *God, that sounded like something my mother would say,* he thought.

"Do you ever curse?"

Is Darth Vader asthmatic? The temptation to lie and be done with it was strong. Or to say something really cliché like, "Never mind what I do; just do what I say." No. That wouldn't do at all. Walsh patted Alex on the head. "Sometimes, Alex. Usually if I get mad about something."

"So I was mad at the FBI for beeping you."

Walsh laughed. He scooped the boy off his feet and held him so they were practically nose to nose. "Let's just say that cursing is an adult ... recreation ... like coffee. Or driving. Okay?" Alex seemed to ponder this answer for a moment. "Okay?" Walsh repeated.

"I guess so," Alex finally said.

Walsh put him down and they continued their walk to the reception building. When they entered the building—an old ski lodge before the owners of Paint Wars had taken it over—the two public phones were tied up and a crowd was gathered around the waiting-room television.

"What's going on?" Walsh asked one of the Paint Wars staff.

"Edwin Moore just got shot," the man said. "It's on every station."

Oh boy! thought Walsh. *This could be like Martin Luther King all over again.* Walsh looked down at his little boy. He was only a kid himself when the civil rights leader was murdered. For months it had seemed like the whole world was going crazy. The public school hallways had cops on patrol, and a few kids still got stabbed and dozens hurt in the racial violence.

Walsh took the beeper from his vest pocket. It displayed Dalton Leverick's home number. Walsh figured his

friend—and partner through many undercover assignments—
had just seen the news reports and had beeped him right away.
Edwin Moore and his United African-American Coalition were
one of the hottest topics at the Bureau. Not because Moore and
his group were suspected of any criminal activity, but because
the UAAC was the fastest growing political movement in the
country: a million-plus members and counting.

"What's wrong, Daddy?" Alex tugged on his father's
arm. One of the pay phones became available, and Walsh
quickly reached for it. He never could get into the habit of
carrying his cell phone.

"A man's been shot," he told Alex as he dialed Leverick's
number. "Edwin Moore. I have to call Uncle Dalton about it."

"Wow," said Alex. "Mrs. Simon has a picture of Edwin
Moore in the library at school."

The phone was picked up on the first ring. "Leverick!"

"It's me. I got your beep."

"Moore's been shot," said Leverick. "He's alive, and a
suspect is in custody."

"Are we in it?"

"Not yet, but count on it. The director called me twice
already. Says he wants FBI representation when the suspect is
questioned and a team assigned to the case right away. You're
it, sport."

"I'm always it."

2

Matthew Pates lifted the couch's cushions for probably the fourth time. His breathing was getting heavy and his pulse was racing. "Damn it!" he thundered, his deep, powerful voice shaking the glass door of the living-room wall unit.

"What is it? What's wrong?" His wife, Elizabeth, ran into the room, a frying pan in one hand, a dishrag in the other.

"The game's about to start, and I can't find the fu ... uh." Pates thought better of it. His wife of twenty-five years always objected to foul language being used in the house. "That kind of talk should be saved for when you're out with your friends," she would say. "Not in a Christian home with a ten-year-old boy living in it." Pates sighed and placed his knuckled fists on his hips, standing there with his huge chest expanded like Superman about to deflect a barrage of bullets. "Liz ... where is the remote?"

Elizabeth smiled that you're-such-a-cute-ol'-teddy bear smile. "You could have just turned on the television one of the ten times you circled the room." She walked over to the couch, threw the dishrag on her shoulder, and reached behind to the window sill. "Where you left it last night."

Pates took the remote from his wife. "Thank you," he said, slightly embarrassed. Before returning to the kitchen, Elizabeth reached up to kiss her husband on the cheek. Pates stood six-foot-two; his wife five-four. She'd once told him that his size and strength made her feel like a little kid snuggling up to her dad for affection. That suited him fine. He loved his wife and he knew that she loved him. He also knew that she feared him. That suited him better. The forty-six-year-old ex-soldier of fortune treasured the fear that he instilled in everyone who knew him the way a new mother treasures the first smile from her infant. People didn't have to know about Pates' ability as a trained killer to be afraid of him. They could see it in his eyes. Small eyes, set close together over a nose with nostrils that seemed to be permanently flared as if he was about to explode into a murderous rage. A tight-lipped smile through grinding teeth often gave people the feeling that he was about to devour them.

He settled into his leather recliner and clicked on the television. The Steelers were playing their first home game, and had the ball on the Vikings' fifteen-yard line. On the bottom of the screen, teleprompter letters read that Edwin Moore had been shot by a yet-to-be-identified assailant ... Mr. Moore's condition was unknown ... Details at six.

Pates yammered for his wife to bring him a beer as the telephone rang. Elizabeth brought him the cell phone. Pates didn't allow any phone wires in his home or anywhere on the compound. Too much of a security risk.

"It's Fred Mills. Be right back with your beer."

Pates took the phone without looking up. "Yeah."

"He's still alive."

"What about Hill?" asked Pates.

"He's shot." There was a long pause. Pates could picture Fred Mills sitting in his worn-out easy chair, twirling the end of his beard—nervous about communicating the bad news. Finally Mills blurted, "They got him at Bellevue Hospital."

18

"Call a general meeting," said Pates. "Six o'clock." He pressed the disconnect button and placed the phone down on a side table. Elizabeth, who had probably been waiting out of sight until he had finished, suddenly appeared with a can of Coors in her hand. "Don't forget you promised Kevin that you'd take him to the batting cage tonight."

Pates gulped half the can, then shook his head no as he wiped his mouth on his sleeve. "Another night."

"A ten-year-old doesn't understand *another night*." Elizabeth folded her arms. She still looked good at forty-three, thought Pates. Her breasts were firm and she had managed to keep her backside from getting too heavy. Only traces of the redhead Pates had married twenty-five years ago showed through her gray hair. He'd let her use a little makeup these last few years. He had taken a fancy to the look after hiring a woman and her twelve-year-old daughter to keep his bed warm while he'd been in Costa Rica, running a training program for a provincial police force. He hated spics but two-hundred-fifty thousand dollars for two weeks of teaching guerilla warfare and tactical response had been hard to turn down.

Pates lifted himself out of his chair with a grunt.

"I'll go talk to him." He kissed his wife on her cheek. She looked at him wryly out of the corner of her eye. "He's young, but he's a soldier," he said. "Kevin understands that the good of his race comes first."

Pates sprinted up the stairs and paused for a moment to check his pulse. He always liked to monitor himself after a sudden exertion. *Still in great shape,* he thought.

The door to his son's room was closed, a vintage flag of The Third Reich hanging from it. Pates knocked, then walked in. Kevin was sitting on his bed with his knees supporting a writing pad.

"Dad!" He looked up.

Pates sat on the bed. "Something interesting?"

"Just a story for school. Mrs. Cowan wants everybody to write a short story." Kevin shoved the pad behind him—under his pillow.

19

"Let's have a look." Pates held out his huge hand.

Kevin shook his head. "No! It's not finished yet." His cheeks turned crimson. He looked genuinely afraid.

Pates held up his hands. "Whoa, boy. Sensitive writer, huh?" He mussed the boy's hair, quickly squelching his son's apprehension. "You can show it to me later. *He* was a writer, too." Pates looked at the wall at the head of Kevin's bed. A picture of Adolf Hitler addressing his troops at Nuremberg hung there, above a picture of George Lincoln Rockwell during a 1967 television appearance. Matthew Pates, a high-school freshman at the time, stood proudly next to the American Nazi Party founder—three months before he was murdered.

Kevin looked up at the pictures, which Pates had hung above his crib when the boy had been just two weeks old. They had been hanging on the wall ever since. "Did he write short stories, Dad?"

Pates snorted a laugh. "I don't think so. He was the greatest man of this century. He wrote of his struggle to preserve the white race." Pates squeezed Kevin's shoulder. "We need to cancel our trip tonight, son. I'm calling an emergency ARCS meeting."

Kevin's lower lip quivered slightly and his eyes became moist. Instead of crying he took a deep breath. Just like his dad always told him. "Do I have to go, too?"

Pates shook his head. "The race war is to begin soon. We have to make plans to keep our families safe."

"Daddy?" said Kevin as Pates stood up, ready to leave. "Why are we better than niggers and Jews?" The young man looked down, almost burying his head between his knees. "I mean, aren't we all just people?"

Pates clenched his fists. Had it not been for the fear that his tightly trained body could cause him to accidentally kill the boy with so much as a slap in the face, he would have struck him. He leaned over and spoke in a low tone that carried more intensity than if he'd been shouting through a bullhorn.

20

"Where in God's name, after all I've taught you, do you come up with such a question?"

"In school ..."

"Your school is funded and run by the Zionist occupational government, son." Pates took his son's head in his hands and eyed him nose to nose. "Even your teacher knows the truth that is the Lord's word. The Christ killers and their nigger soldiers are God's enemies with inferior morals and a desire to extinguish our race from the planet." Pates embraced the boy. "Don't you see," he whispered, gently now. "Your school ... the government ... even many people who claim to believe in Yahweh, will lie to you."

"I'm sorry, Dad," said Kevin, his voice cracking.

"I only want the best for you. By next school year we'll have one of the barracks on the compound converted into a four-classroom school house." Pates kissed his son on the forehead. "Whaddya say we walk over to the range tomorrow and try out my new Glock?"

"I'd like that, Dad." Kevin smiled, a little painfully, but a smile just the same.

Pates returned to the living room and the football game. The Steelers had just scored on an interception and led the Vikings by ten points going into the second quarter. *Might as well flip to CNN to see if they got an update on Moore,* thought Pates.

"Liz," he yammered. "Where's the remote?"

*   *   *

Katherine Jacobson practically fell into the doorway of her studio apartment. The afternoon's workout at the Tao Kwon Do gym had been particularly grueling. Some craphead with something to prove tried to show the rest of the class that a woman, even one with a fourth degree black belt, couldn't possibly score any shots on a man with a second degree who was ten years her junior.

21

She sincerely hoped that his jaw wasn't broken. She also hoped that he was in at least as much pain as she was right now.

A trail of clothing and personal items—starting with her gym bag—followed her from the doorway into the bathroom where she cranked up the shower to steamy-hot. The black-and-blues were just beginning to show through on her forearms and shins. "Why do I bother?" she said, then smiled as she immediately thought about the answer. *You bother because every time people think you can't do something, you have to prove you can. Your whole life is about proving people wrong—especially your parents.*

Jacobson washed her hair under the powerful stream of water. Pangs of guilt hit her when she thought of her mother and father. Last week, she had spent the afternoon before Rosh Hashanah with them. Her mother had wasted no time in asking her if she was dating anyone.

"No, Mom," Jacobson had said. "Work's been busy."

"So, Miss FBI Schmarty-Pants can't get her work done like everyone else between nine and five?"

"The FBI isn't a nine-to-five job, Mom."

"You shouldn't be working. Mrs. Heidelberg's son is a partner at his law firm, and he's coming back to the synagogue. Since his Shiksa wife left him after five years of being treated like a queen."

"Ruth, please!" Her father looked at her mother in that lawyerly way of his. That familiar double chin pressed into his chest as he peeked over his bifocals. The dining room chandelier reflecting off his bald head made him look like a wise, old angel—beaming with goodness. "You don't think Jewish women ever leave their husbands?"

"It's okay, Daddy." Jacobson reached over and placed her hand over his. He lifted her hand to his lips and gently kissed it.

"Let's eat," he said. "Then we'll go to services together."

That night during the beautiful chant of *Kol Nidre,* she felt connected to her faith. Her heart was filled with joy and she experienced such a sense of belonging that she actually thought about letting her mother fix her up with a nice Jewish boy. She even fantasized about pushing a baby carriage to Shabbat services alongside the other wives. She felt that the day of fasting and asking for forgiveness would be a new start for her.

The next day, she ate pizza for breakfast. To make matters worse, she lied to her parents about an emergency at the field office and never attended the Yom Kippur services.

Jacobson watched the water disappear down the drain in a swirl of dirty suds. "I'm sorry," she said to no one in particular.

She lay across the bed, wearing only an open blue silk robe. It felt good to relax. She felt like she could sleep for two days. Maybe she was getting too old for this karate nonsense. She wasn't healing as fast at thirty-five as she had fifteen years ago when she'd first started training. Her chest was sore right above her left breast. She didn't even remember getting hit there.

She reached over and plucked the tube of Tiger Balm that she kept handy on the headboard shelf. She soothed her injury, gently rubbing the analgesic into her skin. If she had a husband, he could be doing this for her right now, she thought. She folded her arms tightly and closed her eyes. An overwhelming feeling of doubt engulfed her and she now imagined herself getting old in this very apartment. She could picture herself, tattered and worn out, surrounded by dusty trophies and plaques that were almost as meaningless as her life had been. The over achiever who had joined the FBI to do something useful for the world, instead spent her days never knowing who she was and always feeling like she had something to prove.

"A research assistant with a gun," she said quietly. "Real important."

Then the muffled sound of her beeper inside her gym bag made her pop up straight and jump out of bed.

Panting all the way over the trail of discarded clothing, she plucked the bag off the floor and violently unzipped it. She grabbed the beeper. "What the hell do you want?"

She pressed the display button and immediately recognized Dalton Leverick's number.

Thanks a lot, boss, she thought bitterly. *You couldn't even let me enjoy a miserable evening at home.*

3

The paramedics worked frantically to stop Edwin Moore's bleeding as the ambulance sped through the streets of Manhattan to Bellevue Hospital. Moore's personal physician, Carl LeGrande, hovered over them and offered whatever advice and assistance he could. A wad of gauze was pressed firmly against the exit wound on the left side of what was left of Moore's jaw. The civil rights leader stared blankly, his dilated pupils showing no reaction to the paramedic's penlight.

"He's in shock," LeGrande said. The doctor checked the heart monitor—no decline. At least that was good news. He was hanging on.

Mental self-preservation placed Moore back in time. Back to the moment when his bodyguards had escorted him to the podium. In his mind's eye he could see the crowd as they had been less than an hour earlier. The boisterous and colorful Reverend Hal Shelton sat in the front row with his contingent of advisors and bodyguards. Shelton had been accused more than once of holding the mayor's office hostage with his threats to organize New York's African-American community to march through the streets in a heated protest of the latest civil-rights violation. In a failed attempt to become Governor, Shelton had gained such notoriety and popularity that his power base was now estimated to reach from Boston to Miami. Some said he could organize a half-million people overnight.

In a recent interview, Shelton had said that he would give up his life for Edwin Moore. He had pledged the loyalty of his own constituency as well. Moore had smiled warmly at his friend as the thunderous applause diminished to a low rumble.

"Thank you, brothers and sisters." Moore held up his hand. The sporadic cheers and applause died down. "Thank you, one and all." He closed his eyes and breathed deeply. Except for an occasional clearing of the throat or a sniffle, the room was haunted with an anticipatory silence. "The vision I hold for the future ..." Moore opened his eyes and held up his right hand as if holding some invisible object, "... on the one hand, is glorious. We are all living together in peace and prosperity. People of every color, race, and religion practicing brotherhood and preparing a paradise on earth for our children."

Moore lifted his left hand, imitating a balancing scale. "But on this side, I see violence. A country ravaged by racism, drug abuse, and crime. Where people only know hate." He brought his hands together sharply and then pressed them into his chest. "Here we have choices. Those choices will carry us toward one of those possible futures.

"If you think racism is an obstacle, you're right. But only if we let it. If you think there are people who want you to destroy yourself and would like nothing better than the total annihilation of every black man, woman, and child, you're right again. But we don't have to cooperate.

"There would never have been a slave trade in Africa if our ancestors didn't cooperate with their captors. While we were weakening ourselves through tribal warfare, the white man was poised and ready to exploit the battle-weary nations of Africa."

Moore smiled and his flesh tingled with a rush of bliss that surged through his body.

"Mother Africa. The cradle of creation. Home of the very first human beings.

"Now if this doesn't tell us that we are all brothers and sisters on this planet, nothing does." Moore laughed. "I was speaking to a gentleman who had called in to a radio talk-show last week where we were discussing this very subject. The man said, 'I ain't 'cendent from no nigger bitch.'"

There were gasps and mumbles from the crowd. Moore waved his hand. He shook his head, smiling again as he did so often during his speeches. The smile that so many governors, mayors, even the President had found so warm and disarming.

"Did you ever watch a group of children left to their own devices? They laugh and play—they cry and fight. Sometimes they wet themselves. Sometimes they say and do mean things to each other. Then, when they grow, they will hopefully become good citizens and put such foolishness—like grabbing toys and hitting just because they're angry behind them.

"My dear brothers and sisters of every race and religion of the world, I assert that we are like children left alone in a huge playroom. We have enormous potential. We just have to grow up right. There will come a day on this planet when the human race will look back and find it hard to believe that we ever hated each other because of the color of our skin." Moore closed his eyes and pressed his hand to his chest. "This I believe with all my heart."

Moore looked up. A reporter had once described Moore, in this part of his speech, as changing from a man with a smile and gentle eyes into a snarling, venomous creature that snorted smoke and spit fire. Even his voice had turned into a harsh, raspy growl.

"Make no mistake. My hopes and dreams are for peace, but I will not stand ... my people will not stand ... for anything less than full integration into American society. I am prepared to love you." He shot his arm straight out, his finger pointed beyond the crowd. "I'm also prepared to kill you if you threaten my life and the lives of my people."

The sound of the applause became so powerful that he could feel the force of the crowd touching his body like a thousand invisible fingers.

He thought he heard several people cry out, "Oh God!" Then he felt a sharp pain on the side of his face before his thoughts faded to black.

*   *   *

On the corner of Eleventh Avenue and Thirty-eighth Street, Martin Walsh and Katherine Jacobson sat in the back seat of a four-door Plymouth, while the two seasoned New York City detectives ran the latest series of license plates through their dashboard computer. It was almost 2 a.m. Monday. The FBI agents had been working with a team of city cops for almost 6 hours, conducting interviews with parking-garage attendants and running license plates on every parked car for blocks in all directions from the site of the shooting.

Walsh glanced across the street and noticed a man walking out of a small deli with a styrofoam cup in his hand. *Coffee sounds good,* he thought. *This night is far from over.*

"You want a cup of coffee, Jacobson?" Walsh offered.

Jacobson crouched forward, peering through the gate-divider at the computer screen. She flopped back in the seat and let out a long sigh. "Sure. When do we finally decide that we're chasing our tails?"

One of the cops, Detective Don Masters, snorted a laugh. Masters was a savvy investigator, the kind of cop who could tell when somebody was full of it just by looking at him.

He also had a reputation for ticking off the suits at the commissioner's office. Walsh liked him the moment he met him.

"How about you guys? Coffee?" asked Walsh. Masters and his partner declined. Walsh handed Jacobson the cell phone. "Call the boss. Maybe the bad guy's talking and we can all go home."

"Tell your boss to get the weight. The perp'll talk quick." Masters' partner slapped the dashboard, laughing. Knowing the two FBI agents weren't in on the joke, Masters offered the explanation. "It's something Bob and I experienced when we first got our gold shields." Bob nodded, still laughing. "We had this loo ... this lieutenant named Sheppard," he continued. "Bob and me were questioning this bad guy who'd stabbed his grandmother. He was being an uncooperative little scumbag. We had the weapon." Masters pointed his index fingers and held them up about a foot apart from each other. "One of these commando-warrior blades they sell in those cutlery shops. Anyway, there was blood all over this woman's apartment— and blood all over this punk's *Air Jordans*. Almost every person in the building swore he'd been there with her that morning.

"So to make a long story a little longer, Sheppard comes into the room with a twenty-five-pound dumbbell and orders us to strip the guy down to balls. He ties a piece of cord around this guy's gonads, the other end around the dumbbell, then walks over to the window. He holds the weight out and starts counting, one ... two ... and that dude not only confessed, he also gave up two of his drug-dealer buddies."

"Great story," said Jacobson sarcastically. "Could you see yourself doing something like that?" she said to Walsh.

Walsh shook his head. "No." He let himself out of the car. "I'd probably drop the weight anyway."

Walsh sprinted across the street. The deli owner was kneeling down, locking the deadbolt at the bottom of the door.

"I guess I couldn't ask you to open up and scare up a couple of cups of coffee."

The man bolted to his feet, startled by Walsh's presence. "I have no cash, mister."

Walsh held up his hands. "Whoa, partner. Just lookin' for some java." He showed the man his FBI credentials for good measure.

"Oh, very sorry, my friend. No, my friend." The man looked at his watch. "My last train leaves Hoboken in twenty minutes. I am late." The man smiled at Walsh and ran down the avenue, disappearing into a PATH station.

Walsh looked across the street at the detectives' vehicle. "I wonder if you guys would arrest me if I broke in and made coffee." He looked again at the PATH station entrance, then started to walk back to the car. He thought about when he had joined the police investigators at the Manhattan Center earlier that afternoon. The suspect had rigged an elaborate harness that had released him to the floor a split second after shooting Moore. He would have escaped through the basement where he had, probably weeks earlier, broken a hole in a concrete wall and then he could have escaped out through a storm drain onto 33rd Street.

Why take the chance of getting caught in outbound Manhattan traffic? Walsh thought. He jumped in the back seat of the detectives' car.

"Closing time?" said Jacobson.

"Let's take a ride through the tunnel." Walsh looked at Masters, who pursed his lips and nodded.

After a thoughtful moment, the cop snapped his fingers. "The PATH to Jersey! Not bad thinking for a Fed," he said. "Let's go."

*   *   *

By 11 a.m. on Monday, the fifth-floor doctor's lounge

at Bellevue had been commandeered and turned into an FBI communications center. Half a dozen televisions, tuned into news coverage of Moore's attempted assassination and its aftermath, were set up on a long worktable.

Walsh scanned the monitors with a sinking feeling in his stomach as he and Jacobson left the lounge and headed toward the suspect's room to join Leverick. Having had only two hours' sleep on one of the lounge chairs didn't help his dreary state.

The suspect had been heavily sedated after the operation to remove the bullet from his leg and the doctors would not permit any interrogation until this morning. Walsh and Jacobson now watched from a corner of the room as Dalton Leverick and a New York detective questioned the suspect. A doctor and a nurse were also present.

"Why did you shoot Edwin Moore?" Leverick asked.

The suspect winced. "I'm thirsty. My leg hurts."

Leverick poured a cup of water from the pitcher on the bedside tray. "I can't help you with the pain but here's a drink of water."

"I'll give you something for the pain in a few minutes," the nurse volunteered.

The suspect gulped the water. The room was silent for a moment, then Detective Masters entered the room and handed the other detective some papers. Masters had insisted on being the one to present their find to the lieutenant in charge. The lieutenant, a large man in his late 40's with white hair and cheeks that were almost crimson, quickly perused the documents. "Hold the phone," he said before handing the papers to Leverick. Leverick glanced at Walsh and Jacobson, nodding his approval. Having a copy of the suspect's photo license to show him would make for good theater.

Walsh admired his superior agent and friend. Fifty-years old and as fit as any man 15 years his junior. Except for a slight bulge around the mid-section, the ex-Marine with the military-style crew cut was hard as a rock and possessed a keen investigative mind.

Leverick leaned close to the suspect's bed, placing his arm dangerously close to the injured leg that the nurse had propped up on a pillow.

"Watch this," Walsh whispered to Jacobson. "Dalton's gonna milk this like he's Columbo."

Leverick slowly raised the papers and held them within an inch of the suspect's face. "Recognize this person, Mr. Hill?"

The suspect glanced at his photo but seemed unfazed.

"I can tell you everything, but I want immunity from prosecution."

Paydirt, thought Walsh. This was shaping up to be the easiest assignment of his life.

"Do you have a lawyer?" Leverick asked.

The suspect shook his head.

"We'll get you one. And as far as immunity ... that depends on what you give us." Leverick leaned closer. "Who sent you to kill Edwin Moore?"

"Sons Elohim."

Leverick straightened up. "You're full of crap!"

The case suddenly took a bad turn. The images Walsh had seen on the monitors intruded into his mind. CNN had shown an aerial shot of a riot in downtown Philadelphia. Another network covered a rowdy march down Pennsylvania Avenue in Washington, D.C. If Moore had died, things would be a lot worse right now. When they had found the stuff in the trunk of the car in Jersey City, Walsh thought he had the whole thing figured out. The driver's license and credit card in the name of Jacob Levine along with the decorative pin of the Sons Elohim. "These guys make Mier Kahane's JDL look like Hari Krisnas," Jacobson had said. Their symbol of the Star of David, with two crossed daggers beneath it, was something its members supposedly wore pinned to their chests in their clandestine meetings. Condemned by almost every Jewish

Group in the world, the Sons Elohim were rumored to be responsible for the death of a JDL representative who had threatened to support the signing of the peace treaty between Israel and the PLO.

It seemed obvious to Walsh at the time that the set of ID belonging to Raymond Hill was real, and that at some point he was going to make his way back to the car just to pick them up and perhaps leave a tip with some local precinct that would conveniently find the car with the phony ID and Sons Elohim pin. Walsh wouldn't have been surprised if right this minute some misinformation were being called into some newspapers and radio stations claiming responsibility for the SE.

Jacobson peered into a small hand mirror. "How do I look?" she asked Walsh.

"Like an ad for wrinkle-free clothing—the before picture," Walsh responded.

"In other words, like crap."

"Pretty much." Walsh turned his fingers toward himself, a gesture that said, 'Me, too.' "It's gonna be a long day."

The doctor ordered everyone out of the room so the patient could rest. The agents and police officers returned to the makeshift command center where they had to push their way through a thicket of media reporters. Dalton Leverick and Carl LeGrande approached the podium of clustered microphones. The men and women gathering around them huddled like a litter of hungry kittens trying to secure a suckle from too few nipples.

Leverick leaned toward the microphone. "Dr. LeGrande will make a brief statement as to Edwin Moore's condition. We will not handle any questions at this time. A press conference is scheduled at six o'clock this evening."

This brought a lot of dissatisfied rumbling from the reporters but they quickly simmered down when LeGrande approached the microphones.

"At approximately 9:30 this morning, Edwin Moore regained consciousness. His condition has been upgraded to serious. He suffered damage to the right maxillary." LeGrande tapped just under his right cheekbone. "Most of the left, lower portion of his jaw—the mandible bone—has been shattered. Mr. Moore is unable to speak, but wrote this statement for me to read:

"'This is a crucial time in the history of our struggle. I am very much alive and very much plan to continue the fight. Do not let this event trigger your anger and force you to take action that you will later regret. This is a time to fight and a time to win. This is not the time for lawlessness. My message of preparedness for loving and preparedness for war is still as true today as it was before the forces of hate and oppression tried to take my life. Preparedness for war does not mean committing random acts of violence and destruction. Please remain true to our cause by practicing restraint. Your brother, Edwin Moore.'"

Cameras flashed, and reporters fired unanswered questions to the doctor, as he and Leverick walked away from the podium.

"Is it true that Mr. Moore was shot by a member of the extremist Jewish Group, the Sons Elohim?" Some of the photographers turned and snapped the man who had asked the question. Others scribbled frantically on their notepads.

Walsh leaned over and spoke quietly to Jacobson. "Now we've got more trouble than we bargained for."

Jacobson shrugged. "Bring 'em on."

4

Since 1925, Pearlman's Custom Furniture has provided Brooklyn's Hasidic community with made-to-order cabinets, bookcases, and dining room tables. Four generations of the conservative, religious people have depended on the Pearlman family's talented craftsmen for their superb furniture. Three generations have, albeit most of them unknowingly, depended on the clandestine activities of Pearlman and the Sons Elohim for their security.

Avi Pearlman, the grandson of the SE founder, sat with his legs outstretched and crossed at the ankles on top of his desk, perusing a copy of KlanWatch magazine. He occasionally glanced up at the security monitors. One displayed the image transmitted from a rotating camera mounted on the workshop ceiling. The mostly black and Puerto Rican crew sanded, cut, drilled and varnished choice pieces of oak, mahogany, and birch, Sunday through Friday afternoon when the shop promptly shut down at 3:00 p.m. for the Sabbath. All personally supervised by Avi's father, Yeheudah. The businessman, now well into his eighties, made all the key

35

decisions that affected the family business. He was also the final authority on all SE decisions.

Avi looked admiringly at the soundless black-and-white image of his father instructing a young man on the use of the table saw. Yeheudah was heavyset, with greying hair and a long, black and grey beard. Even on the warmest afternoons he would wear his *full-length* overcoat and wide-rimmed hat. *That battered old hat,* thought Avi. He could close his eyes and see the story of that old hat unfold as if he were watching an old newsreel. Although the images were always in black-and-white, he could almost feel the biting cold wind ripping through the streets of 1937 Dusseldorf. His faher must have told the story a thousand times. It was a Friday. Ten-year-old Yeheudah ran up the cobblestone street, dropping his package of milk and eggs to the ground. "Mama ... Papa ..." he screamed as two soldiers roughly pushed his parents onto one of six trucks that were lined up along Bohnstrasse 14. It seemed that everywhere children were crying, soldiers were shouting, while the noisy trucks pumped diesel fumes into the air.

"Yeheudah!" his father shouted as he tried to reach for his son over the sides of the cattle truck. A solder smashed his father on the side of his face with the rifle butt. Droplets of blood splattered onto the boy's face, his father's hat falling to the ground.

"Move, you dirty little Jew," the soldier had said as he grabbed Yeheudah by the locks of his hair and pulled hard until he cried out for release. When the soldier finally let go, Yeheudah fell to his knees. He managed to snatch his father's hat before being dragged away from the truck. He looked up, teary-eyed, as the first two trucks pulled away, and he tried desperately to get one last glimpse of his Mama and Papa. He never saw them again.

Before the soldiers could grab him again he slipped under one of the trucks and ran down a narrow street, the screams and the sounds of gunfire behind him muffled as if he was in a slow moving dream. Yeheudah had turned a corner and saw a man slipping into a sewer grate.

Yeheudah slid into the sewer after the man, just like he used to hear about baseball players in America stealing second base. The other people in the sewer had wanted to throw him back onto the street, claiming their little haven to be full. He was saved by the kindness of one person, a woman, who had placed the young Yeheudah behind her and told the rest of the group that they would have to throw her out as well.

There were fifteen of them hiding in the sewer that day. Only four made it safely out of Germany. Three weeks after Yeheudah had been separated from his parents, he and three other refugees crossed the border into Austria. A month after that he was in Brooklyn, taken in and adopted by the Pearlmans, where he began to learn all about woodworking, profits, losses—and the Sons Elohim.

*   *   *

Avi placed his finger under his desk, ready to release the door. He watched the monitor as his father entered the office door with the word 'private' stenciled on it. As soon as he entered the room a motion detector activated another camera that followed his movements toward the rear wall. There he pushed aside a picture, revealing a dial pad with a blinking green light. Before he could enter the code, Avi pressed the release and the paneled door clicked open, its hydraulic hinge hissing quietly.

"Papa, good morning."

Yeheudah waved and nodded his head. A slight smile rose from the side of his mouth. A generous ear-to-ear grin for anyone else, thought Avi. Yeheudah wheeled a chair next to his son, placed his overcoat on the back of it, and sat down. "So, we have a major problem."

"We might," said Avi. "If it's true."

"It's true," said Yeheudah. "I know it in here." The old man tapped his round gut with his fist. He had been rotund since as long as Avi could remember. He was living proof that appearances can be misleading. A harmless-looking old man who was capable of wielding incredible power. Avi had first experienced his father's ability the day he turned eight. When they left the ice cream shop three baseball-bat-wielding teenagers threatened them and demanded money. Yeheudah urged the teenage punks to leave him and his son alone. One of them swung a bat at Yeheudah's head, and in two seconds the old man himself was holding the bat and then hit his attacker on the side of his knee. While that hoodlum writhed on the ground, clutching his knee and screaming, the other two attacked Yeheudah. He ducked the first punch, got behind his attacker, and turned him around so fast the other one's blow came down right on the punk's nose. The last of the young ruffians dropped his bat, turned, and ran like hell.

Avi reached over and patted his father's belly. "If you feel it there, it must be true," he said.

"This is very serious, Avi. If they should have been successful blaming Sons Elohim for shooting Edwin Moore, we would have trouble like nothing you have ever seen." The old man looked up toward heaven and clasped his hands together. "I am very worried about this."

Avi reached over and grabbed a report from a small bookcase next to his desk. "This is an old profile," he said as he thumbed through the pages. "Aryan Resistance Christian Soldiers, at least as of June 1998, was headed by Matthew Pates."

"It still is," said Yeheudah.

Avi shook his head. "Why is it, Papa, that I run the intelligence center for the entire SE with a worldwide computer network and you get more up-to-date information from a trip to the synagogue?"

"Sometimes word-of-mouth is more reliable, Avi. But don't worry on that. You do an important job for us all." Yeheudah looked down for a moment and sighed.

"What is it, Papa?"

"This ARCS will not stop until they have succeeded. I suspect that they will next try to kill one of us and blame it on Moore's group or the New Islamic State."

"What can we do?"

Yeheudah looked at his son, studying him. In an uncharacteristic gesture, he reached out and touched Avi's blond curls. "You were such a beautiful child. Hair golden like the most radiant sunrise. Eyes as blue as heaven's sky." Yeheudah reached into his back pocket and pulled out his wallet. He removed a small snapshot of eighteen-month-old Avi and held it up. "I think your mama's grandfather had blond hair. People used to say that you must be adopted." Yeheudah snorted a laugh, then put the photo away. "You are a very dedicated young man, Avi. A righteous man."

"Of course. I learned from you."

"Then I hope you forgive me for what I am about to ask you to do?"

Avi placed his hand over his father's.

"Anything for you, Papa."

*   *   *

In a small interview room on the eighteenth floor of the F.B.I. building in lower Manhattan, agents Walsh, Jacobson and Leverick sat at a conference with the New York field office's resident expert on hate groups. Jeffrey Anders had passed out copies of a report that all four agents were currently perusing. Anders was only eighteen months from retirement and had worked many years investigating civil rights cases from the Jackson, Mississippi field office. The silver-haired agent spoke with a slight Southern drawl as he briefed the other agents.

39

"This is an old profile," said Anders. "Y'all can bet that Pates is still in charge though."

Walsh closed the report and leaned back in his chair. He recognized Pates from an article he had read in *Black Belt Magazine*. The 1989 story covered an incident at the East Coast Karate Nationals where Pates made a fool out of an Asian karate master who challenged anyone in the audience to try to move him from his 'iron' stance. Instead of trying to push the man back, with cat-like speed Pates reached behind the martial artist's head and pulled him forward, slamming his face to the hardwood floor. Although he had heard plenty about Pates and his Aryan group before, he had never realized until now that he was the same man who had embarrassed Master Nakasima at the Nationals. "If we're planning to interview Pates, I'd love to be the guy to do it," said Walsh.

Leverick and Anders looked at each other, then back at Walsh. "It's a little deeper than that, Martin," said Leverick.

"You betcha," said Anders. "Most of these white power leaders are full of rhetoric and never really pose any serious threat. They usually terrorize the minorities in their own communities, hold rallies with hate-slogan banners, and run military exercises on an organized but irregular basis." Anders picked up another report from the table. "As of last October, there were approximately five thousand skinhead members in the U.S."

"Skinheads?" Jacobson flipped through the report again as she spoke. "I didn't see anything in the report on ARCS about skinheads."

Anders peered over his glass at Jacobson. "That's because, prior to last year, Pates stood clear of the little maniacs."

"Why the change of heart?" asked Walsh. "Cheap muscle?"

"Partly," answered Leverick. "Although the number of skinheads is growing, they haven't been organized into a national movement."

"Not yet," added Anders.

"So Pates is gonna try to succeed where the Metzgers and their White Aryan Resistance failed," said Walsh.

"Organizing a five-thousand-strong-and-growing bunch of racist punks would be a bad thing," said Jacobson.

Walsh looked at Dalton Leverick. "Couple that with pitting certain Jewish and Black groups at each other's throats and we got a real mess on our hands." It was now obvious to Walsh why he had gotten called in after Moore was shot. The Bureau suits must have suspected that the hit wasn't going to turn out to be a case of a lone wolf racist.

"You sure I can't just go down and interview Mr. Pates?" said Walsh.

Leverick laughed.

"I didn't think so."

"What's the joke?" Jacobson asked.

"The direct approach isn't exactly what we have in mind," answered Leverick.

Walsh turned to Jacobson. "If we had someone inside we would have known exactly what they were up to. Instead of all this Monday-morning-quarterbacking. Right, Dalton?"

"That's pretty much it," said Leverick. "We have a directive. Straight from the White House. He wants ARCS shut down and more than a few people are gonna lose their asses if we don't produce."

"This time you don't have to ask, Dalton. If there's such a thing as a divine plan, mine is to serve the cause of law and order and have no life of my own."

Anders' lip quivered a little as if he were fighting the urge to smile. "The Bureau appreciates the work you've done in the past, Agent Walsh. You know, I heard that stories of your deep-cover assignments have been told over coffee as far away as the Anchorage field office. This one is more important to this nation's security than anything you've done before. We're counting on both of you."

"Dalton and I will deliver," said Walsh.

Leverick leaned into the table and tapped Walsh on his arm. "He's not talking about you and me, sport."

"Oh boy," said Walsh.

"Me?" said Jacobson, tapping her fingers on her chest.

"A husband and wife cover. The importance of the operation demands it," said Anders. "You'll arrange to rent or buy a house in Milton, about ten miles from the ARCS compound."

Jacobson let out a long whistle. "That's a big ticket item. The Bureau's going to spring for two-hundred-gees?"

Walsh looked at Jacobson out of the corner of his eye. "Don't worry, dear. I'm sure we'll dump it at a loss once we get divorced."

"Wise guy," she muttered.

Leverick laughed. "I believe your cover already."

The stiff-necked Anders almost laughed too.

"The Treasury Department has enough impounded couches, televisions and tables from all those Colombian boys to furnish fifty new homes."

"I'll only do this if Dalton has to play one of the movers and busts his hump lifting furniture," joked Walsh.

"You're on," Leverick retorted.

Anders held his hands up as if to referee the two men. "We got people to do that. Agent Leverick is going to be busier than a one-legged man at a butt-kicking contest just keeping your cover in order."

"Mr. Anders!" said Walsh. "I do believe that was a humorous statement."

Anders frowned. "Are you understanding the seriousness and importance of this assignment?"

"And are both of you willing?" added Leverick. "Something like this has to be voluntary."

Jacobson raised her hand. "I'd be nuts to pass this up."

Walsh just nodded. "If I thought anybody else could pull it off, I'd refuse."

"Thank God for the ego," said Leverick.

"I'm just getting my courage up," said Walsh. "I still have to tell Amy about this."

5

The vigil outside of St. Andrews Hospital continued through the third day of Edwin Moore's internment after his transfer from Bellevue. Each time one of Moore's four body-guards went off shift, he gave the crowd an update on the minority leader's condition. It was as if the President himself was in intensive care, with all the police barricades and patrol cars outside the hospital.

Outside of Moore's room, Max Smith was just begin-ing his six to midnight shift, having just relieved Huck Perkins. The ex-defensive end folded his arms and leaned against the wall, the door to Moore's room immediately to his right.

Smith glanced at the uniformed officer, a young white kid who looked fresh out of the academy, and nodded. The rookie returned the nod. Two doctors passed in front of them, chatting about gastro intensive something or other. The elevator down the hall pinged and two more uniformed officers emerged around the corner, followed by the mayor and a chubby guy in a suit that fit too tight. The guy was sweating like a pig and talking incessantly into the mayor's ear. The rookie quickly saluted the two officers who casually returned the salute.

"Who's this?" the mayor said, tilting his head toward Smith.

Smith stuck his chin out proudly.. "Max Smith, Mr. Moore's security staff. I don't believe I know this gentleman."

The mayor—a short, slightly-built man with black hair which looked like it was colored with shoe polish—sighed and rolled his eyes. "This is Maurice Lewis, the City's general counsel."

"Thank you," said Smith.

The mayor mumbled something, and then Maurice Lewis knocked on the door to Moore's room. A moment later, the two men were let inside. The three cops gathered into a tight group, excluding Smith from their whispered conversation.

Smith looked at his watch—12:20 PM. Another five and a half hours before Danny Park's shift starts. *At least Danny got to shoot the bastard*, thought Smith.

Then it came again. Like a thrust kick to the pit of his stomach. The doubts; the second guessing; the wishing so hard for things not to have happened the way they did. Smith squeezed the bridge of his nose. *Stupid*, he thought. How could we have been so stupid, so blind? One glance up and I would've seen him. Could've stopped it.

"You okay?" said one of the cops, a tall, bulky man with sergeant's stripes on his leather jacket.

"Yeah," said Smith, looking down at the floor. The black-and-white linoleum tiles reflected the rows of fluorescent lights above so clearly that it seemed like the floor itself was illuminating the hallway. He watched the reflected image of the cop as it came closer. He looked up as the sergeant put a hand on his shoulder.

"Could have happened to anybody, pal." The cop rolled up the sleeve to his leather jacket, revealing a scar on his arm that must have been ten inches long. "Eight years ago. We had formed a blockade by the court steps. Remember the Hollis case?"

Smith nodded. "Hell, yeah. Day care worker accused of poisoning six kids."

"The day she was acquitted the father of one of the kids almost sliced my arm off with a ten-inch butcher knife. Before they dropped him he stabbed her right through the heart."

"I remember that," said Smith. "They caught the guy who really killed the kids about a month later."

"That's right. The wacko broke into the day care's kitchen the night before and used a hypodermic needle to inject arsenic into dozens of ice cream cups." The big cop folded his arms and leaned against the wall next to Smith. He looked straight ahead, as if he could see through the opposite wall and into the distance. "Besides an arm that was cut to hell I felt personally responsible for letting Jane Hollis get killed. Almost quit the force."

"But you didn't," said Smith, glancing up at the other two officers who were still engaged in conversation.

"No. Over the past eight years I've pulled two kids from burning cars, stopped four armed robberies, arrested dozens of drug dealers, pimps and rip-off artists, and even delivered a baby in the back of a cruiser." The sergeant, whose name Smith had just noticed from his name-plate was Stafford, turned and walked back to the other two cops.

"That's it?" said Smith.

"That's it," said Stafford.

A few moments later the mayor emerged from Edwin Moore's room, the sweaty Maurice Lewis in tow. Sergeant Stafford pressed the down button on the elevator. When the doors opened, Stafford held them until the three men were inside. Before stepping in himself, he turned and smiled at Smith. "Stick with it. You might get a chance to make good."

The young officer on the other side of the doorway stared straight ahead. Smith folded his arms and leaned against the wall. It was ten minutes past eight. Four hours left. In Smith's mind he was back at the Manhattan Center, standing close to Edwin Moore. In this version Smith happened to look over his shoulder and see the strange figure suspended from the ceiling, ready to take aim at the man that he was hired to protect. Smith imagined himself propelling his huge frame into the line of fire and catching a bullet in the chest. Then he thought about a later time, in this very hospital, where he would lie recovering from his non-fatal wound, surrounded by well-wishers and reporters.

The sound of Doctor LeGrande opening the door from inside of Moore's room snapped Smith back to reality.

"I'm going to my hotel," he said to Smith. "Mr. Moore is resting." LeGrande pointed down the hall toward the nurse's station. "I'm leaving word for them to check on him every fifteen minutes. Check credentials every time. I don't care if it's always the same person."

"Yes, Sir," said Smith.

The rest of Smith's shift passed slowly and uneventfully. He was glad when Danny Park showed up a half hour early for his midnight shift.

*   *   *

The police officer, a tall, solidly-built woman, looked curiously out of the corner of her eye at Danny Park.

Park stood outside Moore's door with his legs spread wide apart, his crotch almost touching the floor. His hands were clasped in front of him in a prayer-like position. He breathed deep and hard, pressing his hands together forcefully with each exhale. Perfect concentration. Park could not only see the cop's strange looks with his peripheral vision, he could hear every sound around him. Two nurses chatted at their station down the hall. The rhythm of fluorescent lights humming was occasionally broken by the sound of the elevator soaring up and down the shafts.

The officer leaned closer to Park as if trying to study his movements. She then walked over to him and tapped his leg with her tonfa stick. "I assume you got a permit for that."

Park stood up, the leg of his pants once again concealing the holstered Baretta Cougar.

"You assume correctly, officer ...?"

"Rivera," she said. "Natalie Rivera." Rivera tilted her head toward Moore's room. "How's your boss doing?"

"He's gonna be okay." Park smiled at Rivera, noticing for the first time her sleepy brown eyes. She wore no make-up but her soft, pink lips commanded attention. Park wondered if they tasted as sweet as they looked. "I shot the perp," he blurted. Rivera smiled, her lips pressed tightly together. An understanding smile. As if she knew exactly where Park was coming from. He may not have been able to prevent the shooting, but at least he got the guy who did it.

"What's your style?" said Rivera. She stood in front of him, knees slightly bent and her feet a little wider than shoulder width, as if preparing to lunge forward. She held the middle of the tonfa stick firmly in her right hand as she rotated her left hand around the top.

"What?"

"Tae Kwon Do? Kung Fu? You know."

Park realized he was holding his breath. "Oh," he said with a heavy exhale. "Tae Kwon Do—fifth dan."

"Kempo. Third degree," said Rivera. She took off her police cap and shook out her long brown hair. "There's nothing like the hard styles."

"I know what you mean," said Park. "Soft just doesn't have the intention, or the focus." Park cracked the air with a punch.

Rivera swung her leg high above her head, and then brought the heel of her shoe down sharply toward the floor.

Park smiled. "Nice axe kick."

"You'll have to show me *your* stuff sometime," said Rivera. She then stuffed her hair back in her cap, winked at Park, and returned to her post.

The rest of the shift passed quickly for Park. He and Rivera made breakfast plans and talked mostly about martial arts and police training. The duty nurse, still following Doctor LeGrande's orders during Smith's shift, entered the room to check Edwin Moore's vitals every fifteen minutes. Rivera and Park took turns checking the woman's credentials—and listening to her complain. Park almost forgot how depressed he was about failing to protect Edwin Moore.

Lucas Green looked bleary-eyed when he showed up to relieve Danny Park at six fifteen. Officer Rivera had already been replaced by a short, overweight cop who had his nose buried in a newspaper.

"You're late, Lucas. I have a breakfast date."

"Chill out, Confucius. I've been up all night working the door at The Parrot."

"Confucius was Chinese, asshole." Park jabbed a finger into Lucas' enormous chest.

"Chinese asshole, Korean asshole—what's the difference." The cop laughed behind his newspaper. Park rolled his eyes, then turned and walked away.

The elevator pinged and Dr. LeGrande emerged, with two hospital workers at his heels pushing a gurney. Lucas opened the door to Moore's room. "Mornin', Doctor," said Lucas.

LeGrande let the orderlies enter first, stopping for a moment to speak with Lucas. "We're taking Mr. Moore to the O.R. He'll be in surgery for most of your shift and I want you outside that operating room." LeGrande turned to the cop. "Okay, officer ...?" LeGrande leaned closer to read the nameplate. "... Ricowsky."

The cop looked up from his newspaper. "Hey, Doc, I'm not one of your rent-a-goons."

LeGrande reached into his jacket pocket. Ricowsky instinctively took his right hand off his paper and moved it close to his gun belt. The UAAC's second-in-command held a business card under the officer's nose. "This is the mayor's private number. Maybe you'd like to call him yourself and ask him about the cooperation and protection he has promised from the NYPD."

Ricowsky looked disdainfully over at Lucas, then back at LeGrande. "I'll baby-sit your boys. Don't get your panties in a bunch."

"Rest assured, officer, this will be your last day pulling this duty."

LeGrande then entered Moore's room, emerging a few minutes later at the head of the gurney, speaking quietly to Edwin Moore. Moore's eyes were closed and the lower part of his face was bandaged. Bloody shadows crept through the gauze. Lucas walked briskly on the left side of the stretcher as they made their way to the patient elevator. Ricowsky walked a few paces behind and almost missed the elevator to the O.R. floor.

Outside of Operating Room 6, Ricowsky continued to bury his head in his newspaper, barely looking up, even when doctors and other hospital workers would pass within a few feet of the doorway. Lucas stood vigilant and silent, investigating every motion, every sound with what he fancied as cat-like senses. His coach used to tell him that he performed as if he could smell a hole in the offense before it happened. Some of his teammates had ribbed him by calling him The Psychic Psycho because of his ability to predict the opposing teams' strategy.

Bull, he thought. *Some psychic.* He looked at his NFC Championship ring and twirled it a few times around his finger. He sure as hell missed the tackle this time. It was remarkable that Moore hadn't ordered LeGrande to fire all their sorry asses. Lucas hoped that he would get a chance to make it up to Moore. Maybe someone would try to get into the operating room and he could make a stand right here. Take a bullet to the shoulder and take out five or six of the bad guys.

Lucas looked over at officer Ricowsky. *First they shoot him,* he thought. Ricowksy looked over.

"What?" said Ricowsky.

"Nothing." Lucas smiled. Ricowsky mumbled something under his breath that sounded like 'stupid nigger.'

Lucas felt a white hot fury churning in his gut. He walked over to the cop and leaned into him until they were nose to nose. "What's your problem?"

Ricowsky pushed him away. "You could be my problem. Give me a reason and your ass will be locked up and Malcolm X in there will have *nobody* outside his door."

Lucas shook his head, disgusted. "How the hell does the NYPD put somebody like you here?"

Ricowsky laughed. "Easy. You have a scumbag lieutenant who knows you can't stand trouble makers and thinks busting your balls is entertainment."

Now it was Lucas' turn to snicker. "Ain't that a kick in the teeth? I'm pulling guard duty with a racist cop."

Ricowsky threw his newspaper on the floor and took his nightstick out of his belt. "Racist? You and your boss are the racists." He pointed his stick behind him toward the operating room door. "Do you know how many cops were hurt in Sunday's riots? Don't tell me that Moore didn't incite that crap."

"Mr. Moore didn't incite anything. You're not only a racist, you're also stupid."

Ricowksy swung the police club at Lucas' head. Lucas blocked it, twisted the club around and easily disarmed the cop. Ricowsky went for his gun and Lucas pressed the stick with both hands against the man's throat, pinning him against the wall. Ricowsky's bulging, tearful eyes pleaded for release. Lucas took a deep breath, overcoming his urge to crush the cop's windpipe.

Ricowsky sank to the floor, choking and gasping, when Lucas released him. Lucas handed Ricowsky back his nightstick and held out his arms, resigned to getting arrested. Ricowksy snatched the stick and stood up, ignoring Lucas' surrendering gesture.

"Stay the hell out of my face," said Ricowsky. Both men returned to their positions. The handful of hospital personnel that started to gather because of the commotion dispersed. The two men wouldn't so much as look at each other for the rest of their shift.

Three hours later Edwin Moore was moved into recovery. Muscle and bone marrow had been removed from his thigh to aid in the reconstruction of his jaw. By the time Moore was returned to his room, Lucas' shift was over and Henry Perkins took over.

*   *   *

Huck Perkins stood with his chest muscles practically bulging out of his suit jacket. The six-foot-four ex-wrestler had just come from a local gym, where he had been pumping iron for the last four hours. Dr. LeGrande emerged from Edwin Moore's room looking haggard, his shirttail untucked and at least a day's stubble on his face.

"Doc," said Perkins, with a quick nod of his head.

"Doctor LeGrande," the physician corrected.

Doctor asswipe, thought Perkins. "Sorry, Doctor LeGrande," he said. "How is he?"

LeGrande sighed. "Mr. Moore will probably have to communicate using a pencil and paper for a while. I do expect him to recover. Where the hell is the city cop?"

Perkins shrugged. "The last one left when I relieved Lucas. Said he was supposed to leave at noon so at noon he was leaving."

Both men turned to see a uniformed cop running up the

hallway. Perkins noticed the officer's well-defined build as he approached. Body builders check out a man's physique as much as they do a woman's. Sometimes more so. A primal thing, Perkins always thought. An instinctive size-up of the competition.

The cop, a black man in his late thirties, showed no sign of fatigue when he reached Perkins and LeGrande. The man was obviously in good shape.

"The east elevators are out," he said apologetically, then extended a hand to Perkins. "Bill Little."

Strong handshake, thought Perkins. "Huck. Huck Perkins."

The cop then turned to LeGrande and seemed to abandon an attempt to shake his hand. He gave an almost imperceptible nod instead, which LeGrande returned.

"I'm going to wait inside for Mr. Moore to wake up. I'm expecting Terrance Al-Aziz before one o'clock. Knock on the door softly when Mr. Al-Aziz arrives."

"Will do," said Perkins, then rolled his eyes as LeGrande went into Moore's room. "Aziz? Coming here?" said Little.

Perkins shrugged. "I guess so."

Officer Little let out a long whistle. "Can only be something bad."

"My guess is that the good doctor in there is gonna try to replace us with soldiers from The New Islamic State. They've been trying to align with Mr. Moore for a long time."

"Really?" said Little, staring curiously at Perkins.

"What?"

"I can't place it exactly, but you look familiar." Little stepped closer to Perkins, then snapped his fingers. "O'Finn. Huckleberry O'Finn from the WWA."

"Another life. One of many."

"My kids and I never miss Wrestlefest. You last wrestled in ninety four, right?"

54

"Things started getting too weird, even for professional wrestling. After that fiasco—a fruitcake jumping in the ring—I said enough of this." Perkins looked down at the ground, a sudden wave of regret passing through him. "Should have stayed there," he mumbled. *At least I was a success there*, he thought. Nobody got shot there because he didn't do his job. He remembered something that one of his instructors had said during his 'all-for-naught' secret-service training - 'never trust any police department or government agency to secure a site prior to your assignment's arrival. Constantly sweep the room with your eyes for any suspicious movement. It's when you feel safe that you're probably not.'

The sound of Little's voice commanded Perkins' attention. "Either Aziz is here or we're about to be mugged by five brothers in Armani suits."

Perkins looked down the hall to see the imposing figure of Terrance Al-Aziz walking toward them, surrounded by four of his bodyguards. Al-Aziz wore a dark green, double-breasted suit. His bodyguards wore black. When they reached the doorway, the two lead bodyguards stepped aside to let Al-Aziz pass. Perkins stepped in front of the Islamic leader. Al-Aziz stepped back, and with a slight gesture of his eyes, sent two of his guards to confront Perkins. The ex-wrestler effortlessly pushed the two men away.

"Easy, boys."

Little stepped next to Perkins. The big cop slowly and deliberately placed his hand on the handle of his service pistol.

Al-Aziz stepped forward, his entourage surrounding him. Aziz stood almost a head shorter than Perkins. He smiled and gently placed a hand on the huge man's shoulder. "The Honorable Terrance Al-Aziz to see Dr. LeGrande."

Without taking his eyes off Al-Aziz, Perkins reached behind him and gently tapped on the door. A moment later, LeGrande opened the door and let Al-Aziz inside. The bodyguards stepped back and stood four abreast like military police, their eyes staring straight ahead.

Perkins and Little looked at each other and shrugged.

"Something tells me I'm gonna be looking for a new job pretty soon," said Perkins.

Little shook his head. "I don't think Moore will get in bed with Aziz. At least I hope not."

"He will if LeGrande has his way," said Perkins. "Then things could get complicated."

"For all of us," said Little.

Not if I have anything to do with it, thought Perkins. The Secret Service may have found him unfit for duty, but Edwin Moore and the NAAC hadn't. He and the rest of the crew may have blown it the other night, but he wasn't going to sit back and watch the likes of Carl LeGrande sell out on Edwin Moore and ruin Henry Perkins' last chance for greatness.

No, Sir.

6

Amy Walsh looked relieved to see Martin walk through the door. She was running with a bottle of cough medicine in one hand, a spoon in the other. She stopped at the landing to give her husband a peck on the cheek.

"Thank God," she said. "All hell's breaking loose. Alex is coughing his head off; I think he's coming down with an ear infection. Anthony slipped off the steppy-stool while brushing his teeth and bit his tongue. He's in his bed, been crying for the last twenty minutes. He threw his sneaker at Alex and hit him in the eye. Now Alex is crying too." She started to walk up the stairs. "Come on, come on. Let's go."

Am I going to miss this? thought Walsh. *I truly am.* He dutifully followed Amy up the stairs. She pointed toward Anthony's room. "I'll take Alex," she said. Walsh entered his youngest boy's room and found him buried under his covers, whimpering. Walsh sat on the side of the bed and gently touched the spot where he assumed the five-year-old's head was.

"Anthony?"

The boy flipped the covers off and hugged his dad. "I bit my tongue, Daddy." Walsh's tearful son held up a damp towel. Tiny spots of blood stained the white terrycloth. Walsh took the towel and held it up to the light.

"Wow!" said Walsh. "Major blood loss. I can't believe how strong you are."

"Really?" said Anthony, his eyes suddenly bright and wide.

"Sure. Most kids would be screaming. Let's see the damage." Walsh stuck out his tongue. Anthony stuck out his, giggling. "You know what I think?"

Anthony put his tongue back in. "What?"

"I think you're gonna have to eat ice cream for breakfast."

"Really!"

"You bet. But ... you have to be sleeping in five minutes."

Anthony pulled the covers up to his neck. Walsh leaned over and kissed him on the forehead.

"Goodnight, little bud."

Walsh closed the door to Anthony's room, leaving a crack so the hallway light could sneak in. Amy was just closing the door to Alex's room. She looked up at Walsh, smiling.

Then the smile quickly faded. "Let's go downstairs," she said. "I know this isn't going to be good."

Amy bounded down the stairs. Before Walsh reached the landing he could hear Amy moving the kitchen chairs into place. The living room is great for small talk and planning vacations. The bedroom lends itself well to a recap of the day's events. Serious discussions take place in the kitchen. Walsh remembered something a trainer at the FBI academy had once told him about interviewing potential witnesses and informants in their homes. If possible, agents should meet with them in their kitchens where the most important decisions are made.

The look on Amy's face was neutral, non-committal.

She didn't look angry or surprised. Walsh sat opposite his wife. "I'm sorry," he said. "Is it that obvious?"

"I've only seen that look a few times before and every time it was trouble."

"The situation with Edwin Moore has become complicated."

"The news said he was out of danger." Amy examined her fingernails as she spoke. "That true?"

Walsh nodded slowly. "We've got some damage control."

Amy looked up, her hands now folded tightly. Her eyes were moist and some anger was starting to filter through as she spoke. "How long?"

"Three months. I might be able to come home some weekends. My cover could have a business or something that takes me out of town on occasion."

Amy managed a tight smile. "I'll have to thank Dalton next time I see him."

A master in the art of sarcasm, thought Walsh. He was tempted for a second to fight fire with fire, then decided against it. She had every right to be pissed. Walsh had turned down several undercover assignments over the past two years. "Deep-cover assignments are behind me," he had said. "Leave that stuff to the young guys." He reached over and placed his hand on hers. He was grateful that she didn't pull away.

"I'm not sure that I really want to know this. How dangerous?"

"Practically risk free." Walsh found it difficult to look his wife in the eye. He felt like a man who had been unfaithful. The usually distant and quiet thoughts that existed during conversation were now loud and demanding. Amy said something that Walsh didn't quite get. He thought her lips mouthed, "Bullcrap."

"You know I can't tell you all the details. When I'm debriefed they'll polygraph me. If something goes wrong with

BY ANY MEANS NECESSARY

the assignment, one of the suits is gonna ask me whether or not I talked to anyone about the operation."

To Walsh's surprise, Amy walked behind him, placed her arms around his neck, and rested her chin on his shoulder. She rubbed his chest softly as she whispered in his ear. "This is the last time we're going through this."

She kissed him on the cheek and left the room.

Walsh sat back and gulped down the rest of his coffee. *Son-of-a-gun,* he thought. There was no way he could get Amy to understand the importance of this assignment without giving every detail. She was pissed now. Imagine how pissed she'd be if she knew about his partner, Jacobson. Walsh decided he was getting off easy. He'd make it up to Amy some day.

He pushed the kitchen chair in and headed upstairs. *Oh no, he* thought. *Now I have to tell her I promised Anthony ice cream for breakfast.*

*   *   *

Katherine Jacobson placed her right heel high against the closet door and slowly pressed her chest on her thigh. The nightly ritual of stretching had kept her as limber as any of the youngsters at the karate gym. She hoped she would get a chance to work out while she and Walsh were on assignment. She tried to imagine what Walsh's wife would think about her husband living with a female partner. She herself would never stand for it and she didn't see how any woman could.

Jacobson turned to view herself in the floor-to-ceiling mirror. She poked at the tiny bit of flab on her waistline. *No way to avoid it, I guess.* She was wearing a skin-tone leotard that seemed to accentuate all her imperfections. The phone rang as she thought of her mother lecturing her on how she'd better hurry up and marry before her body started to sag.

She took a deep breath and answered the phone.

"Hi, Mom."

"Now you're clairvoyant all of a sudden. Mrs. Millstein's son is supposedly clairvoyant. At least that's what she says every Saturday after temple. 'Michael always knows how to cheer up his mom,' she says. 'Brings me flowers just when I think how nice it would be to have a new bouquet to brighten up the dining room. He stops by with candy on a Sunday afternoon for no reason. He really knows what his mother needs.' Then she says how she's all alone since Murray died and blah, blah, blah ...'"

"Is there a point to this story, Mother?" Jacobson extended a slow-motion kick toward the mirror as she held the cordless phone to her ear.

"So your father tells me you called earlier. What's this about going away for a few months? You're quitting your job?"

Jacobson threw two roundhouse kicks, then retracted her leg and executed a full split to the floor. "I'm going away *for* the job, Mother." She brought herself up to a standing position without using her hands, then walked over and sat on the edge of the bed. "It's an undercover assignment," she blurted, then regretted it immediately. Her mother didn't have to know that. She could have told her anything but that defiant urge took over and ... boom!

"What! You're a *girl,* for God's sake!"

"Yes, Mother. I am a woman."

"Tell them no." Mrs. Jacobson's voice started to break as she called to her husband with what sounded, through the muffled sound of a half-covered receiver, like "Harry, they're sending Katherine on a dangerous job."

"Mother!" Jacobson screamed into the phone.

"How can you do this to us?" She heard a click, then her father's voice, probably from the bedroom extension.

"You didn't say anything about dangerous, Katherine."

Jacobson wanted to slam the phone down and forget the whole thing. Let them wonder where she was. Then she

61

thought of her mother calling FBI headquarters in Washington every day, demanding to know the whereabouts of her little girl Katherine, who, in her mother's mind, never seemed to age past ten in her ability to care for herself. "It's not dangerous, Dad. I really can't talk much about it, but I promise everything is going to be all right."

"How much of it *can* you talk about?" said Mrs. Jacobson, with just a touch of sarcasm in her voice. "Don't say we didn't care when some crazy is following you through a dark basement with a big gun aimed at your head."

Jacobson wondered for a second if she should help spearhead a new law wherein grown children could forbid their parents to watch television. "I'll call you sometimes to let you know that I'm good."

The silence that followed was awkward. As much as Jacobson wanted to shut her mother up, it somehow didn't seem right once she had done it.

"Mom? Daddy?"

"Only if you do it without blowing your cover. They sometimes get caught when they try to call in, you know. You never know who's listening. You have to be careful."

"Yes," her dad agreed. "Make your call from a public phone."

Jacobson wasn't sure if she wanted to laugh or cry. "Look," she said. "I love you. I don't have to report to the office until ten tomorrow so why don't I stop by at eight and we'll say goodbye then?"

"I could come over now and help you pack because ..." Katherine's father interrupted her mom. "Goodnight, Katherine. We'll see you tomorrow."

"Goodnight." Jacobson sprawled across the bed. She fell asleep in moments, not bothering to shut off the light.

* * *

Avi Pearlman sat stiff-necked in an unfinished oak chair positioned in front of a mirror. His father, Yeheudah, and his uncle, Shulman Stein, stood on either side of him. The three men bowed their heads, then rocked gently back and forth as Shulman began to pray.

Grant a blessing for our son—for the time has come.
See him silent and ready—and his eyes glow.
See evening fall, wind in the tree tops. The pine quivers.
There'll be battle soon. And his is just one.
Bless him, my Lord. For the time has come.
Stars are lit and many enemies gather yonder.
For who shall see daylight? And who shall fall and die?
Shall victory be gained or defeat and the grave?
Bless him, my Lord, bless this fighting-man.
Bless his weapons lest they miss ... bless his home.
Bless this people, its youth and fighters,
Until the battle is done.
He has just left silently and his footsteps fade,
Heavy murk and night in mountains,
Bless him—for the time has come.
Grant a blessing for our son.

Yeheudah kissed his son on the forehead, then nodded solemnly to Shulman Stein. Stein was the cousin of a retired Mossad general, and besides being one of the community's most beloved Rabbis, he was also the Sons Elohim's high-tech weapons and surveillance expert. Tonight he would transform Yeheudah's son into something despicable in the eyes of all Jews.

Avi closed his eyes as Stein wrapped a white sheet around him and fastened it behind his neck. Yeheudah kneeled beside the chair, clenched his son's hand, and pressed it against his cheek. He wept quietly, his eyes closed tightly. Avi shut his eyes as well, hoping he could press them closed tight enough to keep the tears from flowing through.

God forgive us, he thought as the sound of the electric shears buzzed around his ears. Rabbi Stein continued to pray as he removed Avi's golden hair. In his prayer he thanked God for the courage of their young soldier and compared him to Gideon and his conquest of the Midianites. Avi prepared himself as best he could before opening his eyes. He hoped to God that they were doing the right thing.

He let his image come slowly into focus. It helped that the person in the mirror wasn't immediately recognizable. Avi would play the role with the detachment of a great stage actor. This hairless man wasn't him. This hairless man was the Sword of Gideon. A temporary shell that would be used to destroy their enemy.

Stein brushed away some hair from Avi's neck and removed the sheet from his chest. "Take off your shirt now."

Yeheudah stood up and helped his son maneuver out of his suspenders and remove his shirt. Avi enjoyed physical labor, always volunteering to haul freight about the warehouse or chop wood for the stove during winter rather than use the power splitter. His muscular body reflected such efforts.

"I'm only going to give you two. One here." He pointed to the left side of Avi's chest. "And one here on your right arm." He then outlined a swastika on Avi's chest using an eyeliner pencil. Avi felt a surge through his body like the force of an electric shock. He quivered and almost lost his breath. Yeheudah buried his face in his hands and let out a long, agonizing wail. Stein then outlined two lightning bolts on Avi's arm—the mark of Hitler's dreaded SS.

With the dispassionate movements of a surgeon, Stein removed a tattooing needle from his bag and plugged the cord into the wall socket. "Are you ready, Avi?"

Avi nodded.

"Yeheudah?"

Yeheudah had walked over to the other side of the room and was sitting on the couch, rocking vigorously and praying rapidly.

"This ink will start to fade by itself in about two months. Hopefully we will have removed these disgraceful symbols before then."

Avi shut his eyes tightly once more. In about a week, when the tattoos healed, he would start his mission as a young man from Bay Ridge, Brooklyn named Michael Dirks—assassin of Matthew Pates.

7

Matthew Pates would often enter the assembly barracks, or "K" building as it was detailed on the compound map, long after all the other members were present and seated. He strode to the podium dressed in a black SWAT assault uniform, an AMT 45 Hardballer pistol holstered to his waist. The Aryan Resistance Christian Soldiers' banner, depicting the silhouette of three soldiers raising a cross, was draped across the wall behind him.

Pates looked out over the small assembly of twenty of ARCS' highest-ranking members. Fred Mills, always stroking his beard, was a former member of a Pittsburgh biker gang called Satan's Chosen. The forty-year-old biker owned the truck rental and repair shop just outside Milton and had a knack for making friends. He was also good with explosives. Pates would use him for recruitment campaigns and to help organize the otherwise loosely-banded skinheads.

Next to Mills sat Brian Hastings, the ARCS lawyer who had masterminded the plot to get, as he put it, "the Jews and niggers to go at each other's throats." Hastings had personally recommended Raymond Hill to effect Edwin Moore's execution. They all shared some regret and pain that their brave soldier was now in the custody of the Zionist Occupational Government.

Pates smiled warmly at the man sitting to Mills' right—Pastor John Hampton. Pastor Hampton returned the smile. The pulpit-pounding preacher could always be counted on to deliver a Sunday sermon that supported the cause of the faithful. In private, and at ARCS rallies, he would often pronounce that the Western Europeans who first inhabited America were the true Israelites and are directly descended from the original twelve tribes described in the books of Moses.

Pates cleared his throat.

"Brothers of ARCS—good afternoon." Some of the men mumbled a response. Others just nodded. "We are nearing the hour of the battle," Pates continued. "Niggers are running wild through the streets of America's cities, murdering, raping and robbing our people while the Jew lawyers make a mockery of everything that is good and decent by creating revolving doors in the country's courtrooms."

Jimmy Price, the youngest ARCS officer, raised his fist in the air. He was seated in the rear of the room, his six-five posture placing him a head above the rest of the members. "ARCS total victory!" he shouted.

Pates held up his hand for quiet. "Our brother Raymond is in the custody of the ZOG. We have to be very careful. Don't be surprised if those stooges of the Zionist government—the FBI—come around to your homes and your businesses asking about Ray. Hold strong, brothers. Remember, no matter what they tell you, there is no proof that Ray wasn't acting on his own." Pates let the last statement sink in. He searched for dissenting eyes and stopped when he got to Paul Hill. "You have something to say, Paul?"

Raymond Hill's brother stood up. Paul was twenty-six, built strong and wiry. His intense loyalty to ARCS was rivaled only by his loyalty to his big brother, Raymond. Raymond had once been mistaken for his younger brother by a witness to the beating of a black soldier, who had the misfortune of walking out of a Burger King with his white girlfriend the same time Paul Hill was passing by in a car with two of his friends. Raymond Hill did two years at Leavenworth.

"Raymond deserves better," was all Paul Hill said.

"Raymond is a soldier." Pates waved his hand over the assembly. "Like all of us. We have all taken an oath to support the cause of white supremacy. To make sure that our children do not have to live like us in a country run by an occupational government that cares more about giving niggers a free lunch than the proliferation of its founding race."

"Say it!" someone shouted.

"White Power!" said Jimmy Price.

Pates again called for quiet. "Providing we can devise a way to funnel the money through, Raymond will get all his legal fees paid through the ARCS emergency fund." Pates meant this message for everyone, but looked directly at Paul Hill. "If an opportunity presents itself, we'll conduct a rescue. Brian Hastings will keep me informed." Pates raised an eyebrow and tilted his head slightly as if to say to Hill, "Satisfied?"

Paul Hill returned a contented look.

"Very well," said Pates. "Jimmy Price will take over for Ray during training." ARCS' compound was so well entrenched in the deeply forested valley of the Western Pennsylvanian Mountain range, that only a low-flying heli-copter would be able to detect it. Pates' goal for ARCS was to have over two thousand trainees within a year.

"This was only a minor skirmish in the big battle," said Pates. "We have set in motion a force that cannot be stopped. We have right on our side. We have Yahweh on our side. The son of Yahweh called all Jews the sons and daughters of Satan and what happened?"

"The despicable Jews crucified him!" shouted Pastor Hampton.

Affirmations rumbled through the wood and aluminum building. "This is the dawn of the new white nation," Pates continued. "The Jews and the mud people will battle each other and we'll be there to wipe up the mess and establish the white nation. The Christ-killers will be executed. Niggers will be shipped back to Africa. Mexicans to Mexico." Pates pointed his fingers as if touching various spots on a huge map visible only to him. "We can dump all yellow, slant-eyes in China for all I care."

ARCS' officers clapped and cheered. Pates took a deep breath, savoring the applause. He could feel the nerve-endings of his skin tingle as if they were reaching out to absorb the power generated by his loyal brethren. Pates pressed a couple of buttons on the podium. A screen lowered behind him and the lights dimmed. Using a small remote control, he activated the slide projector that was mounted on the rear wall. A color-coded map of North America appeared on the screen. Pates removed a pointer from the podium's cabinet and tapped the end on the border between Canada and the United States.

"When we gain control, the borders to Canada and Mexico will be sealed and cut off to immigration. Mexico forever. Canada, until they also become a white nation."

Pates clicked the remote and another slide came into view—a red brick building, taller than the picture frame could capture.

"This is a picture of Jerusalem Hospital on East End Avenue in *Jew* York. In approximately one month two of our most courageous soldiers will drive an ambulance ..." He clicked to the next picture. Two men in dark, paint-covered overalls, wearing goggles and ear-to-ear grins, were posing in front of a vehicle they were obviously customizing to look like a New York City EMS ambulance, "... straight into the emergency room."

70

Pates turned the projector off. "Bill Myrtle says he can mix some body paint from his funeral home and make our boys look just like niggers."

Jimmy Price, one of the goggled men from the slide, raised his hand. Pates nodded for him to speak "We're gonna haul the ambulance inside the rig as far as the New Jersey Turnpike. We unload it, then Fred will drive the rig, and I'll drive the ambulance into the city. The rig gets parked in Harlem near the West Side Highway. Then we drive the ambulance to the hospital and flick the three-minute clock. Two blocks west is an access plate which Ray and I scoped out when we were in New York three months ago. It leads underground to a subway tunnel. By the time they know what hit them, Fred and I will be on the train to pick up our rig and head home."

Hampton started clapping, followed by the entire assembly. Pates called the meeting to an end and said he looked forward to seeing everyone at the weekend maneuvers.

*　　*　　*

Walsh and Jacobson didn't talk much for the first hour of the trip to Western Pennsylvania. Walsh drove and Jacobson relaxed in the passenger seat, sleeping behind her Ray Bans as they cruised on Interstate 80.

It had been a hectic three days. Amy was detached but acting cordial, as Walsh waited around for the kids to wake up before he reported to an anxious Dalton Leverick. Dalton was a little nervous because they had very little time to prepare all the details of their cover and to determine the best way to infiltrate ARCS and arrest Matthew Pates. After meeting for almost fourteen hours with Leverick and Jacobson, Walsh dreamed up a scheme that Leverick liked so much he was ticked he hadn't thought of it himself. Jacobson had gotten up from the conference table to stretch her legs and get some hot

71

water so she could make another cup of that funky-smelling orange tea. The conversation during the breaks got on to karate training, and it turned out that she and Walsh knew some of the same people in the martial arts field.

"That's it," Walsh had said. He waved his hand in the air as if creating an invisible marquee. "The Brotherhood of Yahweh Martial Arts Academy."

Jacobson almost dropped her teacup. "What?"

Dalton Leverick laughed. "Let me guess. Talented martial arts couple ..."

"... let's not forget zealously religious," Walsh interrupted.

"Of course," said Leverick. "Talented and zealously religious couple opens karate studio in Pittsburgh suburb."

"White Christians only," said Jacobson, obviously wanting Walsh and Leverick to know she was on top of things.

Leverick started singing, "I'm dreaming of a white Christian."

Walsh put his hand on Jacobson's shoulder. "The mind is the first thing to go, Jacobson. Dalton will soon be eligible for a mental disability discharge."

"I can't be far behind him," said Jacobson. "My parents were worried about me going undercover. I'll have to tell them I was posing as a criminal. A Goy would be too much for them to handle!"

The three agents had laughed for a long time. Too many hours and too little food had made them light-headed, and prone to giddiness.

Walsh found himself laughing out loud again as he drove down the highway.

"What's so funny?" asked Jacobson.

"You're up," said Walsh, glancing over for a second.

"Where are we?"

"Crossed the Jersey-Pennsylvania border about a half hour ago. Another three hours or so." Walsh looked in the rearview mirror at the U-Haul they had in tow. The agents had agreed that it would be more practical to arrive in Milton with a few essentials, and have the rest of their belongings delivered by moving van once they had secured a house or apartment. Leverick was working on their past lives in New York, creating a trail of two people who never were, complete with high school records, credit histories, and old friends and neighbors who would verify their identities.

"You want to go over it again?"

Jacobson shrugged. "Sure. It'll kill some time." She placed her hands behind her head and leaned back. "You're Edward Hess, thirty-six years old. I'm your adorable wife, Kimberly Hess, thirty-one. Your friends call you Eddie."

"What?"

"I thought I'd add that."

"Why not Kimmy?"

Jacobson slapped Walsh on the shoulder. "Kim. Except you. You call me Kimberly."

Walsh glanced at his new partner and smiled. "Okay, Kimberly." Before returning his eyes to the road Walsh looked down and noticed Jacobson had slipped off her running shoes. Her bare feet seemed to accentuate the shape of her legs, curving invitingly toward her bright yellow shorts. *Damn,* thought Walsh. There are hazards to this assignment that I haven't really considered.

"Where am I from?" said Walsh, pushing his mind back to business.

"Queens, New York." Jacobson placed her foot on the dashboard. "Me, I'm from Albany. We met at a martial arts tournament which was held at my college."

"Married four years later," said Walsh. "No kids."

"Opened up a karate school in Brooklyn shortly there-after. Went out of business when we started incorporating religious and racist teaching into our training."

"The unbelievers literally ran us out of town," said

Walsh. "So here we are to give it another go in Milton, Pennsylvania. What are our educational backgrounds?"

"You only finished high school, then trained as an electrician. I, on the other hand, have a degree in art history."

For the next hour or so they talked about procedural items. They would file their status reports using a laptop computer and a cellular modem line, technology courtesy of the Central Intelligence Agency. Thanks to the new technology they wouldn't have to create opportunities to get to a secure phone line. Walsh had insisted as part of their cover that the Hesses owned a small apartment building in Brooklyn that they would have to occasionally visit. This way, if the assignment dragged on too long, Walsh could squeeze a few quick visits in to Amy and the kids. Since the DEA already owned a building in which they conducted various operations, adjusting the records to reflect ownership by Edward and Kimberly Hess would be a cinch. The closer Walsh and Jacobson would get to ARCS's upper echelon, the more likely Pates would check out their backgrounds.

When the agents arrived in front of the real estate office in downtown Milton, Jacobson slipped on her engagement and wedding rings. Walsh wore his own wedding band. He made a fist and studied it for a moment. He hadn't told Amy that he would be partnering with a female agent. There was a directive from the Bureau not to tell family members specific details about an assignment. Amazing, he thought, how following the rules was easy when it suited his purposes. Part of him wanted to be forthcoming with Amy and tell her. Another part of him, the part that won out, figured, 'why complicate matters?' Jacobson was just another agent. The fact that she was female wouldn't matter. Walsh thought this just as his partner walked from the car toward the red brick building, which housed the tiny real estate office. Two men turned their heads to look at Jacobson as they passed. Walsh could swear one of them said something about her attractive rear end.

74

Mr. Van Dickinson introduced himself to the couple and welcomed them to Milton.

"Edward Hess," said Walsh, shaking the man's hand. Van Dickinson had a weak grip, and a disturbing gaze. The kind of look that said 'I trust nobody.' His blue, badly-wrinkled sport coat was about two sizes too big. He was beardless now. Gone was the goatee in the FBI file surveillance photo taken of him at an American Nazi Party rally in South Carolina. Van Dickinson was suspected of being a member of ARCS, though one of low rank. "This is my wife, Kim."

"A pleasure, Mrs. Hess." He invited the couple to sit at a small conference table in a corner of the office.

"Your letter said you wanted to see some storefront space as well. If you don't mind me asking, what kind of business are you in?"

Walsh removed a business card from his shirt pocket and handed it to the real estate agent. "It's our old address in New York City, but the name will be the same."

"Interesting logo," said Van Dickinson as he placed the card down on the table. "We have a listing on Montgomery Street. I can't think of a more appropriate location for a ..." He tapped his finger on the business card, "... The Brotherhood of Yahweh Martial Arts Academy. Very unique concept."

"We think so," said Jacobson. She leaned forward slightly and whispered. "Unique and exclusive."

"There's nothing wrong with white Christians desiring to be with their own, Mrs. Hess. I think you'll find plenty of support here for your school."

"Brooklyn wasn't ready for it," said Walsh.

Van Dickinson shook his head. "I could see how that would be a problem in any part of New York."

Walsh looked at Jacobson. She was nodding her head like she agreed with every word that Van Dickinson had said. "Maybe you'd like to take an introductory lesson once we get set up," she said.

Van Dickinson laughed. "I don't know about myself, but I have an eighteen-year-old who might want to."

"It would be our pleasure, Mr. Van Dickinson," said Walsh. "My wife and I are looking forward to becoming part of the community." Walsh stood up. "Shall we find ourselves a home, Honey?" He held his hand out for his partner. *Don't enjoy this assignment too much, Martin*, he thought. Things are bound to get ugly.

8

Edwin Moore dreamed that things were different. In his dream, he looked in the mirror and saw a gray-haired and wrinkled man smiling back at him. He was smiling because the world was different now, more than thirty years after his United African-American Coalition had taken to the streets, airwaves, computer networks and courts. In the early 2000's, movements promulgating respect and equality among all people had taken the country by storm. Citizens by the millions had poured into their churches, synagogues, mosques and temples to pray for peace, security, and prosperity for all nations under God. The murder rate, which for a typical city like New York had been three people a day in the late nineties, was now down to a few dozen for the entire country. People cared about the environment like never before, and most of the world's energy was being supplied through the harnessing of solar power. Police departments had been trimmed by eighty percent, and millions of firearms had been melted down and recycled into lawnmowers and power tools. Life was good.

Moore smiled wider, admiring his still brilliantly white

teeth. He suddenly thought about how strange that was. He remembered his teeth yellowing at some point in his life, and they seemed to magically accommodate his thoughts, changing color first to yellow ... then green ... then black. Then, as if being ground down by an invisible grindstone, they began to disintegrate, millimeter by millimeter. The searing pain mainlined from his jaw to the base of his skull, and he tried to wail in excruciating agony, but could not utter a sound. The invisible gnasher tore apart his gums and lips, sending streams of metallic-tasting blood down his throat. *Help,* he thought. *Help,* he tried to scream, but could manage only a long, agonized groan.

"Edwin." He could hear Dr. LeGrande's voice calling from a distance. "Edwin." Closer now. "Edwin." Near him. "Edwin." Right in his ear.

Moore opened his eyes to the dimly lit hospital room and the very real pain in his jaw. He looked pleadingly at LeGrande, who knew exactly what he needed. LeGrande was already preparing a shot of Demerol, which he poked into Moore's arm seconds later.

Although it was much too soon for the drug to have actually taken effect, the pain seemed to recede the moment the syringe pinched his flesh. Moore nodded a thank you.

"Try to relax, Edwin," LeGrande said. "I expected after all that sleep that you'd wake up hurting."

Moore held up his arm and tapped an imaginary timepiece.

"It's one o'clock Friday afternoon. You've been sleeping for almost sixteen hours."

Moore pointed to the laptop computer on the end table, and LeGrande handed it to him. Moore had ordered the PC hooked up to a larger monitor suspended from the television rack on the wall. Tired of writing on a notepad, Moore could now take part in conversations even when a few people were in the room. He had first used the keyboard during Tuesday's meeting with Terrance Al-Aziz.

Diary. Where is it? Moore typed.

"Don't worry," LeGrande assured him. "Your heirloom has been shipped home and is locked in your safe."

Good. Who's outside now?

"Perkins ... until six o'clock." LeGrande laid his hand on Moore's arm. "I wish you'd reconsider the agreement with Aziz." The doctor pointed toward the door. "You'd have three men—professionals—outside that door at all times."

City guaranteed officers to support my men. Are they doing it?

LeGrande nodded his head. "Don't count on that continuing once you're released."

When?

LeGrande stood up and poured two cups of water. "You're changing the subject, Edwin," he said, offering Moore a cup with a straw in it.

No, no, no, no. Al-Aziz wrong for us!!

LeGrande plopped back into his chair and sighed. He leaned his head back, looking toward the ceiling. "Edwin, Edwin. Can't you see that the movement has peaked? An alliance with Al-Aziz would breathe new life into the organization. Think of the political influence we could wield. Besides, an alliance with the Muslims will send a message to the Sons Elohim that any attempt on your life will have dire consequences."

Moore's heart thumped heavily in his chest and felt like it had jumped into his throat. Not only because the reality and memory of the attempted assassination had hit him again, but also because he saw, for the first time, something perfidious about LeGrande. They had been friends for more than twenty years. Differences of opinion were nothing new, but a serious ideological split was occurring, and he was in no shape for a fight.

FBI says wasn't Sons Elohim.

LeGrande shook his head. "Disinformation. Al-Aziz

says he has proof that the FBI is withholding information that confirms the SE's involvement." He then turned toward Moore, his hands held out in front of him. "Please, Edwin. The Muslims can provide new direction for the organization."

Al-Aziz is no Muslim. He's a fraud. Most Islamic leaders dismiss Aziz as a nut who has twisted the teachings of the Koran to fit his own anti-white, anti-government, anti-Jewish, anti-everything-the-hell else-he-does-not-like agenda. NO!!!

LeGrande placed his hand on Moore's. "Let's leave it alone for now. We have to get you back to health." LeGrande reached into his pocket and pulled out a small calendar. "You have a meeting scheduled with Governor Watkins in three weeks. You need to practice your typing."

Moore would have smiled if the lacerated muscles in his jaw allowed it. Instead, he simply nodded. At that moment, he dismissed his earlier doubts and clung to the hope that he and LeGrande could work out their differences. He had no choice. LeGrande stood up and grabbed his briefcase from the side table. "I have some work to do at the office. I'll return around ten o'clock. Can I bring you anything?"

Moore shrugged. *Some news magazines. And a big steak ... RARE!*

"I hear you, friend. You'll get there. I'll tell the nurse to check on you."

Moore stared at the door for almost ten minutes after LeGrande had walked out. He was no longer certain that he could trust Carl LeGrande.

LeGrande used the pay phone on the sidewalk outside the hospital lobby to call Al-Aziz. He took a deep breath of the early evening air. The humid air and smell of the Manhattan streets were a welcome change from the antiseptic smell of the hospital room.

The vigil across the street had dwindled to about a dozen hard-core supporters. Four of them were huddled in a tight circle, praying over a bunch of lit candles.

Idiots, thought LeGrande. *Kiss-ass, rich-kid whites wanting to show the world how liberal they are in supporting the great black leader of our time. What a crock.*

Al-Aziz answered on the second ring. "All praise be to Allah."

"Moore will not consider the alliance."

"I wish him good fortune then," Al-Aziz said. "I trust he is recovering well and will be released soon."

"Yes. I've rented a house—very quiet and very private—in Pine Hills, New York."

"Will it be safe, my friend?" Al-Aziz asked. LeGrande could picture him grinning as he spoke.

Sometimes it's necessary to deal with the devil for the sake of a people, LeGrande thought. "We'll have his four bodyguards in the house at all times. I'll be there myself when I return from my trip to Philadelphia on the nineteenth but I'm sure Mr. Moore will be in good hands until then."

"With his *four* bodyguards."

"Yes," said LeGrande, noticing that Max Smith was crossing the street toward the hospital entrance. "Smith is going in the hospital right now to relieve Henry Perkins. You remember Mr. Perkins?"

Al-Aziz grumbled something that LeGrande couldn't quite understand. Al-Aziz had been furious after the confrontation with Perkins outside Moore's room. He didn't rant about it at the time, but LeGrande had seen the fury burning in those eyes like tiny incinerators. "I'm sure Mr. Perkins and the other three will do a fine job on the ... nineteenth?"

"That's right. Besides, I doubt the Sons Elohim will be able to find out where they are."

"Hopefully. Well, I guess there is nothing more to say, Dr. LeGrande. All praise be to Allah."

LeGrande slowly placed the telephone on its hook. Although it was almost 70 degrees outside, he suddenly felt cold. He shivered as if someone had stuffed an ice cube down

81

his back. What would the price be, he wondered, for a heart turned to stone and the betrayal of a friend?

*   *   *

Pates liked to occasionally spring a surprise attack on his son, Kevin. "Readiness is next to Godliness," he would often tell the boy. "Be on your toes physically and mentally because you never know when the enemy is going to attack."

Pates crouched outside the boy's room with his ear to the door.

Silence.

Light glowed from under the door. Pates concentrated for the sound of heavy breathing—sleep breathing. No sound. No shadow either. Kevin was clear of the door.

He grasped the doorknob, moving his fingers one at a time like the legs of a spider. He fought the urge to chuckle as he slowly turned the knob, holding his breath while he moved it a millimeter at a time.

Almost there. The latch was retracted.

Now!

Pates burst through the doorway. "Gotcha!" he roared.

Kevin jumped behind his bed and emerged a second later with his paint pistol aimed at his father's head. "Your move, dipstick."

Pates put up his hands and feigned trepidation as he inched closer to the weapon. "D ... d ... don't shoot." With a quick swipe of his hands, which must have looked like a blur to Kevin, Pates disarmed the boy and pointed the weapon at him.

Pates chucked the gun onto the bed and gently cuffed his son on the ear. "Never let your prisoner get close."

Kevin looked down, dejected. Pates mussed the boy's hair. "No sweat, son—you did good. Fast response. Authoritative tone."

82

"Thanks, Dad." Kevin sat down on his bed. "I have some schoolwork to finish. Okay?"

Pates sat next to his son. "Whatcha working on?"

"Just something for English. A book report."

"What on?"

Kevin looked away. "Actually, we had a choice. She said we could read a book or write a short story."

Pates held out his hand. "Let's have a look."

Kevin shook his head and attempted to move his hand surreptitiously to the side of the bed. "It's not ready."

Pates reached over, and plucked the paper from between the mattress and box spring, ignoring his son's protests.

"Survival of the Fittest," said Pates. "Good title." Kevin buried his head on his knees. Pates patted him on the back as he continued to read the story. It described a character named Roger Ford, whom Pates cheerfully thought resembled him. Ford was a soldier, a white supremacist who ran his household like a military base and forbade his family from association with anyone outside of their race. One night, while Ford was on the way home from a rally, a spaceship beamed him aboard and brought him to a distant planet where he was dumped in a forest with blue and red vegetation that glowed like neon lights. Before long, the aliens told Ford that he was being hunted for sport and if he made it to the other side of the forest, he'd be returned to Earth.

Pates looked up from the paper. "You've got some imagination, son." Pates continued to read, smiling during the next couple of pages. Until the character Roger Ford met up with Henry Morris, a black man from Earth who'd been dropped in the forest the day before. At first, Ford and Morris didn't get along, but soon realized that their only chance for survival was to work together against the aliens. Something the aliens hadn't counted on. Kevin ended the story with the two men being returned safely to Earth, vowing to be friends for life.

Kevin was peeking up at his father with pleading eyes when Pates looked down at him. Pates clenched the papers in his fist and shoved them in the boy's face. "What the hell is this nigger-loving garbage?" Pates stood up. Kevin followed him and tried to grab the papers.

"That's my project. It's due tomorrow."

Pates held the paper up out of Kevin's reach. "Well, you'll just have to sit down and get busy writing another one. One with a realistic ending like Mr. Ford killing the nigger and feeding him to the Martians." Pates ripped the pages in half. Kevin looked at him, shocked. Then the boy tried to jump up and snatch the papers. Pates effortlessly pushed him out of the way. Kevin hit the floor hard, banging his head against the baseboard and crying out. Pates knelt beside him. "Shake it off, son. Don't let a little pain get the better of you."

Kevin curled up in a ball. "I hate you. God is gonna punish you for being mean to people."

Pates coiled his fist and somehow found the strength not to strike the boy. He threw the ripped papers at his whimpering son, and stormed out of the room and down the stairs. He stomped his way through the kitchen and then through the basement doorway. Elizabeth yelled, "What's wrong?" as Pates darted down the steps and to his gun room. He grabbed one of his assault rifles and ran up the stairs three at a time. The fury was burning a hole in his chest as he kicked open the back door, and jumped to the ground. He aimed the rifle at a tree stump twenty yards away and fired off more than fifty rounds. Two guards appeared seconds later, their own rifles trained on the source of the gunfire.

Pates sank to his knees, clutching the weapon in one hand, the other covering his eyes. He stayed that way for almost a half-hour until one of the bodyguards gently coaxed him to return to the house. He spent the night in his gun room.

9

It was hot in downtown Milton as Avi Pearlman parked his pickup in front of the Montgomery Lumberyard. He left the windows open and kicked the door shut with his Dr. Martens boot. Uncle Shulman had told him that a skinhead without a pair of Dr. Martens was like a zebra without its stripes. You just didn't see it.

He caught a glimpse of himself in the storefront window as he stepped onto the sidewalk. White T-shirt, blue jeans, with holes torn near the knees, black boots and a clean-shaven head. Sons Elohim had provided his alter ego, Michael Dirks, with a job lead at the business owned by ARCS member John Dubois. Avi was impressed with the way his people had manipulated Dubois into providing the job. A Sons Elohim agent had invested in a Pittsburgh contracting company using an assumed identity. Dubois was happy to promise a temporary job should a certain nephew of a certain contractor show up at his door one day. The very grateful contractor could practically guarantee another ninety thousand dollar order in the near future.

Avi pushed open the door, which tripped a loud buzzer. He recognized Dubois from a photo as the burly owner held up his finger and said he'd be with the young man in just a minute. Dubois waddled to the rear of the store where the showroom connected with a huge warehouse of wood and other building materials. In the main part of the store, shiny new lawnmowers and power tools were haphazardly displayed. A chain saw sat atop a lawnmower. Several cans of paint served as the base for bags of grass seed. *What a mess,* thought Avi. He wondered how such a disorganized shop managed to stay in business.

Dubois disappeared into the warehouse. "Lazy bastards!" Avi heard him yell. "Why the hell isn't that sheet rock stacked yet?"

Avi laughed. He remembered the first day that he had been allowed to work in his father's shop. The then twelve-year-old Avi had watched open-mouthed as his father strolled through the woodworking shop, gently but firmly giving orders to his workers. Yeheudah Pearlman could whisper as effectively as some men shouted through a bullhorn. He always looked people in the eye and never spoke until he was sure that he was commanding their full attention.

Avi wiped some sweat from his brow, running his hand over the fuzz that used to be his hair. He took a deep breath, telling himself that this would soon be behind him and he'd be back in Williamsburg, growing his hair and running the Sons Elohim's information network computers while the closed circuit-monitors panned over his father's furniture shop.

The buzzer sounded as another customer, a man in overalls and a white T-shirt, walked through the door.

Dubois appeared and slipped behind the counter. "Well, Ken Hooper," Dubois said enthusiastically, looking past Avi to the man in the overalls. "I expected you a week ago."

"Had some trouble with the truck, John. You got my propane?"

"Got three fresh tanks in the back. Browse around a little."

Hooper gave Avi a brief looking-over and shook his head. Avi wondered if the man was disgusted at the sight of the skinhead. *Not bad,* thought Avi. He held up his fist. "White Power," he said, just for the hell of it.

Hooper disappeared into the power tool aisle, but not before giving Avi another strange look.

"Now what can I do for you?" said Dubois. The store's owner didn't seem to object to Avi's appearance. *Small wonder,* thought Avi as he eyed a photograph on the wall behind the counter. He recognized Dubois wearing army fatigues, a hunting rifle slung over his shoulder as casually as an English gentleman might carry an umbrella. Avi suddenly felt as if a grapefruit was lodged in his throat. Standing right next to Dubois in the eight-by-ten color photo was Matthew Pates—unsmiling and wearing sunglasses, but unmistakable in his arrogance, with his chin held up and his left hand on the butt of a holstered forty-five.

Dubois snapped his fingers in front of Avi's nose.

"Wake up, kid. I asked what I could do for you."

Avi took a deep breath. "Sorry. I'm Michael Dirks. My Uncle Sammy said I could see you about a job."

Dubois showed his yellowed teeth with the tightest smile Avi had ever seen. Uncle Shulman used to say, "They smile like they have shofars stuck up their tukus'es," whenever he looked at the newspapers and saw the phony smiles of politicians, lawyers and actors.

Dubois held out his hand. Avi shook it firmly.

"Strong grip," said Dubois. "You'll do well in building materials, Michael." Dubois looked around the shop. "I can't promise you work for more than a few months. But I gave your uncle my word, kid. When do you want to start?"

Avi shrugged. "Today?"

Dubois shook his head, laughing. "Tomorrow. We open at seven. You start at six."

"One more thing, Mr. Dubois. You know anybody with a room to rent?"

"You got any money, kid?"

"A few bucks." Avi actually had more than six thousand dollars locked in the glove compartment of his truck. In case Dubois went back on his word to the fictitious Uncle Sammy, he would still have to set himself up with a place to live until he could get close enough to Pates to carry out his mission.

Dubois grabbed the phone. "A good friend of mine is in the real estate business. I'm sure he'll find you a place."

*   *   *

For almost two weeks, Walsh and Jacobson worked sixteen-hour days sanding and varnishing the floor, installing stretching bars, safety mats, two heavy bags, mirrored walls and weight training equipment. With the help of a couple of hired men from The Mongomery Lumberyard, The Brotherhood of Yahweh Martial Arts Academy was almost ready.

The property was ideal. A six-hundred-square-foot storefront with two apartments overhead. They could live separately and no one would be the wiser. One of the apartments was small, nothing more than a bedroom and bath. They set up the large apartment as if they were both living there. After a brief dinner of take-out Chinese, pizza, or sometimes sandwiches, Walsh would slip off to the smaller apartment for the night. So far, everything was going smoothly.

A horn beeped, and the two agents trotted out to the street and met the delivery truck from the sign company. Walsh wondered how Leverick was faring with the bean counters, over the $450 price tag for the customized sign.

Walsh and Jacobson stood across the street, arms folded, each wearing sunglasses as they watched three men hoist and position the huge placard. The school's logo, a yin/yang insignia with tiny crosses—white ones on the black side and black on the white—was placed in the middle above the boldly printed lettering THE BROTHERHOOD OF YAHWEH MARTIAL ARTS ACADEMY.

"Not bad," said Walsh. "I can't help feeling a little pride right now."

"Pride, my butt," said Jacobson. "I'm just glad we're finished breaking our backs."

"We've only just begun, Jacobson. Now we have to drum up some business. Did you talk to the printer today?"

Jacobson tapped her head in true I-coulda-had-a-V8 fashion. "Damn. I'll do it in a few." The electric drills whirled as the men secured the sign to the face of the building, just under the apartment windows. "Did you remember to order the Bibles?"

"Two dozen. New King James versions. Should be here tomorrow," said Walsh.

"Looks like we're ready to start teaching some God-fearing people to kick, punch and hate anyone who's different." Jacobson jabbed the air with a one-two punch.

"Hopefully nail some angry white guys in the process," Walsh added.

The workers completed the installation, and the agents walked back across the street to the storefront. Walsh signed the work order, and the men piled into their truck and drove away.

"Well, Mrs. Hess. Our doors are officially opened."

Both agents swung around as a car screeched to a halt near them.

"It's Van Dickhead," said Jacobson.

Van Dickinson jumped out of his blue Mercedes, enthusiastically waving to the couple. He had someone in his car with him who remained seated in the front passenger side.

"I'm glad I caught you," he said, out of breath after

trotting across the street. "I have a young man in the car who needs a room. The small apartment upstairs would be perfect."

"Wait a second," Walsh objected. "We've gotten kind of used to it for storage."

Van Dickinson held up his hands. "But I thought you'd be happy to have the extra income." He signaled for the person in the car to get out and join the group in front of the karate studio.

Jacobson and Walsh looked at each other incredulously, then back at the young man approaching them. He appeared to be in his early twenties. The muscular youth's head was shaved, and he wore a white T-shirt and denim pants. If this kid was for real, maybe this could work to their advantage in getting to Pates, he thought. He knew Jacobson would agree.

Van Dickinson made the introductions. Walsh noticed what appeared to be a swastika tattoo on Dirks' chest. It was showing through like a light shadow on his shirt. *He's the real thing, all right*, thought Walsh. Dirks and Walsh shook hands. The skinhead held Walsh's stare fearlessly, which made the FBI man wonder about his initial judgment of Dirks as just another Nazi punk. Perhaps he was more dangerous than that.

"Interested in the martial arts, my friend?" Walsh asked.

Dirks walked closer to the storefront and peered in the window. "A little," he said. "I have an uncle who taught me a few moves."

Walsh walked up to Dirks and placed a hand on his shoulder. Dirks flinched a bit and gave Walsh a curious look. "Maybe you'd like to come to our open house on Saturday. Free lessons and a chance to win a new Bronco."

"What?" Dirks smiled.

So, thought Walsh, *it can smile*. "Just kidding about the Bronco. The free lessons are true."

Dirks turned slightly, freeing his shoulder from Walsh's chummy touch. "Maybe," he said. "Do you have to believe in Yahweh?"

"I'm assuming that you already do," said Walsh.

Dirks snorted a laugh. "I'm not much of a churchgoer, Mr. Hess."

"But your background is Christian."

Dirks nodded. "So you don't let Jews in your academy?"

Before Walsh could answer, Van Dickinson came between them, tapping on his wristwatch. "I have to get to the office, Mr. Hess. Your wife went up to the apartment. She said it would be empty inside of an hour." The real estate agent turned to Dirks. "Is that all right with you, Mr. Dirks? Shall I drive you back to your truck?"

"No, thanks," said Dirks. "I'll walk over and get it later."

Walsh opened the door to the karate studio. "You can browse around if you'd like, Michael." Walsh tossed him the key. "I'll go help my wife clear the stuff out of your new place."

Dirks thanked Walsh. Van Dickinson trotted back to his car, happy for the tiny commission he'd be getting from the Hesses for their sub-rental to Dirks.

When Walsh entered the small apartment, Jacobson was carrying two shopping bags and had several folders and magazines tucked under her arms. "Don't think I'm moving your dumbbell," she said.

Walsh was amused. That statement reminded him of Amy. She and Walsh always argued about that 45-pound weight. Walsh insisted on packing it in the car when the family took its yearly jaunt to the lakes region of New Hampshire. He remembered a hellish fight one weekend when he took the weight to a cabin on the Jersey shore and didn't even move it from a spot on the corner of the floor the whole time they were there.

Walsh carried the weight into the larger apartment and placed it next to the couch. On the way back to the other apartment, he met Jacobson in the hallway. This time, she was carrying two boxes in her arms and had the black leather case containing the laptop computer strapped over one shoulder.

"Don't bother, Mr. Hess. This is the last of it."

"I'm sorry, Mrs. Hess. Let me help you." Walsh unclipped the strap from the case and tucked the leather cover under his arm.

Unfazed, Jacobson raised the two boxes overhead and pumped them up and down a few times before continuing to carry them down the hallway toward the apartment door. Walsh again caught himself admiring her physique—shoulders and back cut and muscular but not bulky; a Barbie-doll waist; tight rear end and long, well defined legs. For a moment he imagined himself following her into the apartment and rubbing those finely chiseled shoulders. She would not offer any resistance. *After all, what's the harm in a little backrub between co-operatives*, thought Walsh. She would moan her approval as Walsh brought his fingers to the back of her neck and through her hair. Then he would lean closer and kiss her softly on the cheek, perhaps blowing softly in her ear just before gently biting the lobe. He imagined himself kissing her neck as he placed his hands around her breasts, massaging them as he worked his thumbs and forefingers toward her nipples. She would suck in air sharply as he pinched her nipples and pressed his teeth into her neck.

"What are you waiting for?" he thought he heard her say. "Don't tell me you've worked up a sweat carrying that little computer."

Walsh handed her the case. "I'm going to go down and tell our new neighbor that his apartment is ready. I'll be back in a half hour or so. I feel like pounding the crap out of the heavy bag."

"Have fun," she said, then disappeared through the doorway.

Walsh jogged down the stairs and out to the sidewalk. Inside the karate studio, he found Dirks throwing some pretty decent side kicks into one of the heavy bags.

"Not bad," Walsh commented. "Bring your knee a little further away from the target before executing the kick. That'll give you a little more power."

Dirks tried it, and the bag bent in half with the impact. "Not bad is right," Dirks said. "Maybe I'll take you up on those lessons. No Jews, right?"

Walsh looked Dirks squarely in the eye. *This is as good a time as any to practice the racist facade,* he thought. "No Jews. No niggers. If you want to join up after the free lesson, it'll cost you sixty bucks a month. Sign-up includes a uniform and a Bible. Ever read the Bible?"

Dirks looked as if he was suppressing a laugh.

"Parts of it."

"Good. We feel the Good Book is very clear about racial segregation."

Walsh found the skinhead disturbing. He expected to find fiery, irrational hatred behind those intense blue eyes. Instead, he found intelligence and perhaps some uncertainty. Not his idea of a racist skinhead punk. Walsh knew better than anyone that what lies beneath the surface is often quite different from the outward facade.

Dirks left the studio.

Walsh slipped on a pair of bag gloves and started pounding away.

10

The driver of the brown Ford van painstakingly kept the speed at 55 and at least five car lengths from any vehicle ahead of him. Ahmed Farzi would do nothing to draw attention to the vehicle, lest a routine spot check and the opening of the van's rear doors reveal its cargo. How unfortunate it would be for the unsuspecting trooper when he opened the door to find five men dressed in black jump suits complete with hoods, goggles, gloves and automatic weapons. More unfortunate than the corpse of some young trooper who would never see his family again, lying riddled with a hundred rounds of bullets torn through it, would be the fact that they would have to abandon their mission.

"Edwin Moore is a traitor and must not see another sunrise," Al-Aziz had told them before they'd hunkered down to a two-day planning and training session. It would be a simple cleaning operation. Four bodyguards, minimally skilled, and the now-debilitated Edwin Moore in a two-story colonial house. Dr. LeGrande had been courteous enough to provide detailed information. At eleven thirty in the evening, Moore would

would be in the middle room on the ground level. He would be propped up in a hospital bed, reading. One of the bodyguards would be sitting in a chair on the porch. One would be in the front room—a den with a couple of couches and some bookcases. A third bodyguard would be near the rear door, watching TV or playing solitaire in the kitchen. The fourth would be sleeping upstairs.

Every few hours, the guards would rotate their positions to break up the monotony and give one of them a chance to rest. Farzi laughed out loud at the thought that they would all be resting forever in less than an hour. It wasn't the first time Farzi and his team had cleaned up for Al-Aziz. He had sent them to Philadelphia a year earlier to wipe out eight drug dealers as they were packaging their goods and counting their money in a Phillips Street apartment. The raid took only seven minutes, and Farzi and his men split more than fifty thousand dollars in cash. What Farzi didn't know was that Al-Aziz's real motivation wasn't the elimination of the devils who were trying to poison the community's children, but the elimination of competition for that part of South Philly's drug business.

Farzi spoke into his headset. "Get ready. Twenty minutes before target."

All five men looked up as Farzi's voice came through their receivers. One of the men, short, muscle-bound, with light brown skin, was known simply as Mix. Mix was the detail man of Al-Aziz's death squad. He would make sure there were enough bullets to kill everyone five times over. All except one bodyguard. Their orders were clear on that subject—leave one alive. Shoot up his legs and arms so he'll never walk or be able to do so much as lift a cup of coffee, but leave one alive to tell the world that the Sons Elohim were responsible and had set out to finish what they had failed to do that night at the Manhattan Center.

Mix surveyed the faces of the other four assassins. Each man was pumped, ready to strike hard and fast. They each had two Mac 10 machine pistols strapped in specially made holsters at their sides, as well as a 9mm in a leg holster. In case of the almost impossible occurrence of finding oneself without a weapon, each man had been trained in unarmed guerrilla tactics—strictly throat-crushing, joint-breaking and eye-gouging techniques. Mix thought this job was like sending a SWAT team to break up bingo night at church—a real cakewalk.

Mix opened a jar of theatrical makeup and applied it around his eyes, lips and wrists. He passed the jar, and the others followed suit. Although the raid would be fast and furious, the lucky one—whom Farzi had decided would be whomever was sleeping in the upstairs bedroom—would not see any dark skin under the masks or gloves. The squad was a perfectionist outfit. Nothing was left to chance.

The house was located a quarter mile up a winding, tree-lined gravel road. Farzi killed the light just before turning onto the road, and the moonless night provided a blanket of darkness with which to make their way. They left the van and walked slowly, three on either side, in single file, the sound of their footsteps drowned out completely by the endless chirping of crickets and other night creatures.

Farzi gave the order to stop with two quick "sssst" noises as the house came into view through the trees. Three more "ssssts," and the men spread out along the overgrown lawn that surrounded the house.

They crawled on their bellies a few inches at a time, barely making a sound and never taking their eyes off the house.

Farzi could now make out the silhouette of someone sitting by a dim lamp in the front room. The image appeared to be that of a very large man. *Probably the wrestler,* thought Farzi, remembering the image of Huck Perkins from the photos he and his squad had looked over every day for the past week.

As organized on paper and discussed probably a hundred times, Mix took two men to the rear of the house and waited for the sound of Farzi's voice, who simply said "Go!"

In an instant they kicked the front and rear doors open and the entire house erupted like a Fourth of July fireworks finale. The figure in the front-room chair exploded as a torrent of bullets engulfed it. It took only a few seconds for Farzi to realize they'd been had. The figure that now lay torn to pieces on the floor was nothing but an old mattress tied with ropes, with an extra-large suit jacket and a football for a head. Farzi spat on the shreds of cotton and cloth. His cheeks burned with a humiliation from which he knew he would never be able to liberate himself.

He wasn't sure at that point whether LeGrande had simply underestimated Moore and his bodyguards or was himself a traitor to Al-Aziz.

Mix trotted into the room from the staircase. "Upstairs is empty."

Fools, thought Farzi. *We have been turned into a bunch of fools.* "If they knew that we were coming, I wonder why ...." It was only then that he noticed the thin, white wires strung along the base of the doorway and into a small hole in the floorboards. Without saying another word, Farzi threw himself out the door and rolled down the porch steps and onto the grass. Mix was right behind, but only about half of him landed on the grass next to Farzi. The rest of the squad didn't have a second to scream as the house turned into a ball of flame, and the force of the bomb ripped through and destroyed it like it was built with matchsticks.

The explosion pushed Farzi almost to the edge of the woods. Mix's legless body landed a few feet away. He moaned, looking at Farzi pleadingly. Farzi crawled closer to his colleague while flaming pieces of what used to be a pretty nice country house landed all around them.

Farzi smiled at Mix. "Don't worry, brother. You'll be

with Allah soon." Farzi then put his pistol to Mix's temple and fired a single shot through his brain.

*   *   *

Jacobson clicked open the laptop computer and raised the tiny antenna. The device had been given to her and Walsh to electronically file their 302s and other updates on the investigation. They could also use the computer to connect to the information center in Washington DC. The computer hub, nicknamed WizKid, provided field agents with links to any Motor Vehicle Bureau, police department, university, or airline-reservation system, as well as hundreds of other sources of information.

It was nearly midnight, and Jacobson was sprawled out on the couch, the computer on her lap. Walsh sat across from her at a card table next to the window. He made notes on a legal pad as he perused the Bible in preparation for the introductory class the following morning. Thirty-one people were signed up for the very first Bible-based karate lesson in Milton county history.

"That's the last one," Jacobson said with a sigh. "No Michael Dirks with a driver's license in Oregon." She placed a finger on the screen where she had set up a notepad window. "I got two Michael Dirkses in Michigan—no photos."

Walsh looked up from his papers. "Nothing in Pennsylvania?"

"Six, actually. All of them had photo scans. None of them our boy."

"Send Leverick an email. Ask him to secure a warrant to bug our little neighbor's apartment."

Jacobson nodded. "Good idea." She clicked to another window and a list of names appeared. A second later, she highlighted Leverick, and a double-click later was in a text-entry box. Within a minute the request was typed and delivered—all through an untraceable cellular transmission sent over a frequency unavailable to the citizenry at large. In fact, a person could get twenty years behind bars for even attempting to build a communications device capable of reaching it.

Jacobson put the computer on the floor and tucked her hands behind her head. Walsh, although trying hard to concentrate on his work, couldn't miss, out of the corner of his eye, Jacobson alternating a stretch of each leg. *It's funny,* he thought. Amy had always complained about his endless stretching routines, punching and kicking the air, pounding his knuckles on a tree or cement. *Martial Arts nuts are all alike.*

Walsh grabbed the Bible and pulled his chair opposite his partner. She sat up on the couch to face him.

"What do you think about starting each class with a reading from First Kings?" Walsh asked.

Jacobson put her hands over her ears and pretended to faint. "Can't ... stay ... awake ... early ... childhood ... trauma ... of ... forced ... Hebrew ... lessons."

Walsh slapped Jacobson on the thigh with the Bible. "Don't think I didn't do my time in religious school, Jacobson."

Jacobson sat up and held out her hand. "Don't tell me. Irish-Catholic. Taught by nuns. Am I right?"

"Close, but no cigar. My grandparents were from Belfast and very Protestant."

The two agents were silent for a few moments. As much as Walsh had been estranged from the religion he was brought up on, he did have some pleasant memories. He wondered if she was thinking along the same lines.

"I wonder what happened?" Jacobson finally said.

Walsh shrugged. "We changed? I know I did. I started believing that God was nothing more than Santa Claus for adults. I felt that way for a long time. Now I'm not so sure. I haven't been to church since shortly after my son Alex was born."

Jacobson leaned forward a bit, her eyes locking for an instant on Walsh's. "What was it?"

"Something my sister said. She invited me to ask myself if there was a God the next time I held Alex in my arms and looked into his face." Walsh suddenly felt sad. It must have shown because Jacobson asked him what was wrong. "Nothing. I've never told her that what she said had an impact on me. I think I will as soon as we finish this assignment."

Jacobson pointed to the computer on the floor. "Does she have email?"

"I couldn't say. She's hooked up with a small church called the Christian Universalists."

"Never heard of them. But let me guess. LA?"

"Where else?" Walsh stood and walked to the window. "You'd like Diane, Jacobson. She's got a lot of heart."

"Maybe she could help us with our quickie Bible education."

Walsh laughed. "I don't think Milton is ready for Christian Universalism. It's a bit unorthodox."

Jacobson sat up straight. "You've piqued my curiosity. Do they think Jesus was born of extraterrestrial parents who artificially inseminated a young virgin?"

"Cute, Jacobson. Not quite, but they do believe in reincarnation of the spirit. Diane used to tell me that we are all reincarnated until we become good enough to completely merge with the universal energy called God. As long as we are attached to the world, we keep coming back. If we're good, we get a better life the next time around. A love for worldly pleasures—this is where sin comes in—binds one to the cycle of reincarnation and death."

"Sounds like an Asian religion," said Jacobson.

"Except that they believe that Christ was one of the great liberators. They also believe that Buddha, Krishna, Mohammed are all reincarnations of the same spirit."

101

Jacobson shook her head. "I don't buy it. If they're all reincarnations of the same person, why are the religious beliefs so different?"

"I asked that same question," said Walsh. "Diane reasoned that the followers caused the distortion when they attempted to put the universal message to paper."

"You're right," said Jacobson. "We'd better stick to run-of-the-mill, Bible-toting, Jew-hating Christianity."

"Groups like ARCS don't represent Christianity."

The expression on her face turned sour.

"Oh no? What would you know about it? You said yourself you hadn't attended much since you were a kid. Now all of a sudden you're the defender of the faith. You have no idea what the Jewish people have had to contend with at the hands of so-called Christians."

"That's the spirit," said Walsh. "Maybe you should wear a Star of David around your neck if we ever get near Pates and his little army."

"What the hell is that supposed to mean?"

"It means neither one of us are here to defend our faiths. We're on the same side. We're the good guys. Pates and his bunch are the bad guys."

"It's easier for you. You're not Jewish."

Walsh was wondering if they had made a critical mistake using her. She had no strong religious convictions, and had stated herself in an earlier interview with Leverick that she was not so passionate about her Jewish roots that it would prevent her from playing her role in the undercover assignment. "Look, I'm sorry, Jacobson. Maybe you should get some sleep. I'll prepare for the class myself."

"I apologize too," said Jacobson. She stood up and walked over to Walsh. "I think meeting that skinhead punk today rattled me more than I expected. A couple of skinheads once defaced the synagogue where my parents worship. For weeks my dad looked sad ... beaten down. I guess I'm more Jewish than I thought."

Walsh put his hand on her shoulder and looked her in the eyes intently. "It's okay. I'm probably more Christian than I thought. Besides, no one ever said life for God's chosen people was going to be easy."

Jacobson smiled.

Walsh returned a grin. "Although I once heard that the Jews were God's second choice after the Chinese turned him down."

Jacobson pushed Walsh hard on his chest. "You creep," she said, laughing.

Walsh put up his hands and baited her by tapping on his chin. "Come on, Special Agent. Let's see what you got." Jacobson threw three rapid punches—left, right, left—which Walsh skillfully blocked. Off the third punch, she threw a well-placed roundhouse kick to Walsh's thigh. Walsh caught her leg and threw her back onto the couch. He took a half step forward, and she sprang up, kicking him squarely in the gut, then attempted a knife hand strike toward his head. He sidestepped the attack, and blocked her while grabbing her wrist and twisting her arm around her back. While Jacobson attempted to twist out of the hold, the agents' legs got wrapped up together, and both fell to the floor.

Of all the times Walsh had faced life-and-death situations where he'd had to dig into the depths of his being for courage and determination that he never thought he had, this moment was the toughest. He felt that he would die—that his pounding heart would cease to beat in his chest—if he didn't kiss this woman right there. They stared at each other for a long moment, practically in a lovers' embrace on the floor. Walsh closed his eyes and inhaled as if he was about to dive into deep water.

A second later, they disengaged. Without saying anything, Jacobson got up and walked into the bedroom. Walsh sat there for a moment, eyes closed and breathing deeply. Before getting up himself, the FBI man shot off a set of eighty pushups.

He sat down at the table and opened the Bible to Kings. The computer beeped, demanding Walsh's attention. On the screen was an indication of an electronic message. He walked over and picked up the laptop, punched in a few commands and a password, and found a message from Leverick. Another attempt had been made on Edwin Moore's life. The situation had just become a little more complex.

Too close for comfort, thought Jacobson. She sat on the bed with her legs crossed and practiced some relaxation techniques. She knew that she must clear her mind of any sexual thoughts and her body of any sexual desires. *Walsh is married. He's a senior agent. He's my partner. We're on a very important assignment.*

She vowed to be more guarded from that moment forward.

11

It was times like this that Dalton Leverick wished he had taken his cousin's offer to go into the fried-chicken business ten years ago. He'd be sitting pretty on a lake in Virginia right now instead of walking into a scene of carnage and southern-fried body parts.

He clipped his FBI badge to the outside of his jacket and walked up to a state trooper who was barking orders at several firefighters. The smoldering wood that was once a house pumped out billows of smoke that mixed with the early-morning fog. The flashing lights of a dozen cruisers and fire trucks seemed to make the thick air swirl like ghostly dancers. Leverick heard intermittent static and an occasional muffled voice over some of the radios. The air was rank with the distinctive smell of burnt flesh and hair. The dense fog was holding the grisly reminder of slaughter down to the earth.

The trooper turned toward Leverick with an impatient look on his face, which subsided once he saw the FBI badge.

"Agent Leverick. Lieutenant Miller." Miller switched his cell phone to his left hand and extended Leverick a firm handshake. Miller had a scowl that must have scared the hell out of more than a few suspects. Leverick liked him immediately.

"You called the New York field office."

Miller nodded. "Yes. You're wondering why."

"I admit I'm curious," Leverick said.

"I trust you've heard of Dr. LeGrande—Carl LeGrande." Miller tilted his head toward the smoldering debris. "He rented this place. I've seen enough of him on the news these days. I also understand that the Bureau is giving this case some priority since the Sons Elohim might have been responsible for shooting Edwin Moore."

"We have our doubts," Leverick said. "It doesn't look like Sons Elohim was involved."

Another trooper jogged up to them at that moment. She saluted Miller and tipped her hat slightly to Leverick. The nametag on her uniform read J. Paris. "The body by the edge of the grass has a bullet wound to the head," she reported.

"Let's have a look," Leverick said.

Leverick, Miller and Paris walked to the edge of the grass before the thicket that surrounded what was once an eight-room country home. A man in a brown leather jacket was examining the legless corpse. The examiner was bald except for a patch of hair near each ear, and he wore round, wire-rimmed glasses.

"This is Dennis Chang," Miller said. "The best medical mind in Wellington County." Chang looked up briefly, then continued to speak softly into a micro cassette recorder. He clicked the recorder off and placed it in his jacket pocket. "The implosion of the head speaks about a nine-millimeter from about two inches away." Chang pointed to streams of dried blood in the grass. "The evidence speaks that he was thrown from the structure, then crawled here."

"Where someone put a bullet in his head," Miller said.

"Precisely," Chang said, now standing and looking at Miller.

Miller rubbed his temples and sighed. "Do you think this is Edwin Moore?"

Chang shook his head. "This man was in his late twenties. Of course, without an examination in the lab, that's only a guess."

Miller cuffed Chang on the shoulder. "Chang's guesses are more accurate than the lab work of many others." Chang smiled shyly and crouched down on one knee. He removed the recorder from his jacket and continued his examination of the crime scene. Paris excused herself and joined several other officers and a photographer near the remains of the dwelling. Miller and Leverick left Chang to his work and walked over to Miller's cruiser.

Leverick declined Miller's offer of a cigarette. Miller leaned against the car, letting out a sigh along with a stream of smoke.

"This is going to be messy," he said. "I was in high school when King was shot. You know this is going to make that seem tame by comparison." On cue with the end of that sentence, a news van appeared, and a reporter and cameraman jumped out before the van stopped completely, the reporter struggling to stay on her feet. She walked straight up to Leverick and Miller, her little cameraman trotting at her heels. Miller turned toward the news people and held out his arms. "Whoa. This is a hot crime scene." Miller unclipped the phone from his belt, and after pressing a couple of buttons, started barking orders at the cops who were stationed at the bottom of the hill. He made it very clear to whomever was on the other end of the conversation that if another vehicle was permitted up the road that five years of enforcing the pooper-scooper law was certain. Miller then turned his attention back to the reporter. "Please return to your vehicle, miss."

Ignoring Miller, the reporter turned and shoved a microphone in Leverick's face. "There is a rumor that Edwin Moore was in this house, Mr. ..." She squinted to make out the name on the FBI man's credentials, "... Leverick?"

Miller placed his hand over the microphone. "I want

you clear and away from this crime scene in one minute, or I'm going to lock up you *and* your buddies."

"Wait a second," Leverick said. "Edwin Moore was not in the house." Leverick pulled a business card from his jacket pocket and handed it to the reporter. "I give you my word that you'll get the information first when we identify the bodies."

She took the card and considered it for a long moment. "Turn off the camera, Smitty." With that, the light clicked off, and Smitty held the camera at his side. "What do you want from me?" she asked.

"Don't mention Edwin Moore in your report," Leverick said. "Let the public continue to believe he is in hiding."

The reporter, whose name Leverick could now see from her press credentials was Allison Friedman, shook her head. "You've got to prove to me that Moore's not here. Carl LeGrande rented the house a week ago. Moore left St. Andrew's Tuesday with his four bodyguards sometime during the night without police or FBI escort. Now the house that Dr. LeGrande rented looks and smells like a Texas barbecue pit the morning after a Jeffrey Dahmer picnic."

Two officers had spread a huge tarp on the lawn, and several workers from the medical examiner's office started placing body parts on it. Dennis Chang was crouched next to what looked like a torso with one leg attached to it, still murmuring into his recorder. "I'll tell you what," said Leverick. "If Lieutenant Miller and Dr. Chang agree, you can cover the whole investigation. When they discover something, so do you. Up to the minute."

Leverick looked at Miller, who seemed to be thinking real hard about the FBI man's proposal. Leverick guessed that he was thinking about the impact the news of Moore's murder would have on an already uneasy constituency. Leverick also suspected that Miller shared his gut feeling that Moore and his bodyguards never spent a day in that house.

"Let's go talk to Chang," said Miller.

108

Leverick breathed a sigh of relief as he watched Miller and the two news people approach Chang. They had bought themselves some time. Now they needed to find out where the hell Moore was and just how many people were trying to kill him.

*　　*　　*

Danny Park trotted into the study juggling a box in one arm, a computer keyboard in the other, and a collection of wires and plugs strung from his neck like a high-tech necklace.

Max Smith and Lucas Green jumped to their feet, Green reaching for an M16 rifle he had kept at his side since they had come to the safe house.

"Damn it, Danny," Green said sharply but quietly, careful not to wake Edwin Moore as he slept on the hospital bed in the corner of the room. "You scared the crap out of me, fool! Where the hell is Perkins?"

Park placed the box on the floor and piled the other stuff on top of it. "Perkins? He said he had another meeting with his Secret Service bud last night. About watching the other house."

At that moment, it became very clear to Park by the looks on the faces of Green and Smith that something was very wrong. Perkins had volunteered to organize surveillance of the first safe house. Moore wasn't convinced that he had been betrayed by Carl LeGrande, his longtime friend and advisor, and who could blame him? Perkins had promised to bring Moore the proof he needed before he would agree to go to the police, and now Park had a sinking feeling in his stomach that Perkins had done something terrible. Before he could ask what had happened, Smith clicked on a small monitor and queued up a tape of the morning news. He held out a pair of headphones for Park.

"This is gonna be bad, isn't it?" Park muttered.

Smith grunted, definitely indicating that "bad" was an understatement. Park held his breath for a moment, then slowly breathed through his nose as he focused his eyes on the television monitor. There was a young newswoman speaking into a microphone. Park listened carefully to her words but looked past her to the background where the smoldering remains of a house were being sifted through by firefighters and police. He stood transfixed by the carnage, as he listened to her tell how the police had not yet identified the bodies, but that a preliminary examination by the county medical examiner revealed at least four people were dead. The reporter promised to provide a full report at six.

"Perkins has lost his mind!" yelled Park. Smith reached over and ripped the headphones off his ears.

"You don't have to scream, stupid." All three men looked over at Moore, hoping they wouldn't disturb his sleep, yet feeling too anxious to even think about leaving his side.

"Sorry," Park said when he realized that Moore was now awake. Moore's face was still bandaged, although the blood stains, so prevalent during the first couple of weeks after the shooting, no longer forced their way through the gauze.

Danny Park nodded at his employer. "Hello, Mr. Moore."

"He knows," said Smith, reading Park's mind. Moore lowered his gaze. The sad, defeated look in his eyes made Park feel ashamed, and he knew that Smith and Green shared his guilt. Moore had wanted to confront LeGrande right away after Green had spotted him using the pay phone outside of the hospital. *Perkins,* thought Park. *That big dummy conned us all. All that crap about Secret Service connections and surveillance teams!*

Smith pulled a chair over to Moore's bedside. "What should we do?"

Park suddenly remembered what he had been excited about before getting hit between the eyes with the revelation that Huck Perkins was a murderous psychopath. "Hold on," he said. "I got this from my Uncle Sihak's shop." Park quickly

110

opened the boxes, and in less than three minutes, he'd assembled on the bedside table a voice synthesizer that looked like a space-age boom box. He connected Moore's laptop computer to the back of the synthesizer, pulled a disk from the pocket of his blazer, and after a few clicks, a couple of whirls and a flicker or two on the screen, it was ready to go.

Park handed the computer to Moore. "Move the arrow here and click. You can type what you want to say, then press F5 or click on Send. Then *voila,* it goes round and round, and comes out here." He tapped on the synthesizer box. "Give it a try."

Moore stared at the screen suspiciously for a long moment, then began to rotate the trackball. He hunted and pecked a few keystrokes, then turned to look at the synthesizer. A robotic-sounding voice droned, "Test ... test ... test." Park wasn't sure, but he thought Moore's eyes betrayed some pleasure at what he had just heard.

Moore pecked at the keyboard a few more minutes, then pressed the F5 key.

<<Where is Henry Perkins>>

Smith looked at Park and shrugged. Park looked at Green. Green sat on the edge of Moore's bed with his huge arms folded across his faded Buffalo Bills T-shirt. The man whom Park used to rib by calling him Black Hercules didn't look ready to take on the world anymore. He looked liked they all felt—sad and defeated. Park squeezed Green's shoulder, then pulled a chair next to the bed.

"He never came back," said Green.

"He told us last night he was meeting his surveillance team," offered Smith. "I'm having big-time trouble believing Perkins blew up that house. Not that I give a crap about those suckers anyway."

Park leaned in closer to Moore. "What do you want us to do?"

The three bodyguards looked at the tiny speakers.

<<Call the police ... no ... the FBI ... mayor's counsel ... Lewis ... gave me a card>> Moore reached over and tapped the

drawer handle of the bedside table. Park jumped up and opened it. He pulled out a pile of papers and fished through them until he found the card: "DALTON LEVERICK, SUPERVISOR."

Green unclipped his phone from his belt and flipped it open. After holding it to his ear for a second, he stared at it curiously. "Just static."

"Are you sure you paid the bill?" asked Park.

Green snapped the phone back in its holder, then flipped his middle finger to Park.

"I love you, too," said Park. He pointed across the room to a beige rotary phone, which sat on an old William and Mary tavern table, a yellowed doily hanging from the edges like an intricate spider's web. "That working?"

"It was last night," Green said.

Park walked over and lifted the receiver to dead air. The young Korean was suddenly struck with the feeling that at any moment life for him and the rest of the people in that room was about to take a turn for the worse.

Park crossed his arms, shoving both hands inside his jacket and coming out with twin 9mm pistols. He turned to face the others, his guns pointed at the floor. "We're in trouble."

"Shit," said Green.

"Shit," said Smith.

The tiny speaker emitted its robotic voice, <<Shit>>

*   *   *

Ahmed Farzi rested his back against the trunk of a huge oak. He stood with his knees bent and his machine pistol held against his shoulder, pointing toward the treetops. He spoke into the tiny microphone of his headset. "Hold your positions." Farzi thought he saw some movement from the trees about six yards in front of him. He pointed his rifle sharply, then realized it was just his tired eyes playing tricks on him. Eyes that hadn't rested in almost two days. Eyes that Terrance Al-Aziz had threatened to gouge out with an ice pick unless his soon-to-be-ex-chief-of-security gathered up a new team and found Moore immediately.

Sometimes Allah provides, thought Farzi. Allah and a brother-in-law who had access to police computers. That in combination with the employee records that Dr. LeGrande had in his files which provided full dossiers on Smith, Perkins, Green and Park. It took Farzi's contact a little less than an hour to narrow it down to four addresses in upstate New York. Farzi thought the slant-eyed Park should have been smarter than to put Moore in his Uncle Sihak's country house. *I think I'll kill him first, just to say, 'thank you'* thought Farzi. *When Al-Aziz gives his blessing, of course.* For now, his orders were clear—nobody would die until Al-Aziz was sure of what Moore and his crew knew and whom they had spoken to in the last 24 hours.

Farzi took a deep breath. "Get ready to move in," he said, holding his hand in the air like a military commander.

"GO!"

12

Walsh pointed his finger like a pistol at the buzzing alarm clock. "Bang. You're dead," he said, squinting through one eye across the room. Since his college days, more years ago than he cared to think about, he'd always placed his alarm far away from the bed (or in this case, the couch). As he sat up, the pain in his lower back sent home grim reminders that he was on the losing end of the sleeping-arrangement agreement.

After taking a few seconds to stretch his back and work out all the kinks in his knees and elbows, Walsh walked over to the desk and silenced the alarm. The sound of the running shower then filtered its way through the apartment and helped create in Walsh's mind a very pleasant image of his partner. He vigorously shook his head. After last night's awkward encounter, he wondered whether this operation was going to prove to be too much for him to contend with. He had been shoulder to shoulder with members of the country's most notorious bike gang, and had gone one on one with maniacal killers in other deep-cover assignments, but had never felt this uncertain of his ability to handle himself.

He looked down at the Bible that he had been studying last night to prepare for The Brotherhood of Yahweh Martial Arts Academy's first day of business. After hours of flipping through scripture and planning an opening prayer guaranteed to offend ninety-nine percent of the American population, he had finally tossed the book on the table and practically nose-dived onto the couch.

The shower abruptly stopped. He could hear Jacobson's muffled singing.

Walsh closed his eyes and pinched the bridge of his nose. He conjured up an image of Amy and the kids. He thought about a recent Saturday morning when Alex and Anthony pounced on him and Amy in their bed, asking to go downstairs to watch cartoons. The parents had pretended to be mad at being woken up, enjoying every second of the two smiling faces, knowing well that the time with them as small children would be very short.

Walsh opened his eyes. The Bible was opened to Mark. He looked down at the phrase, "Therefore, what God has joined together, let not man separate." *Amen,* he thought. He remembered a situation in Florida about five years ago where two agents were thrown out of the Bureau for having an affair while they were working the Mob in Dade County. The female was single, and the male agent married with three kids. The stiff lost everything—wife, kids, house, and career. Last Walsh heard, the guy was working the rope outside Planet Hollywood in Minneapolis.

"Good morning, Agent Walsh."

Walsh turned around to find Jacobson dressed in a blue silk karate uniform. Her belt was so old that most of the black around the knot was worn away to the color and condition of an old and stringy mop head.

"Looks like you've tied that on a time or two," said Walsh. He lifted the end of her belt, which had four white stripes embroidered on the tip. "Not bad."

116

"It's been a bit of an obsession for me. Been at it since I was fourteen."

Walsh stood up and stretched toward the ceiling. "Since I'm only a first degree, maybe you should run the school."

"Bull! Leverick told me a few stories about you, pal."

Walsh folded his arms and looked curiously at his partner. "Leverick has a tendency to exaggerate."

"You are so full of it, Walsh. Your fight with the Wrestlemaniac perp is must-see-TV at the academy. I personally watched it a dozen times."

Walsh snorted a laugh. "It's not every day you get to fight for your life on a pay-per-show event."

"You sure as hell didn't pick up that kind of skill in the do jahng," said Jacobson.

Walsh shook his head. "Ever hear of a civilian named Charlie Red?"

Jacobson looked surprised. "Charlie Red is a real person?"

"Sure is. Retired now, I'd bet, but the Bureau used him to train agents for about ten years. It had to be unofficial because the suits would never admit that basic hand to hand wouldn't cut it if the situation went extreme." Walsh gently rubbed his throat. "When Dalton was training me for the Henchmen operation, Charlie Red almost broke my neck. After the biker case was over, I hired Charlie Red to train me privately for almost a year." Walsh opened a suitcase, which sat on the floor next to the table. He pulled out a pair of black canvas pants and a short-sleeved shirt. A pair of black wristbands completed the ensemble. "Very basic," said Walsh. "No belt."

Jacobson untied her belt and removed her uniform top. Walsh held his breath for a second before he realized that she was wearing an undershirt. "Basic?"

"Very."

"Did you get everything finished last night?"

Walsh tapped the Bible. "To tell you the truth, I'm a little nervous. I dreamt last night that I was back in my Sunday School class, and Pastor Richie was looking at me with those accusing eyes." Walsh laughed, then picked up the Bible and raised it high above his head. He pointed his index finger hard at Jacobson's face. "'Some of you children are *not* saved. You say you believe, but you do not.'" Walsh held the book at arm's length, admiring its black leather cover. "He used to scare me to death sometimes but I think even he would be shocked at what I'm going to say today. He may have been all fire and brimstone when it came to his salvation message, but there wasn't a racist bone in him. He and his wife adopted and raised more than twenty kids—some black, some Asian."

"Believe me, I can relate. Imagine if my nice Jewish parents could see me now." Jacobson positioned herself into a fighting stance. "Okay, students—or should I say, little Nazi creeps."

There was a loud knock at the door. "We prepaid two months' rent," said Walsh. "So it can't be the landlord."

"Speaking of little Nazis," Jacobson bantered, "it could be our tenant from across the hall."

Walsh breezed past his partner and opened the door. He focused his eyes immediately on the swastika tattoo on the young man's chest that was partially exposed under his sleeveless undershirt. Michael Dirks' weightlifter arms were folded tightly across his chest.

"'Morning, Michael," said Walsh. The skinhead's hateful stare was bothersome. Walsh wondered if that was how Dirks looked at everyone, since the FBI partners were putting on a show that should get the little Nazi's respect and admiration.

"If the offer is still good, I'd like to work out with you this morning." Without waiting for an answer, Dirks turned and walked away.

"Ten o'clock!" Walsh yelled as Dirks disappeared down the staircase.

"Well, Mr. Hess," said Jacobson. "It's an hour till show time. We might as well open up shop."

Walsh gestured for his partner to walk through the doorway. "After you, Mrs. Hess."

*   *   *

A few minutes before ten a.m., a tall, bulky man with a shaved head knocked on the door of the storefront. He appeared to be in his late forties, and tattoos covered his arms. He had two young boys with him who he introduced as his sons Sam and Jimmy. As soon as Jacobson had signed them up and handed over their uniforms and Bibles, another customer arrived. This time it was a short, grandmotherly type, with a teenage girl and a young boy. By ten-thirty, fifteen young people and four adults had become members of The Brotherhood of Yahweh Martial Arts Academy.

Walsh and Jacobson stood at the front of the training floor, and after going over the rules and procedures, they ordered the students to line up in rows of five.

Here goes nothing, Walsh thought.

"Welcome to The Brotherhood of Yahweh Martial Arts Academy," he said. "I'm Mr. Hess, and this is Mrs. Hess." Jacobson bowed slightly. "This school stands for purity." A couple of the students looked at him quizzically. "A pure mind A pure spirit. A pure race."

Walsh took a moment to look around at the students' faces. Some looked confused, some eager. Dirks looked confident, almost amused by it all. He seemed to be enjoying the mumbling and grumbling of the other students' friends and relatives who were standing to the side of the training floor.

Walsh instructed the students to sit down and close their eyes for the opening prayer.

119

"I don't believe it," someone whispered from the sidelines.

"Father Yahweh," said Walsh. "We ask for your blessing as we begin to train in the martial arts today and pray that you will keep us safe as we take part in the struggle for a racially pure country."

"Oh, my God!" someone shouted. Walsh opened one eye and spied the sidelines, fully expecting to see a grin on the face of the bald, redneck-looking guy. Surprisingly, the grandmother was smiling. Four parents, including the burly redneck, darted onto the training floor and took their kids by the arm. Walsh jumped to his feet, as the gym suddenly became a whirlwind of confusion, angry parents demanding refunds. The big man pointed a finger in Walsh's face.

"You should be ashamed of yourself calling this a Godly school." Walsh took a step back, ready to fight the big man who just shook his head in disgust. "My children and I will pray for you, Mr. Hess. May God forgive you."

Jacobson announced that anyone wanting a refund could have it. The old woman walked up to Walsh and extended her hand. "It's high time, young man, that someone had the courage to say what needed to be said. My grandchildren will be proud to learn from you."

"Thank you, Ma'am." Walsh looked over at the woman's grandson. The boy was standing soldier-like, although he shifted his eyes nervously from side to side. Only about six students remained in place, the rest having either left on their own or been taken out by angry parents. A woman, who was dragging a young boy out kicking and screaming that he wanted to stay and do karate, paused in the doorway long enough to threaten the couple with lawsuits, civil complaints, newspaper reporters and a visit from the Anti-Defamation League. As she slipped out to the street, her muffled threats could still be heard.

Walsh looked at Jacobson. She leaned over and whispered in his ear. "What a mess."

"Yeah, perfect, isn't it?" Walsh grinned at her.

Jacobson shook her head. "You're a nutcase."

They warmed up the class with calisthenics and stretching. Jacobson demonstrated at the front of the class while Walsh worked the floor, correcting the students' form and position during a basic punch and kicking drill. Two more spectators entered the gym. One was a short, hairy biker type. The other was tall—at least six-three. Walsh continued training the students, feigning indifference to the two men, but an unspoken understanding passed between him and Jacobson.

I hear you, partner, thought Walsh. These guys looked like some of the mugs in the photos of ARCS members that he and Jacobson had been shown at one of the briefings. Walsh felt a familiar surge of exhilaration. He relished the pleasure of drawing in the prey. Especially when many of the suits who thought they knew it all about undercover disapproved of the hide-in-plain-sight tactics that he and Jacobson were employing. Whoever said that fishing wasn't fun when the fish jumped in the boat had never experienced it.

The tall guy looked disdainfully over the class. The kind of look that said "This is crap and all black belts in these gook arts are a bunch of wussies."

Walsh ordered the students to pair off.

"You will learn a lot of deadly self-defense techniques here."

One of the men laughed contemptuously, just loud enough for Walsh to hear. Walsh's sense of imminent chaos moved up another level. As a young man learning his ABCs in the martial arts, his instructor, Master Eugene Cho, drilled into him that chaos could break out at any time, in any place. He likened it to nuclear readiness, telling the then eighteen-year-old Walsh that he should always be as alert as if at Defcon 4. He could move down a notch at a time if circumstances

121

permitted, but he had to be able to jump immediately to Defcon 1 and total war when necessary.

"If you ever find yourself in a situation where you need to defend yourself or a fellow Aryan ..." The biker grunted something that sounded like a tone of approval. "... I want you to take all the techniques we are going to teach you in this academy and toss them out the window and just fight. What you really know will work for you."

Jacobson picked up a Bible from the corner of the training floor and opened it. "First Kings 20:11 says, 'Let not the one who puts on his armor boast like the one who takes it off.'" She closed the book sharply and placed it on the floor. "Nobody is going to be scared of you anymore because you say you know karate."

"That's for sure," said the tall guy, whom Walsh was now sure was ARCS member Jimmy Price.

"Please don't talk while class is in session," Walsh said firmly.

Price held up his hands. "Sorry, Bruce Lee. But let me ask you one thing first. What *should* be used in a street fight?" Price looked to his companion for approval of his questions.

"Yeah," the biker said. "Is it the double-twirl, spinning, snapping hook kick?"

Jacobson walked over to the two men. She leaned down until she was nose to nose with the hairy troglodyte. Walsh inched a little closer to the sideline—just in case. "No," said Jacobson. "It's the single bite-your-frigging-nose-off-your-ugly-face maneuver."

"Easy, Mrs. Hess," said Walsh. "We have a class to run."

Price placed a heavy hand on the biker's shoulder. "Relax, Fred," he said, then looked at Walsh. "You always let your woman do your fighting?"

A few other spectators grumbled. One woman jumped onto the floor, and grabbed her son by the hand and took him away. Walsh took Jacobson by the elbow and led her back onto

122

the training floor. "Only my light work," Walsh said, adding further insult by turning his back to the intruders.

"Son of a bitch," Fred said as he jumped toward Walsh. Jacobson spun around and hook-kicked the attacker's leg from under him. Someone gasped at the sound of the man's head smashing against the hardwood floor. Surprisingly, he jumped up to his feet, his face a bloody mess, snorting like a wild bull. Price remained on the sidelines with his arms folded, probably confident that his buddy would wipe the floor with the two martial arts instructors.

Fred went straight for Jacobson, his arms extended as if he intended to strangle her. The rest of the students darted to the sidelines. Walsh dove at the back of Fred's legs, catching his ankle and slowing him down, but not stopping him. Walsh looked up, worried that Jacobson was about to get trounced, when seemingly out of nowhere, the skinhead Dirks came crashing against Fred's skull with a thunderous elbow strike, knocking him out cold.

Walsh jumped up and confronted Price as the big man moved in toward Dirks and Jacobson.

"I'll give you one opportunity to leave." Walsh pressed a strong hand against Price's chest and pointed a finger at his nose. "One opportunity." Walsh could sense that Price was a very capable fighter. He hoped that Price would sense the same from him.

Price turned away from Walsh and helped the now semi-conscious Fred to his feet.

Walsh apologized to the students and dismissed them early. The next scheduled class would be in two days, and Walsh was sure the school would be the talk of the neighborhood by then.

"Hell of a first day," Walsh said to his partner.

"We made new friends and everything." Jacobson tilted her head toward the locker-room door where Michael Dirks was now coming out. "He's no beginner."

The two agents walked over to Dirks. "Thanks for helping out," said Walsh.

"It was a pleasure," said Dirks, delighted with himself. "I haven't had an opportunity to stomp anybody in a while."

Walsh decided to work him a little. "Would be a lot more fun if it had been a nigger or a Jew, wouldn't it?"

Dirks' eyes shifted and he tensed for a moment. Walsh could see the veins in his neck start to pop up. The skinhead just nodded, biting down on his lower lip. He turned and walked silently away and out the door.

"What was that all about?" Jacobson asked.

"I haven't a clue." Walsh shrugged.

The wall phone rang on line two. The agents had installed a line for the school as well as for their upstairs apartment. It was Leverick. Ever cautious about speaking on an unsecured line, he simply said that the deal had gotten very complex, and a business meeting would be necessary: "Call when you get back to the apartment."

*   *   *

Matthew Pates slammed down the phone so hard the base cracked. "Idiots," he said. It never ceased to amaze him how two grown men who were sent somewhere to simply observe and report could screw up the whole thing. They were really sorry, Price had said. He and Fred Mills had gulped a couple of beers before heading over to the karate place, and they had just gotten a little carried away.

Serves the dummies right to get their clocks rearranged, thought Pates. He was in his office at home, working on the ARCS newsletter—*When Freedom Rings.* The Brotherhood of Yahweh Martial Arts Academy and the Hesses intrigued him. There's truth to the adage of doing it yourself if you wanted it done right, he thought. He would invite the Hesses over for a friendly night of dinner and conversation.

Then he'd know if they were true believers.

124

13

Danny Park crawled along the floor to the rear of the house. He reached up and unlocked the door, inching it open to try to get a view of the rear perimeter. The wood of the doorjamb immediately splintered at the height where his head would have been.

Bad idea.

Inside the front of the house, Smith and Lucas weren't faring much better.

"I think I hit one of them," Lucas shouted. "But I got no idea how many are out there." A front window crashed in, and a smoking metal cylinder hit the floor and rolled against the wall. Greenish smoke quickly engulfed the room, making it hard to get to the source. Lucas held his breath until he almost passed out, all the while groping and pawing around the floor for the noxiously spewing canister.

"Lucas!" Smith yelled. "Where the hell are you?" Smith had quickly assembled a bulletproof panel and positioned it in front of Moore's bed. Henry Perkins had arranged for its manufacture six months before the shooting, insisting that it would one day come in handy when Moore started addressing huge, stadium-size crowds. He was at least half-right, but right now, Smith would have traded the $8,000 hunk of plastic for a couple of gas masks.

Lucas reached the canister and howled as the hot metal seared his flesh. His eyes burned and he could hardly see through the tears as he struggled to toss the menacing cylinder out of the window.

Smith lifted Moore out of bed and held him in his arms. "Don't breathe deep, Mr. Moore. We got to get you to the rear of the house." Smith ran down the narrow hallway, almost knocking over Park on the way.

"They've gassed it," Smith said, blowing out a deep exhale.

Another crash came through a front window. Another canister twirled on the floor, spewing its green gas.

Trapped in the middle of the house with both sides filling up fast with noxious vapors, the men could see that their options were practically nil.

"Let's give it up," said Smith, his arms tiring from Moore's weight. Moore nodded, his eyes betraying defeat.

"Forget it," snapped Lucas, maintaining a tight grip on his pistol. "Let's take as many down with us as possible."

"They wouldn't be gassing us if they wanted to kill us, fool," Smith shouted in his face. Moore reached up and grabbed Lucas' shirt. He nodded, looking up imploringly.

"Wait," said Park, pointing toward an access panel in the ceiling. "Attic storage."

"Oh, great idea, Park," said Lucas. "After we hoist Mr. Moore up there, and the rest of us get killed, I guess they'll all just forget the whole thing and go away."

The hallway was starting to fill with gas. Someone could be heard shouting orders outside the house. The attackers were rapidly closing in on them.

"Look," said Park. "One of us goes up and out. I don't

care who. If they wanted us dead, we'd be there already."

"I agree," said Smith. "Park, you go."

Sighing, Lucas opened the panel and then locked his fingers together to give Park a leg up. In a second, the agile Korean was up and inside the attic. Once the panel was shut, the only light came from the louvers on either end of the long room. Park could hear muffled shouting and scuffling below as he crawled toward the cracks of light, the sauna-like heat of the attic sticking his shirt to him like an extra skin. He flipped onto his back and kicked out with both feet, easily popping out the brittle wooden louver. The opening was small—about eighteen inches in diameter. Park placed his right arm through the opening, contorting to fit his shoulders. Once his arms and torso were outside he reached up and grabbed the asphalt shingles, ignoring the searing pain from the sun-baked roof. He hoisted himself up, his arm strength waning as he pulled himself through the narrow opening. Uncertainty engulfed Park for a moment, as he realized that if he slipped, he would fall thirty feet to the ground. He managed to maneuver his fore-arms onto either side of the peak, and with a painful groan, hoisted one leg over. He had to press hard on the rough shingles to keep from falling back, his chin scraping painfully against the asphalt. *This is it, Danny,* he told himself, and with one final burst of energy, threw the other leg over. Resting there for a second, squinting against the bright sunlight, he wiped his bloodied chin with the back of his hand. Keeping his back flat against the roof, he slid down to the edge.

The rear of the house was now clear, unguarded—a lucky break, or he would never had made it so far. Car doors slammed shut around front, and someone barked orders to move out. Then came the sound of engines turning over and the popping sound of tires pressing into the loose gravel. The young Korean hung over the edge of the gutters by his fingertips, his feet still about twelve feet from the ground. With hardly a thought, he let go, bending his knees sharply when he hit the ground, then rolling out to absorb the shock of the fall.

The blissful satisfaction of coming out of a treacherous situation alive was short-lived when Park realized that he was on the wrong end of a gun barrel.

"Slowly," said a man who looked like he had just returned from deer hunting. He wore camouflaged pants, a green hunting vest and an orange cap. Park figured that since the sound of gunshots in the distance was nothing strange in these woods during hunting season, their assailants were confident that they could conduct the daylight raid without fear of someone calling the police "Up. Keep your fingers locked and pressed against your chest."

Park eased his way up, studying his captor. He was alert—not the kind of man who could be easily disarmed. Smart, too. When a man was in front of you, he could be very dangerous, even with his hands in the air. The masked man also stayed just out of range of a surprise sweep or kick. Without taking his eyes off Park, the man reached into his vest pocket and flipped open a cell phone. "I have the Korean ... no—no sign of *him.*"

As the man nodded, Park wondered if the orders for his execution were coming through the airwaves at that very moment. As Park thought that the time was now to make a move, another man, outfitted almost identically to the first, emerged from the woods. Any opportunity to disarm his captor had just vanished. The man placed his phone back in his vest pocket, and as if sensing the approach of his comrade, took two steps back from Park. He then glanced quickly over his shoulder at the approaching figure before returning his gaze to Park.

"So what now?" Park asked.

"Now you tell me where the other one is."

"Pal, I wish I knew."

"Wrong answer." He took a step closer to the Korean,

128

training the machine pistol on Park's face. The other man was on them now. "Enjoy the last five seconds of your life."

Park had been in tough spots before. Dangerous spots. He had always felt that he would come out of them okay. Not this time. He was convinced that this was it. He didn't see his whole life flash before his eyes. He didn't even feel scared out of his mind. He just felt sad.

Park closed his eyes, bracing himself for the last sound he would ever hear. The gunshot came. Park shuddered hard but he wasn't dead. He wasn't even shot.

Like someone about to test the sunlight after spending a week in a dark cave, Park slowly raised his eyelids. There he was, the crazy bastard. Standing there with an ear-to-ear grin and holding a bloodied hunting knife in his hands. At Henry Perkins' feet lay the body, the throat cut so deeply that the spinal cord was visible through the bloodied mess of ripped muscle and flesh, dead finger still curled around the pulled trigger.

"Ain't you gonna thank me, Park?"

"Thank you ... and screw you." Park poked the big man in the chest. "What the hell did you do?"

Perkins returned the huge hunting knife to a sheath on his belt. Ammunition belts and weapon holsters crisscrossed the front of his way-too-small hunting vest. He looked like Rambo the Mental Patient.

"We're at war, Park. No prisoners."

Park got right up in the big man's face. "Perkins! You gotta wake up, you dumb son of a bitch. We have to go to the police." Park remembered the business card he had shoved in his pocket earlier—an FBI agent named Dalton something or other.

Perkins pushed him back. "No way. They'll just get us killed."

"What do we do then, Perkins? Start knocking on doors: 'Excuse us; we're looking for a kidnapped African-

American leader and his two bodyguards; are they by any chance in your basement?'"

Perkins smiled. A dangerous, I-just-can't-wait-to-kill-somebody-again grin. "We visit good old Dr. LeGrande, and he tells us where they took Mr. Moore."

It was the craziest idea Park had ever heard. But the more he thought about that traitorous pig LeGrande, the better it sounded. "Let's do it," he said, hardly believing the words came out of his mouth.

"Yes!" Perkins said as he kicked the bloodied corpse for punctuation. "Follow me, Park. My jeep is hidden about a mile through the brush. We'll drive back to the city and catch a few winks before hunting down LeGrande." Without waiting for a response, Perkins turned and started walking toward the woods.

Although part of his mind screamed not to, Park followed.

*   *   *

Bob's Big Boy was serving Mexican buffet for dinner. Walsh was tempted, but finally decided to pass on the complicated task of building tacos and ordered a sandwich. Jacobson ordered a bowl of soup.

The restaurant was crowded and noisy. Leverick had doubted very much that anyone would be following the two agents, but always on the better side of caution, he had set up the meeting ready with a cover. He would soon arrive, ready to play the role of a media salesmen for KaratePlus, a martial arts supply wholesaler. Ready just in case someone from Milton happened to run into the Hesses or in the unlikely event that they were followed.

Jacobson winced as she examined the knuckles on her right hand.

"Problem?" Walsh asked

"Just one of those bruises that show up hours later."

"All in all, not a bad first day, though," said Walsh. "We got noticed by the bad guys; we won a fight in front of our students; and Dalton gets to pay for dinner."

"You don't think we should have waited for him before we ordered?"

"It'll be okay with Dalton. He'll probably just want coffee."

The Mexican food bar suddenly became noisy as a horrified waitress confronted two small boys as they concocted taco-like abominations on their precariously held dishes. They had left a trail of shredded cheese, lettuce and chopped tomato on the carpet. After a desperate call for the boys' parents and a quick cleanup by two busboys, order was once again returned to the festival of fat and grease.

Jacobson cracked her knuckles, shaking her head and laughing. "So what do you think? Fifty lashes with a wet noodle for each boy?"

"At least," said Walsh. "They're an absolute menace to society."

"Let me ask you something." She leaned in a little closer, just in time for the waitress to plop down the dishes of food. The waitress mumbled a half-hearted apology with her back turned, then disappeared through the kitchen doors.

"I'll remind Dalton to stiff her," said Walsh. "You were about to ask me ...?"

"You've got a take-no-bull reputation at the Bureau. I won't tell you who, but one of the agents on my old squad in Newark said you had a higher body count than *Die Hard I, II,* and *III* put together."

"I had to take a few out. I try not to think about it much."

Jacobson waved her hands in the air. "No, no. That's not what I'm getting at. I wondered after seeing those kids how a man like you treats his own children."

"You mean how often do I beat them?"

"Do you?"

Walsh smiled. "If a tenth of what you've heard about me is true, it would be a pretty sad case if I were to use violence against a six- and a ten-year-old."

"I wasn't talking about shooting them."

Walsh laughed. "You know what the Bible says. 'Spare the rod and spoil the child.' Actually I think I spanked my little guy twice in his life. Once for kicking me in the groin."

"So you do have a weak spot?"

"Yeah. My family." Walsh tilted his head toward the entrance to the restaurant. "The boss is here."

Leverick was dressed in a blue sports jacket with beige pants and brown shoes. He placed a leather briefcase on the table.

"Sorry I'm late." Leverick flipped open his briefcase and removed two thick, spiral bound books. Each book cover mimicked a catalogue of martial arts equipment. He then placed a small metal cylinder in the center of the table and flipped a tiny switch on its side. "Those are the most recent profiles of ARCS members and their families as well as some aerial surveillance shots of the compound."

Jacobson looked around nervously, obviously concerned with the ears around them.

Walsh picked up the metal cylinder. "What is this?"

"It's the latest thing from R & D. Creates a sort of sound vacuum around us. We are free to speak."

"Who are you ... Agent Q?" Walsh placed the device back on the table.

"We've come a long way since the cone of silence, you've got to admit," said Leverick.

The waitress appeared with her order pad ready. Leverick waved her off with a request for a cup of decaffeinated coffee.

"You don't look well, Dalton," said Walsh. He wasn't used to seeing Leverick looking every bit his fifty years and then some. Walsh guessed that this was to be expected after almost three decades with the Bureau, Dalton-Leverick-style. If many street cops and most thugs thought all FBI agents were pencilnecks who never got their hands dirty, they'd never met Walsh's friend and mentor.

"Rough day," Leverick said. "Edwin Moore was moved by his bodyguards to a supposedly safe house. This morning, I helped sift through what was left of it."

"Moore?" asked Walsh.

"That's the thing. There were five dead. None of them were Moore or his bodyguards."

"ARCS people?" asked Jacobson.

"Not unless they've taken their 'Whites Only' sign off the clubhouse door." Leverick sat silent for a moment. The waitress plopped the cup of coffee on the table. "Moore's shooter is still claiming to be an assassin for Sons Elohim. Other than that he's clamped up so tight we couldn't pull a pin out of his butt with a tow truck. Bottom line is that the trail to ARCS is getting cool."

Walsh suddenly lost his appetite. He pushed his half-eaten sandwich away from him. "You're not telling us that our assignment is being shut down?"

"Shut down?" said Jacobson. "We're about to get off the ground! Two ARCS guys even came to the school and started some trouble. You couldn't ask for a better launch."

Leverick formed his hands into a T shape. "Time out, kids. It's not that bad. Yet. But it does look like we could be barking up the wrong tree."

Walsh could tell when his friend and partner of many years was insincere. "You're full of crap, Dalton. ARCS shot Moore. Raymond Hill is an ARCS guy—no doubt about it."

"The director is starting to think that Hill, although obviously having ties to ARCS, might have acted on his own. Since the director also has the President's ear, what he thinks carries a lot of weight. *The New York Times* is about to make

Edwin Moore the Jimmy Hoffa of the nineties. Which means that 'Where's Moore?' takes over as the Bureau's driving theme, and white-supremacist-world-dominance-conspiracies become somewhat less of a priority."

"Wait a second," said Jacobson. "We can get cold on an operation just like that?" She snapped her fingers in the air. "The wind blows in a different direction this morning and the chief changes his mind? Screw him!"

Walsh couldn't blame her for being incredulous. She had a chance to sink her teeth into a good deep-cover assignment, and it looked like it could be snatched away. Walsh remembered how anxious he was his first time out. If the plug had been pulled on him before he had a chance to prove himself he would have been devastated.

Walsh placed a hand on her shoulder. "It just means we justify ourselves. Pronto." He looked over at Leverick. "Give us a week. We'll come up with something good."

Leverick agreed to sing, dance, evade, beg, borrow and steal to buy the assignment some more time. He also picked up the check.

14

The streets outside Carl LeGrande's apartment were deserted. The doorman of the Jamaica Heights apartment building was taking advantage of the early morning hour, slumped over in his chair, a magazine dangling from his limp hand.

Danny Park watched the clock on the dashboard blink to 3 a.m. He tapped his fingernails against the glass, occasionally glancing over at the man whom he had voted most likely to get all his friends killed. Perkins continued to stare out the window. He hadn't said a word for the last hour and a half, except to tell Park to shut up and wait. When it felt right, they'd go in. He had instincts for these kinds of things. Just like his instincts told him that LeGrande would not be guarded. The last thing he would suspect was for the hunted to become the hunters. Perkins sat, staring and motionless like a crocodile waiting in shallow water.

It was almost funny, thought Park, singing in his mind to the rhythm of his tapping fingers, *"I'm an idiot, for going along with this psycho."* At least they had taken the time to change into some clean street clothes. Perkins looked a little less crazy in his blue suit than he did as *The Deer Hunter.*

Without warning, Perkins got out of the car. Park followed, right on his heels.

"You're really starting to worry me, Huck," said Park. "Maybe we should rethink our position with the cops."

Perkins kept walking.

"Guess not," Park said as both men entered the doorway. Perkins placed a finger on his lips, signaling for silence as the pair slipped by the sleeping doorman and through a door at the end of the lobby that read "STAIRS/FIRE EXIT."

Once inside, they quickly and quietly trotted up the nine flights to LeGrande's floor. Park barely broke a sweat. Perkins looked soaked, his face tomato-red.

"Coulda been worse, Huck," Park quipped. "Coulda been the penthouse floor."

Perkins didn't acknowledge the comment. He slowly opened the staircase door and stuck his head out. A second later, Park followed him into the hallway. The two men headed down the corridor toward apartment 9W. The click of a door latch froze them. Someone emerged from an apartment only two doors away from LeGrande's. Perkins spun around, grabbed Park by the shoulder and threw him against the corridor wall. He pressed the palm of his hand hard against Park's mouth. "Don't move, Danny," Perkins ordered, his face pressed tightly against the back of his own hand.

Park couldn't see over the hulking Perkins, but could hear a man's voice mumbling, "friggin' queers," as he passed them on his way to the elevators. Perkins didn't let up until the elevator pinged and the doors had closed.

Park shoved Perkins away. "You're a jerkoff, man," he hissed.

Perkins tilted his head toward the elevators. "I would

136

have had to kill him if he'd seen our faces," he chortled. "Quiet. Let's go."

A second later, they were at LeGrande's door.

"What now?" Park whispered. "Do we ring the bell and claim to have his pizza?"

Perkins pulled out a key from his jacket pocket. "Never leave your house key on the ring when you park your car." He slid the key into the lock and slowly turned it. In the dead silence, the click of the latch seemed to reverberate down the hall. The two men slipped inside the dark apartment, where LeGrande's breathing was audible in the otherwise eerie quiet.

Perkins removed a cloth from his pocket as he entered the bedroom. Park moved catlike to the side of LeGrande's bed nearest the window. A few muffled horns and an occasional siren could now be heard from the street. LeGrande's breathing was still the most audible sound in the room. The doctor slept on his back, the covers pulled tightly around his neck. Tiny slits of white were visible from the corners of his eyes. He looked more like a man suffering from a seizure than someone peacefully sleeping. Those white slits bulged open as Perkins slipped a gag around the doctor's mouth with the speed and skill of a rattlesnake handler. The big man ripped the covers from LeGrande and pulled him by his collar to a sitting position. Park yanked their victim's arms behind his back and slapped on a pair of handcuffs. LeGrande's eyes bulged even more, straining as if to curse his captors.

Park took a deep breath. Now it was his turn to sweat. He was nervous as hell, and Perkins looked cool as an afternoon in November. The sadistic bastard was enjoying this, Park thought.

"Hello ... Doc," said Perkins. "In a moment or two, I'll take off the gag and give you an opportunity to speak. You will not yell for help. In fact, you will not raise your voice. That would upset me." Perkins reached inside his jacket and whipped out a small pair of tin snips. "Each time I'm upset,

Doc, you will lose something. It could be a finger. Maybe your earlobe. Maybe an eyeball."

LeGrande tried to jump from the bed, and Perkins slammed him back. Perkins then backhanded the doctor across the side of his jaw. "Consider that a favor," Perkins growled.

"Take it easy," Park protested.

Perkins glared at Park. This wasn't going to go well. Park was sure of that now. He reminded himself that if LeGrande had his way, the whole bunch of them would have been killed. That's *if* Perkins was right about LeGrande.

Perkins grabbed LeGrande by his green striped pajama top and pulled him up so they were nose to nose. "I'm going to take off the gag now. Speak very low so we don't disturb the neighbors." For a few moments after Perkins pulled down the gag, the only sound in the room was LeGrande's heavy, panicked breathing.

"You're both dead men," LeGrande finally spit through clenched teeth.

Perkins clamped his powerful fingers around LeGrande's throat. The doctor's eyes bulged, and he thrashed furiously. Park shivered as if a cold, evil presence had just entered his body. Instead of ripping Perkins' arms away, Park thought of all the reasons why LeGrande was a complete scumbag and deserved to die. Watching LeGrande desperately convulse for air actually excited a part of him that craved retribution. He had been seduced by the satisfaction of revenge and the thrill of cruelty. He had once read that the only thing that separated Joe Citizen (who never so much as took 11 items to the 10-item express lane) from the most sadistic killer is the reason they do it. He never really believed it. Until now.

Perkins released his grip and let LeGrande fall back onto the bed.

"This may prove to be more difficult than I'd thought," Perkins said flatly. He put the gag back around LeGrande's mouth and slapped him lightly to revive him. Holding the tin snips in front of Park's face, Perkins smiled. "It's time to use a little persuasion."

Park offered no protest.

*   *   *

When Walsh walked into the living room, Jacobson was sitting on the sofa, staring at the phone.

"You alright, Jacobson?"

Jacobson nodded. "You'll never guess who that was on the phone."

"J. Edgar Hoover?"

"Stranger than that. Elizabeth Pates just called to welcome us to the neighborhood."

Walsh set the laptop on the table. He had been planning to file their report electronically, but that would have to wait. "I love it when a plan comes together."

Jacobson tossed the portable phone to one side. "There's more. We're invited to have dinner with the Pateses tonight."

Walsh clenched his fist in the air. "Yes!"

"I have to admit it, I had my doubts," said Jacobson, still looking amazed by the latest development in their deep-cover assignment.

"It happens like that sometimes, Jacobson. The first time I went deep-cover ..."

"... two members of the Henchmen biker gang knocked on your door on Saturday morning."

Walsh shook his head in mock disgust.

"You forget that I've read everything the Bureau has on file about your undercover work, agent Walsh. Like when you actually volunteered to be placed inside a prison cell to buddy up with a member of the country's most notorious biker gang."

"Agents do a lot of strange things when they're young, ambitious, and ignorant." Walsh raised an eyebrow, implying that he was describing Jacobson's current attitude.

"I resent the implications of that remark," she responded. "I'm not that young anymore."

"One thing you won't read in the files is how I sat there in that prison cell not sure if it was a great beginning to the operation or the end of my life."

"What do you feel about our opportunity to get into the compound tonight?"

"There are a few possibilities. Don't get me wrong, partner, I'm as pumped up about this as you are. However, although Pates could have bought our cover hook, line and sinker, he could also be suspicious and wants to meet us face to face to make up his own mind."

Jacobson punched the palm of her hand. "Big deal. I'm ready."

Walsh looked around the apartment and gestured with an open hand. "Or in spite of our daily sweeps of the place, they could have managed to install a sophisticated snoop device and are planning to kill us tonight."

"Maybe Mrs. Pates is going to serve us poison pigs in a blanket."

"My favorite," said Walsh. "We live for danger, Jacobson." He looked at his watch. "We'd better get ready. What do you bring to a white supremacist's dinner party anyway?"

"The usual: Spanish rice and matzoball soup."

"I think I'm going to lose my position as the biggest wiseass in the Bureau."

"I try."

*   *   *

After a while, it gets hard to tell what day it is when you've been deprived of natural light, clocks or any TV or radios. Lucas' best guess was that they'd been locked up for about two days. He surmised that they were in a basement

140

stronghold, probably a homemade fallout shelter of some kind. The room was about 300 square feet with stone walls, painted white, and a solid, white-plaster ceiling with two rows of caged fluorescent lights. A single vent in the middle of the ceiling fed the room with a comfortable flow of air. They had been served food twice. A few tuna salad (or maybe it had been chicken) sandwiches had been dropped off, maybe yesterday. Today, they had eaten rice and fish. The food had been cold, but he and Smith had attacked it like wolves.

Edwin Moore had slept most of this time, waking only once to drink his liquid meal through a straw. He had no way of communicating with Smith and Lucas. The bastards hadn't left them so much as a pad and pencil for Moore to write with.

Lucas looked over at Smith, who was ever steadfast in his search for a way out, touching every stone on the walls and examining the lights and air vent for the hundredth time.

"You're gonna lose your mind, Maxwell. You look like a friggin' crazy tiger at the zoo," Lucas said.

"Shut up ... and my name's Max."

The familiar hum of the descending elevator ended the verbal joust. Even Moore was stirred by the ominous sound. The three men stared at the thick steel door as the elevator rumbled to a stop. *Now,* thought Lucas. *As soon as the guard opens the door, before he gets a chance to train his machine pistol on us.* The hard rhythm of the militaristic stepping on the other side of that steel door echoed in Lucas' head like a bass drum. In his mind, he leaped up like a leopard and pounced on his prey, easily disarming the guards and placing a bullet in their skulls. He then led Smith and the helpless Moore to freedom. In reality, he sat defeated as two men with their now-all-too-familiar Mac 10 pistols entered and took up positions on either side of the door.

Lucas stood. Smith joined him, both men instinctively shielding Moore.

Terrance Al-Aziz emerged through the doorway, one of his cronies trotting behind him with a small chair. Al-Aziz sat without thinking about it, the chair placed beneath him with perfect timing.

"Please sit," Al-Aziz said. Although said politely, it was an order. Lucas and Smith looked at each other, then sat down on the metal bench.

Al-Aziz leaned over and sighed, shaking his head as if he had nothing to do with their predicament and was about to lecture a couple of misbehaving children. Lucas looked over his shoulder at Moore whose eyes were open wide, his body alert, propping himself up on his elbow to hear Al-Aziz speak.

"I am very sorry that you have been treated so poorly," Al-Aziz offered.

"Screw you," Smith spat. Al-Aziz raised his hand to prevent his henchmen from moving on Smith.

"I'm sure you're sorry," said Lucas. "Sorry that we're not all dead."

Al-Aziz chortled in that cliché mad scientist way of his. "Mr. Green. Do you really think that you'd be alive if I didn't want you to be?"

"Then why the attack on the safe house?" Lucas hissed.

Al-Aziz flared his nostrils and clenched his fists.

Lucas shrugged. "Something I said."

"You killed men who were trying to protect you."

Moore mumbled something through his wired jaw that sounded like, "You're full of it." Lucas and Smith turned around to see Moore waving his hand as if to warn them not to believe a word this lying snake said.

Al-Aziz opened his arms and managed a tight smile. "My poor misguided friends. Don't you see? The very people who failed to assassinate Mr. Moore have now won." Al-Aziz stood up and began to walk away. After a melodramatic pause, he turned around. "I'd like nothing better than to let you go, but until we find Perkins and the Korean, there is just no way to know how deep the conspiracy goes. Did you know that

Henry Perkins has ties to the Secret Service?" He turned again to leave.

Lucas bolted up. Two machine pistols immediately honed in on him as if they had minds of their own. "Wait! I may be able to help you find Perkins and Park."

Smith looked at Lucas, astonished. "You're not buying this crap, Lucas?" He grabbed Lucas's arm.

Lucas yanked his arm free. "He makes sense, man. Don't you see? Perkins set everything up. Think about it. He was trying to get us away from official protection."

Moore collapsed on his back and let out a long sigh. "No ... no," he said through his wired-up jaw.

Al-Aziz gestured for Lucas to join him. Lucas stopped momentarily at the doorway to look back at his friend, and his eyes were met with a look of hatred for what Max Smith could only see as betrayal.

"This is the right thing to do," Lucas said.

Smith looked away. Lucas stared at him as long as he could until the steel door clanged shut. He hoped he would see them again. He knew his only chance of escape was coming up soon.

15

Until today, Walsh and Jacobson had seen the ARCS compound only from aerial surveillance. Driving through the thickly wooded roadway, it was hard to imagine that there was really going to be a house within the burgeoning forest.

Jacobson tapped her fingers on the white cake box, occasionally plucking the tightly wrapped cord like a guitar string. She suggested something Jewish, like a cinnamon loaf or rugelach, just because she desired to say in her own small way, "Screw you, you racist pig," to Mr. Pates. After some discussion and negotiation, they had decided on devil's-food cake.

The road curved at such an angle that it seemed as if they had driven in a complete circle. They found themselves in front of a huge gate with a sign reading "PRIVATE—TRESPASSERS, ESPECIALLY NON-WHITES, WILL BE SHOT." On either side of the gate was a metal and barbed wire fence that stretched deep into the woods. Wires running through it suggested high-tech security. About twenty feet inside the gate was a guard tower. A man in green fatigues spoke into a headset mike, an automatic rifle hung casually over his shoulder.

"I'll bet he doesn't have a permit to own that," said Walsh, eyeing the outlawed assault weapon.

"We don't give permits to own that anymore. Let's arrest him," said Jacobson. "Do you think Leverick would settle for a simple weapons violation for one of Pates' men?"

"Cute," Walsh muttered.

A red light on top of the gate started to flash and spin as the gate rolled open. Walsh guessed they were under surveillance via several tree-mounted cameras that sent images back to a command center within the compound. Instructions would then be radioed back to the tower guard to open the gate.

"Welcome to Jurassic Park." Walsh eased the car through at about 10 miles an hour. Three men in heavy camouflage were suddenly in front of the car, forcing Walsh to stop short.

"Are we in trouble, Mr. Hess?"

Walsh kept his eyes on the men, but could see with his peripheral vision Jacobson reaching under the dashboard for her Colt 380. She and Walsh had measured the risk, and decided that a handgun under the seat would not be an unusual thing for the Hesses to have should Pates' men search the car.

"Don't. I think we're ok." Walsh lowered the window.

One of the men walked to the car window and saluted the couple. Jacobson sat back with the cake box on her lap and smiled. "Dessert," she offered, holding it up by the string.

"I'm sorry to have to do this, Mrs. Hess," the young guard said gently. "May I please see that box?" Jacobson passed it to Walsh, who held it up for the guard. The young man produced an eight-inch combat knife and clipped the strings. He pushed the top open with the blade. Satisfied that there was no explosive device hidden in the cake, he thanked them for their cooperation. He instructed them to follow the road past the row of barracks and make a right where the road forks. They would find the Pates house at the end of the second road.

146

Walsh tapped his forefinger to his temple, a signal for Jacobson they had discussed beforehand. It meant "Stick to the script—no more talking freely." They were without their anti-bug gizmos, and there was no way of telling how many sophisticated listening devices Pates had installed in the compound, or to what degree he was suspicious of his guests.

In front of the two-story, brick-faced home, was a paved parking spot, large enough for a half-dozen vehicles. Walsh parked between a black Cherokee Sport Jeep and a silver Lincoln Town Car.

Two more guards greeted them as the agents stepped from their car. After a quick frisk and another inspection of the cake box, they were permitted to approach the house.

The front door bore the ARCS emblem, and the tiny brass doorknocker had Third Reich emblems embossed into the metal. Jacobson rang the doorbell.

A young boy answered. He was about 10, with dark hair, and was wearing low, baggy jeans and a Pittsburgh Penguins jersey. Without introduction, the boy turned and trotted off, yelling to his mom that more visitors were here. Elizabeth Pates emerged a few moments later, the little boy in tow.

She smiled warmly.

"Welcome. I'm Liz Pates. You must be the Hesses."

"Yes," said Walsh. "I'm Ed and this is my wife Kim."

Jacobson shook hands with her. "A pleasure, Liz. A little something for dessert."

Elizabeth Pates took the cake box and handed it to her son who then scurried off.

"I'm so glad you were able to join us on such short notice. Please come in. My husband is very anxious to meet you."

Liz Pates ushered them inside and into a cozy living room that would have betrayed nothing of the couple's political beliefs had it not been for the many pictures hanging from the walls. One in particular caught Walsh's attention. It was a panoramic shot of a 1925 march in Washington with 40,000 hooded KKK members parading down Pennsylvania Avenue.

Matthew Pates caught Walsh looking at the old photo and took the opportunity to introduce himself.

"My grandfather marched in that rally. Those were the days when the Klan had over four million members. That was when Americans actually occupied the White House. Before the Klan lost its nerve." Pates extended a hand to Walsh. "Matthew Pates. Welcome to my home."

"Edward Hess." Walsh turned to introduce his wife but Jacobson had already been escorted by Elizabeth Pates to meet two women on the other side of the room. Pates presented the ARCS lawyer, Brian Hastings, and another senior ARCS member, Pastor John Hampton, and introduced them as his closest and most trusted friends.

"I heard some good things about you, Ed," John Hampton said cheerfully as he pumped Walsh's hand. "I wish more people would take a public stand for segregation and white supremacy." Hampton had three strands of hair that looked as if they were glued onto an otherwise bald head. Large liver spots dotted his forehead and cheeks and his snake-like smile reminded Walsh of the sleazy televangelist he used to see on late night TV encouraging people to send $50 for their two 'lucky blessings.'

Brian Hastings was not as cordial. When he shook Walsh's hand he stared at him with distrust and made no attempt to hide his disdain. Hastings, a small-shouldered man with a bit of a paunch, wore round glasses that magnified his suspicious gaze. His wrinkled forehead and stiff mouth made him appear to be locked in an angry frown. "I'd be very interested to know all about your experiences in New York, Ed," said Hastings. "Believe me, I'll verify it all."

"It's a pleasure to meet you, too ... Brian."

148

After a few moments of awkward silence, Matthew Pates politely ushered his guests into the dining room.

*   *   *

Pastor Hampton and his wife Sarah sat to the right of the Hesses, and across from them sat Brian Hastings and his wife, Lynne. Pates sat at the end of the table. After bringing family-style servings of chicken, mixed vegetables, and boiled potatoes, Liz Pates took her place at the other end.

Hampton stood up and folded his hands across his chest. "Let us pray," he said, bowing his head and closing his eyes. Walsh and Jacobson did the same. "Thank you, Lord," Hampton continued. "Thank you for the opportunity for fellowship with new members of our community. We ask your blessing over our race. Teach us to love. Teach us to hate. Help us to win the struggle. Amen."

There was little conversation for the first few minutes. The room was filled with the clicks, pings, and tinks of serving dishes, glasses, and silverware. Pates served himself a generous pile of chicken pieces, then passed the dish to Jacobson, smiling warmly as he did so.

On the wall behind the Hastingses and the Hamptons hung an unusual painting—a very life-like rendering of Adolf Hitler on one knee in full Nazi regalia, supporting a huge cross on his shoulders. The words "Help With the Master's Burden" were hand-lettered in black ink on the clouded sky.

"A nephew of George Lincoln Rockwell gave me that painting," Pates said. "You like it?"

"It's a fine piece,"—*of crap,* thought Walsh. "Don't you think so, honey?" he asked Jacobson.

"It says so much about us all, doesn't it?" Jacobson answered.

Pates pointed at the picture. "I liken him to the second coming of Jesus Christ and myself to the apostle Paul," he said proudly.

149

"Hallelujah and praise the Lord!" Hampton shouted. "The Fuehrer wasn't allowed to finish the great work he started, and it's up to us to see it through."

Jacobson's mouth immediately dried up, and the piece of chicken she was chewing suddenly tasted like shredded cardboard and chalk powder. Afraid that she was about to choke, she grabbed her glass and gulped a drink of water.

"You alright, Kim?" Lynne Hastings asked with the tone of a caring mother.

Jacobson patted her chest. "Sorry, almost went down the wrong pipe." She tried desperately to pull herself together. She was blowing it, and she was sure her face betrayed her as if she had a Star of David tattooed on her forehead. *It's now or never, Katherine,* she told herself. "We could have used people like you in Hymietown New York," she said to Pates.

Pates slapped the table. "Tell me about it. The only truth that Nigger Hal Shelton ever spoke was calling that cesspool Hymietown."

"I don't know how you could have lived there." Sarah Hampton placed her hand over her heart. "Negroes running wild, murdering whites in the streets and breeding like mosquitoes in a wet July. Jews controlling all the banks, schools and news media. How did you manage?"

"We didn't." Jacobson turned to Walsh. "The bastard sons of Satan drove us out."

Nice recovery, thought Walsh about his partner. He had had his eye on the huge carving knife Pates had left in the chicken, and if things went sour, he wasn't going to give Pates a chance to snatch that pistol out of his holster. "I feel like I can trust you folks," said Walsh. Heads immediately starting bobbing in agreement. "The reason we had to leave ..."

"... Honey, don't," said Jacobson right on cue. She touched Walsh's knee, while her face and eyes pleaded for his silence. *Academy Award nomination for certain,* Walsh thought.

"Sweetheart, there comes a time when you have to take

a leap of faith in your fellow human beings." He smiled at her.

"Amen," said Hampton.

Pates tilted back in his chair, picking his teeth with a fork. "So why *did* you leave?"

Walsh took a deep breath and let it out slowly, hesitating just the right amount of time before baring his soul to his new friends. "A group of men came to the school—Jews who had nothing better to do than parade around all day handing out Kike propaganda about the threat of another holocaust and telling everyone not to tolerate our behavior."

"Imagine that," said Jacobson.

"I had the gym wired with an alarm system that triggered a buzzer in our bedroom. It had gone off one night and when I came down, I found this little bastard—couldn't have been more than seventeen—fixing to burn down the place. I broke him up pretty good and dumped him in a trash container about 10 blocks away. Before he passed out, he warned me that he was part of Sons Elohim, and they would avenge him." Walsh looked directly at Pates. "He died in a hospital three days later."

Jacobson looked at Sarah Hampton, who looked back sympathetically. "They burned us out a week later," said Jacobson.

"So I taught privately," said Walsh. "Did a little body-guard work for a year or so, then came here."

"Ed, I'm sorry about the trouble at your school the other day." Pates laughed. "Good help is hard to find."

"Forget it. Though I do hope the men guarding your compound out there are more capable than the two you sent to the school."

Jacobson elbowed Walsh in the side and spoke through gritted teeth, "Manners, dear. We're guests, don't forget."

"Nonsense," said Pates. "I like a man who speaks his mind. Jimmy and Fred are loyal patriots. But maybe a little more training as soldiers is in order."

Hastings glared at Walsh. Since they had first shaken hands, Hastings had made no secret of his distrust toward Edward Hess. While Pates himself was all smiles, Hastings stared fiercely at Walsh and practically grilled him on every word that came out of his mouth. Walsh didn't doubt that this was exactly the way Pates had planned it. It was their equivalent of a good-cop/bad-cop interrogation.

"Do you fancy yourself a soldier, Mr. Hess?" Hastings was getting better at delivering sarcastic questions and remarks as the night went on.

Pates intervened. "Now, Brian. Ed is obviously very good at what he does. There's no need for any hostility." The ARCS leader then looked directly at Walsh. "You'll have to forgive Brian. He's a lawyer."

The comment actually got Hastings to smile.

"I'm sorry, Ed," Hastings muttered. "It takes me a while to warm up to new people. Especially since we're always living with the threat of ZOG crawling up our backs. Matthew has good instincts when it comes to a man's character so ..." Hastings held up his glass. "... welcome to Milton, Pennsylvania."

Walsh took out his wallet and flipped it open. "FBI, you're all under arrest." The look of horror on his partner's face quickly faded as she saw that he was holding nothing more than his Edward Hess driver's license.

Pates pounded the table. "On what charge?" he managed to blurt through hearty laughter. Hastings joined in the merriment, and the infectious mirth spread around the table. Even the normally stoic pastor joined in the fun.

Hastings saluted Walsh. "Very funny. All kidding aside, do you think that stuff you teach is effective in real life?"

"That depends on what real life is, Brian," said Walsh.

"I don't mean the usual 'can you stop a bullet' line. What if you're against two experienced, combat-trained knife fighters? What are you going to do?"

Jacobson looked as if she wanted to jump across the table and smack Hastings upside his head. *Good,* thought Walsh. She was right in character with the situation. Walsh had to be also. He was being challenged in front of his wife and couldn't back down. It reminded him of being undercover with the outlaw biker gangs. It seemed every other day some guy was getting in his face accusing him of being a cop. He had to fight back then as he was going to do now.

"I'm going to kill them both. Unless, of course, they're friends. Then I'll just put them in the hospital long enough to learn their lesson." Walsh grinned at Pates.

Pates let out a long whistle. "Can you really walk that walk, Ed?"

Walsh stared at Pates' empty eyes. Eyes that indicated nothing but a cold heart and cruel mind. Eyes that said, "I only know one way, and that's all the way."

"I think maybe you can," Pates finally said. "I have a little proposition for you. If you would like to train with us and run some hand-to-hand drills right here at the compound, I'd guarantee you that within the next two months, you'll have more new students at your karate academy than you can handle."

"What's the interview like?" Walsh quipped.

Pates grinned. "You disarm two of my best, and you're in."

"And if I can't?"

Pates leaned forward, and spoke low and intensely. "You'll bleed."

*   *   *

It was a warm night, so after praying in his room, Avi took a walk. He wore his Dr. Martens and a pair of coveralls. He was shirtless with one strap of the coveralls over his shoulder, the other dangling freely at his side. He modeled this look from pictures they had on file of skinheads at white power rallies. He stopped for a moment to look at his reflection in the window of a closed dry cleaners. The skinhead with the Nazi tattoo who looked back wasn't him. It felt as if he had borrowed this strange and ugly body, and he would be able to simply discard it when he had accomplished his mission. In a way, that was true. His uncle could remove the tattoos, and his hair would grow back. His soul might even heal.

The downtown streets were cluttered with people going in and out of Milton's ice cream shops, bars, and coffee spots. Avi found himself enjoying the strange, sometimes fearful, looks he received from people as he sauntered past with his high-stepping, tough-guy attitude. He thought that this must be how an actor feels when a part is played so perfectly that the audience actually thinks the actor is the person he's pretending to be. He felt a little ashamed that he allowed himself to enjoy the effects that his despicable persona had on people. But at least he was convincing.

On the other side of the street, in front of a bar with no name, just a flashing sign that read "BEER," two young men leaning against a parked car were having a smoke. One had on a leather bomber jacket, despite the heat of the lingering Indian summer. He was shirtless, wore straight-legged jeans and a pair of black Dr. Martens identical to Avi's. The other wore a white T-shirt with a white power fist on the front and a pair of khaki shorts. In his true life, Avi would have pretended not to see them and kept right on walking, ignoring any slurs or provocation they might have tried to assault him with. He would have done it despite the fact that he could probably beat them both silly—thanks to the training regimen he started when he was a boy. Along with that training came a lot of practical advice. His father used to tell him to remember that sticks and stones may break your bones but words would never harm you, with such enthusiasm, that you'd think the old man just made up the saying at that moment. That was his true life. This wasn't.

He crossed the street.

16

For the sixth time that evening Dalton Leverick promised himself he'd give it another fifteen minutes then go home. He swung his chair around and looked out at the city lights, wondering what it must be like to have a real life. He didn't want to look again at the piles of paper littering his desk, or the extra-wide marker board that hung from the side wall completely filled with notes, charts and cross references. The director had called earlier that evening and told Leverick to call him with any news about Moore, no matter what the time.

Leverick swung his chair around, snatched the eraser from the desk and attacked the marker board with it. He stood there a few seconds, staring at the board he had just cleared. *Okay, Leverick, let's start from scratch.* On the left side of the board he wrote a list of names beginning with Edwin Moore. He included Moore's security team, Matthew Pates, Terrance Al-Aziz, Carl LeGrande. In the middle of the board he listed the names of the organizations: ARCS, UAAC, Sons Elohim, New Islamic State. On the right he listed events as they had unfolded—the attempt to kill Moore; the still-tight-lipped suspect who they thought to be a member of ARCS; the disappearance of Moore; one flattened house that had been rented by the UAAC's second in command, Carl LeGrande; the aftermath of what looked like a small war at a remote country house belonging to Danny Park's uncle.

Think. Moore and his bodyguards are missing. Al-Aziz and LeGrande announced a new alliance of the United African-American Coalition and New Islamic State. Terrance Al-Aziz threatened to march on Washington if the government did not do something to punish Israel for their support of the Sons Elohim. Al-Aziz was making the most of the rumor that the radical Jewish group was responsible for the attempt on Moore's life. There wasn't, of course, any evidence to backup Al-Aziz's ranting.

Al-Aziz. Leverick flipped open a folder on his desk to a photo of Al-Aziz taken at a Washington reception for the finance minister of Sierra Leone several months earlier.

Where does he fit into all this, thought Leverick, turning the pages of a recent report on the NIS leader. The FBI had run a cursory investigation on him before, and like a Teflon Don, he had insulated himself well, occasionally ranting about his religious freedom and persecution by the Judeo-Christian tyrants. Perhaps it was time to investigate him a little deeper. He had to be getting something out of this besides creating the facade that he actually cared about Edwin Moore's cause.

Leverick finally decided to pack it in for the night and get some rest. He would think long and hard about Al-Aziz. He tucked the file under his arm and left the office.

As the door clicked shut he heard his telephone ring. He looked at his watch—2:25 a.m. He wanted to ignore it and get some sorely needed shuteye. About a dozen "what ifs" raced through his mind and then before he could say damn it all to hell he whipped his keys from his jacket pocket, opened

156

the door and dove over his desk to snatch the receiver from its cradle.

"Leverick!" he panted.

"Sir, I didn't think you'd be there but I figured what the heck, man like you always working might just be there so I figured I'd give it a shot and ..."

"... please get to the point, Henderson." Leverick was actually more amused than agitated. Henderson was annoying but efficient, even though he said about ten times more than he had to in order not get the point across. He also read ten times faster than any agent Leverick had ever met and could function one hundred percent on only two or three hours sleep. Henderson even sported a Pee Wee Herman bow tie and haircut.

"Well, Sir, we ran those profiles you ordered on Mr. Moore's bodyguard team and I think your hunch was right, Sir, that we should be focusing on Henry Perkins. Did you get my fax this afternoon? Anyway, we checked Perkins' apartment in Stamford and the place looked as if it hadn't been lived in for a while. It was pretty bare, Sir. Unusually sparse. I mean no photos, few clothes, no television or radio ..."

"... bottom line, Henderson."

"Yes, Sir. We went through the phone records and interviewed a female subject—a Ms. Emelia Milo. She had a relationship with Perkins that she ended two years ago because she was afraid of him. She said he used to take her to his apartment in New York City and show off his weapons collection. She changed her phone number three times but Perkins keeps getting the new one ..."

"... wait a second, Henderson. New York City?"

"Yes, Sir. The subject must have used Stamford as his official address. I took the liberty of getting a search warrant. It's a basement apartment on 93rd street."

Leverick looked at his watch again. "When did you get the warrant?"

"Two hours ago, Sir. My uncle is a Judge. Not that I would ever abuse that privilege, Mr. Leverick. No, Sir, this was a legitimate request."

"Have you searched the apartment?"

"No, Sir. That's really why I'm calling. I believe the subject is inside ... with another male who could be Daniel Park."

"Where are you calling from, Henderson?"

"I'm sitting in my vehicle about fifty yards from the residence now. I saw two of them enter the apartment a few minutes ago."

"Listen carefully, Henderson. Do not move from that vehicle. I'm going to arrange for backup from the police. I'll be there in half an hour. If they leave the apartment, follow them and call me."

Leverick ran from his office toward the elevator, not bothering to close the door behind him. As he rushed down the hall he quickly dialed the dispatch office in Washington. They would connect Leverick with one of six special assistants to the Police Commissioner who would have a police team to the scene in less than ten minutes.

"This is Leverick, Dalton, L ... E ... V ... Seven ... One ... Four. A40 clearance." There was a short pause as the attendant verified Leverick's authorization to request local force mobilization.

"Okay, Sir. Just a moment while I transfer you."

*   *   *

Park thought that Huck Perkins' apartment looked normal enough. Sitting on a braided rug was a worn leather couch, a light oak coffee table with intricate carvings of leaves on its legs, and a television stand with a TV-VCR combo. A closer look at the artwork hanging from the walls revealed Perkins' bizarre character. On the wall behind the couch was an oil painting of a victorious Roman gladiator, pressing one

158

foot on the chest of his headless opponent, and holding the severed head high above his own. On the opposite wall was a series of pictures depicting scenes of a special-forces deployment of Paratroopers, Navy Seals, and Green Berets. There was even an old black and white photo of two French Legionnaires standing on either side of a dead prisoner who was hanging by his feet like a prize tuna.

"This one's my favorite." Perkins pointed across the room to a wall-size blow-up of a photo of himself in the professional wrestling ring during his short stint with the WWA. "Come on," Perkins beckoned Park to follow him to the poster. He lifted the picture off its frame and placed it carefully against the couch. A dial pad with a flashing light had been hidden behind the poster. Perkins quickly pressed in a code and after a few short clicks of lock tumblers releasing, he pressed his hand against the wall and slid the facade to the right.

"I don't believe it," said Park.

"Believe it," said Perkins. "My personal collection. I got six AK-47's, four UZI's, a couple of Hi-Point niners, a MAC-10, four Bersa 380's, three double barrels and a dozen grenades."

"We're gonna die today. You know that, don't you?"

Perkins grabbed the MAC-10 machine pistol and stuck it in his belt. "We're going to liberate Mr. Moore is what we're gonna do." Perkins handed Park one of the Hi-Point's and a Bersa.

Park looked at the two pistols, checked the clips and safeties, then tucked them in his belt. "Let me get this straight. We're going up to a hundred thirty fifth street and we're gonna waltz into Al-Aziz's office, which may or may not be two floors above a Halal food store. Then we're gonna hold a gun to Aziz's head and he's gonna happily hand over Mr. Moore, Lucas and Smith to us and we'll walk out like we just finished breakfast. Is that the plan?"

"Precisely."

"Okay, let's do it."

It took them about five minutes to gear up. Perkins grabbed the two AK47's and clipped four grenades to his belt. Danny Park wrapped a shotgun in plain brown paper. This was suicide. This was also war so screw it—might as well go down fighting.

Perkins led the way out of the apartment, stopping to hold the door for Park so he could lock the three deadbolts. Perkins had stuffed the assault rifles into special pouches, made for the inside of a full-length, oilskin raincoat. *Psycho Man From Snowy River,* thought Park. It was almost four a.m. LeGrande had sworn (before Perkins shot him up with enough Phenobarbital to keep a gorilla out cold for two days) that he didn't know for sure they were keeping Moore, Lucas and Smith there, but that Al-Aziz arrives at his office every day before dawn. He also told them that the basement of that building contained a fortified bunker that would be an ideal place to confine someone. Perkins had figured that since the Halal store wouldn't be open yet they would have a minimum of bodyguards to deal with. Park hoped to hell he was right.

Perkins' girth filled the stairway as he walked up, blocking the light from the streetlight. Park was beyond scared to the point where he couldn't wait to get the job done. As crazy as it all seemed, part of him believed they could pull this off and rescue Moore. Maybe he and his big old buddy Henry Perkins would be famous heroes.

As if he was being shaken awake from a dream, he heard someone shout "Police. Don't move."

Perkins flew back. Park instinctively reached out to catch him and before he could say 'that was stupid,' they both hit the concrete hard. There was no gun shot, no blood. Perkins moaned. "Thanks, Danny."

"I can't breathe, Huck. Get off me."

Perkins rolled off Park but kept him pinned to the floor

160

with his arm. "This could be it. Our last stand without a chance for glory." Sounds from the street of scuffling and car doors closing echoed through the dark stairwell.

"What are you talking about?" Park pushed the big man's arm off and sat back in a crouched position with his back against the wall. "It's over. We give ourselves up."

"You think those are real cops up there? You're a dumb ass if you think you're not gonna get a bullet in your face the second you poke your ugly mug up there." Perkins eased his way around Park and fumbled for his apartment keys, all the while keeping watch above him like a soldier in the jungle, vigilant for snipers.

Park wanted to give it up but he was sure Perkins was so paranoid that he would kill him before he got up two steps. If he followed him into the apartment they would probably be killed in some crazy attempt to hold off an attack by throwing Perkins' entire little arsenal at them.

Perkins was about to open the third and final lock. The footsteps above were getting closer. Park couldn't tell how many there were but he imagined them scampering for position and closing in. He gripped the handle of his pistol. It would only take a second to draw and shoot Perkins. Just a shot in the leg to give him a second to save both their lives.

Park flipped open the holster clip with his thumb. *Sorry, Huck,* he thought.

"Freeze!" Park relaxed his grip at the sound of the thunderous voice. *Thank God,* he thought, pressing his arms high above his head. Perkins dropped his keys and turned to look up at the half dozen S.W.A.T. cops pointing automatic rifles down at them.

Perkins crossed his arms and came up with an AK47 in each hand. Defying the gravity that his huge frame imposed, he pushed his body up using his powerful legs. The AK's exploded with firepower and were answered six-fold with a hundred bullets ripping through Perkins' body. Park crouched in the corner, showered by splatters of Perkins' blood, flesh and clothing. Perkins' lifeless body hit the concrete with a dull thud.

Park shut his eyes tightly and kept his hands high and in plain sight as he listened to the footsteps coming down the stairs.

Leverick could see the flashing lights in the distance as he turned up 93rd street. "Henderson, I hope you didn't screw this up." Leverick reached under his seat, pulled out the cherry and placed it on the dashboard, flipping the flashing light on with his thumb.

A few seconds later he arrived on the scene. A frantic Henderson ran up to him waving his arms like a signalman on the tarmac.

"I see you, Henderson. You can put your arms down."

"There was nothing we could do. They were about to leave and the S.W.A.T's were there for backup, just like you ordered, but the suspects fired." Henderson looked as if he was about to bleed from every pore in his face.

"Whoa, boy. Slow down. Didn't you learn about punctuation in school?" Leverick placed his hand on the young agent's shoulder. "Slowly, Henderson. Has anyone been killed?"

"Henry Perkins. Daniel Park is in the back of a NYPD cruiser. That's another problem. The captain ..." Henderson pulled a small notebook from his jacket pocket and flipped through the pages, "... Captain Denton says Mr. Park is NYPD's prisoner and the Bureau can go ... screw themselves."

"Thanks, Henderson. Get yourself a drink of water and sit down for a minute."

Leverick clipped his credentials to his jacket and approached the melee. It was obvious even before the captain's bars on his uniform became visible who was in charge. Denton was barking orders to the pathology team and to the officers assigned to keep the growing crowd of citizens at bay.

Denton took a step back as Leverick reached into his pocket for his phone. The police captain, well in his fifties, was as solid as a rock. His wide jaw and weatherworn face projected the image of a man who has seen all that the mean streets of New York could puke out.

"You must be Leverick. Poindexter over there has been up my rear end to release the Korean kid. I think you'd ..."

"I think you'd better take this call," Leverick interrupted, sticking the phone in the cop's face.

Denton snatched the phone. "Denton ... yes, Sir ... I understand ... yes, Sir, I will ... Thank you, Sir." He tossed the phone back to Leverick. "Screw you."

Denton ordered an officer to take Park out of the cruiser and release him into the FBI man's custody. "Just a second," said Leverick. He walked over to the stairwell, where at least a dozen officials were gathered, and looked down at the twisted, bloody mess that used to be Henry Perkins. Having taken a mental photograph of the carnage, he claimed his prisoner from the officer and escorted him back to the Bureau car. Park was silent, looking down at the ground. He seemed docile but Leverick still kept a firm grip on the young man's arm. The FBI car didn't have a cage separating the back and front seats or any special door locks. Leverick sat Park in the back seat with his arms handcuffed behind his back. He pulled the seat belt and shoulder harness around the young man and buckled it tight. It would have to do.

Leverick got behind the wheel and, before pulling out, called Henderson over and ordered him to get some sleep, then file a report in the early afternoon. Although, knowing the hyperactive agent, the reports would probably be finished and a copy would be on Leverick's desk in both his New York City and Newark offices by 9:00 a.m.

Leverick glanced in the rearview mirror. Danny Park remained silent, pressing his chin in his chest.

Night construction had caused a backup at the Lincoln

Tunnel in spite of the early hour.

"Mr. Park?"

Park looked up. "Yes, Sir."

"Do you know the whereabouts of Edwin Moore?"

"Yes, Sir. I do, yes."

"Care to tell me about it, son?"

Park nodded.

Leverick sighed. The director was going to be very happy to get a 4:00 a.m. wake-up call.

17

Lucas Green was left alone in what he could best determine was a storeroom. He felt his way through the dark, touching rows of metal shelving jammed with cans, cellophane bags and canvas sacks. He soon settled down on a couple of sacks of what felt like rice and rested. There had been no opportunity to disarm Aziz's thugs and run, so in a desperate attempt to buy some more time, Lucas had given them Henry Perkins' address in Stamford. Perkins used to joke that that address was his speeding-ticket address and that he never so much as spent one night there since he rented the place.

Lucas' mind felt so full of noise and the room was so dark that he couldn't tell whether or not he had fallen asleep. But if the footsteps he now heard outside the door were Aziz's men returning from their wild goose chase in Connecticut, then he figured at least two hours had passed, and he'd better think quick.

They pointed a blinding light into his eyes.

"Stand up, please," a guard said. "The Honorable Al-Aziz wishes to speak with you."

Lucas said nothing as he was escorted into Al-Aziz's office and told to sit on a wicker chair facing the desk. The guards never turned their rifles away from Lucas' head as they stood on either side of him. Al-Aziz entered from another doorway and plopped behind his desk into a cushy high-backed chair. For a long time, he sat back, staring at Lucas and tapping his bony fingers on the leather armrests.

Lucas broke from the stare and glanced around the room. It was decorated in a Caribbean style with lots of wicker and green plants. He could see from the beams of light trying to invade the room through the slats in the closed shutters that it was daylight. He wished he knew which day.

"Would you like something to drink, Lucas?" Al-Aziz asked.

Lucas shook his head. He could feel tiny beads of sweat forming on his forehead.

"Maybe we should get started." Gone was the NIS leader's trademark grin. He looked dead serious, and Lucas was beginning to understand what it meant to be between a rock and a hard place. "You and I both want the same thing, you know," Al-Aziz continued. "I hope you realize that."

Lucas remembered something one of his old football buddies had once told him: "If your woman hears that you've cheated—deny it. If she says her best friend saw you—deny it. If it *was* her best friend you were screwing—deny it. 'Til the day you die—deny it."

The ex nose tackle sat up straight. He figured dumb was the smartest way to be. "I assume you found Huck and Danny in Stamford," Lucas stated. He studied Al-Aziz's face. He thought he saw some of the anger disappear from his eyes. Al-Aziz hadn't gotten what he was after, but he didn't know he'd been conned either.

"No. The apartment was empty. In fact, I'm told it looked like no one had lived there for a long time."

"Mr. Al-Aziz, all I want is to survive. I want Mr. Moore

166

to be let go, and I want to go home and call my ex-wife and ask her if she's interested in having a Blockbuster night."

Al-Aziz laughed. He waved his hand, and the two bodyguards shouldered their weapons. It was now or never for Lucas Green.

Lucas raised his open hand as if to plead with the great Al-Aziz for mercy. "You are a great leader of our people, Mr. Al-Aziz. I can speak to Mr. Moore. He once told me that he trusted me more than any of his security crew. I just need one thing, Sir." Lucas held his arms apart wider and before Al-Aziz could ask what that one thing was, the football star clenched his huge hands into hammer fists and struck both guards squarely in the gonads. He then drove the inner ridge of his hand into the throat of the guard to his left, smashing his windpipe, and simultaneously hit the other guard with a back kick to his knee. Lucas reached down and snatched the weapon from the writhing guard as he fought a losing battle to suck in air. Lucas spun around and fired before the other guard could get to his feet. Al-Aziz disappeared behind his desk. Lucas could hear him fumbling through the desk drawers.

No sense waiting around, thought Lucas. The gunshot would no doubt bring more NIS thugs, and Al-Aziz sure wasn't looking for his stapler in that desk.

Lucas swung open the door and stood flat against the wall. He fired a quick burst into the wall behind Al-Aziz's desk, then ducked and low-rolled out onto the hallway carpet. He could hear footsteps coming up the staircase at the end of the hall. He looked quickly over his shoulder, then fired at the open doorway just as the silver barrel of a pistol appeared from Al-Aziz's office. The footsteps behind the staircase were getting closer, just about to the door now. The windowless storeroom at the end of the hall was the only choice besides going back into Al-Aziz's office. The staircase door burst open, and two NIS guards appeared with machine pistols blazing.

Lucas fired. The men fell back, probably an instinctive retreat because Lucas doubted he'd hit anything with his spray of bullets.

Lucas whispered to himself, "I hope you don't handle a pistol well, you crazy bastard," and jumped back into Al-Aziz's office, firing in a wide arc. The NIS leader was crouched behind a Hawaiian stone carving. He fired and missed Lucas by a mile. Lucas leaped over the desk, hitting the floor hard.

"Mr. Al-Aziz?" a guard shouted from the doorway. "He's in here. Help!"

Lucas popped up and fired, hitting one of the guards in the chest as he entered the room. The other guard fired blindly into the office, then ducked away. Al-Aziz also fired. The bullet ripped through Lucas' side, spinning him around before he collapsed on his back.

"Damn." Lucas painfully felt around for his gun. His body was quickly cramping up, and he couldn't so much as lift his shoulders off the floor. He was suddenly thirstier than he could ever remember. Not even during that double-overtime game in Oakland when it felt like 150 degrees in the shade. *It's over,* he thought. He'd taken his shot and blown it. He heard shouting and more gunfire. He could feel the vibration beneath him before he heard the heavy footsteps. Someone might have yelled, "Don't move." He wasn't sure. He wondered how many more seconds he had to live. *God, I'm hurtin'.* He covered his eyes with his forearm. It was almost over. They were walking softly now, barely making a sound. Getting closer. Directly over him now.

"Sir?"

Lucas peeked over his arm, the person over him a blur in the dimly lit room. "Who ... who are you?"

"Relax. Don't try to speak anymore. My name is Dalton Leverick. I'm with the FBI."

Lucas covered his eyes again and closed them tight. No matter how hard he squeezed them shut, he couldn't stop the river of tears.

168

*   *   *

The speakers blared so loudly that Avi could hardly hear himself think. He sat on an old mattress, one of about a half-dozen lying around the barn's loft, pretending to get drunk on Wild Turkey. He clenched his teeth and stiffly bobbed his head to the shrills that these despicable creatures called music. Every now and then Slick, a tall kid who had stripped down to his boxer shorts and Dr. Martens boots, would look over and give Avi the thumbs-up.

Thumbs-up your ass, thought Avi. Slick was dancing wildly, alone in the center of the loft. He and his dopey friend, Rolf, had invited Avi to their little skinhead party. Rolf's uncle let them use the loft as a clubhouse, and all of them, the whole pile of drek, were excited about the big weekend at the ARCS compound.

Avi slipped the bottle of whisky behind him and spilled a little on the floor. Finch, a squat and muscular kid—one of the few skinheads who had long hair—sat low in a cushioned armchair directly across from Avi. Finch had SS lightning bolts tattooed on each cheek. His hair was drawn tightly into a ponytail and he was dressed in a blue, tiger-striped field outfit complete with dog tags and a canteen on his belt. He held up his own dwindling supply of Wild Turkey, and Avi returned the gesture.

Another punk, whose name Avi didn't remember, was standing in front of a picture of Adolf Hitler, yelling accolades and raising his rifle in the air. As loud as the music was, this freak's voice broke through it: "You are the father of us all! Yeah! The greatest man that ever lived! I pledge my life to you! Yeah! Yeah!"

It would be so easy, thought Avi. In his mind, he smashed the whisky bottle against the floor, and dove across the room, plunging the broken glass into the punk's neck.

169

Before anyone knew what was happening, he would grab the rifle, spin around and shoot everyone in the room. He imagined a dozen bloodied corpses sprawled over the loft floor, even the two sluts the big man, Marky, had brought up.

More skinheads poured into the loft. It seemed that every punk and his brother who joined the fiasco, brought a Nazi poster or flag, and fastened it to any available wall or support post.

The music suddenly stopped.

There were a few mumbled protests before shouts and applause filled the room. "Heil Frederick!" was chanted as the figure emerged from the staircase. The cone of a Klan wizard came into view first. *Frederick Cicone,* thought Avi. *The organizer of the Northeast KKK.* Cicone looked ridiculous in his red silk cape, robe and cone-shaped headpiece. He wore the robe open, and his pumped-up chest brandished a skintight T-shirt with "White Power" stenciled in red over an even redder swastika.

Cicone walked, with his mindless entourage in tow, to the picture of Hitler where he waited until Rolf wheeled over a television. Avi walked to the edge of the crowd to get a better look.

Cicone raised his hands, calling for silence.

"Hello, my brothers!" he shouted, punching the air.

"Heil, Frederick! Heil, Hitler!" The punks shouted back.

"Heil, Hitler!" Cicone was beaming as though he had just been elected king of the world. "Are you ready for the war?"

The skinheads cheered and stomped their thunderous response.

Cicone nodded, and Rolf clicked on the TV monitor. "This is work that we must complete." Avi squeezed in tighter with the rest of the crowd. The room became so silent that only the whirring of the VCR could be heard. When the black and white image of the Third Reich insignia appeared, the skinheads roared again. Avi felt light-headed and didn't even realize that he was holding his breath as he watched the all-too-familiar images of the emaciated men and women paraded to their deaths by firing squads, shot two and three thick to save on ammunition. Each time a poor soul fell back into the pit of death, the group in the room would cheer and applaud.

Cicone shouted, "Six million more! Six million more!" Most of the room joined in and sustained the horrid chant until Cicone called again for silence. Rolf clicked off the television.

"Your race is your nation, brothers. The Zionist bankers who have control of this country are scared of you."

"You said it, brother," shouted a skinny kid with the words "white power" tattooed on his back.

"That's right, little brother. They're scared of you because you're not like the boot-licking, race traitor, homo-loving white people who have all but surrendered this country to Jews and niggers.

"This ..." Cicone tapped his robe, "... this represents the beginning of an alliance among all the white loyalists in this country. Some of you have come here from as far away as Seattle where your little groups of 10 or 20 throw bottles through Jews' windows. Maybe crack open a few nigger skulls. Maybe even do some jail time, but the Zionists don't take you seriously, and they call you isolated and frustrated youths. Bull! Aryan Resistance Christian Soldiers has promised to unite us. This weekend, we will have the leaders of almost fifty groups." He paused and took a deep breath, dramatically closing his eyes as though he was savoring the moment. "Fifty skinhead organizations training together for the first time in the history of the struggle for our race's survival. Is Hitler dead?"

"No!"

"Where does he live?"

"In our hearts."

Cicone turned around and saluted the picture of Hilter,

shooting his hand out from his chest again and again. "Seig Heil! Seig Heil!"

Avi was frozen. He would be the only one in the room not participating in the disgraceful salute. He trembled and clenched his teeth so tight it hurt. There were too many of them now. He would never survive a fight. If he turned and ran down the stairs, the mission could never succeed. He would never get near Matthew Pates, and this madness would never stop.

"SEIG HEIL ... SEIG HEIL ... SEIG HEIL." The sounds hit him like a knife in his chest. His head pounded, and he was trembling. He was blowing it. Like a pressure cooker waiting to explode, the frustration was choking him. He had to do this. For the Sons Elohim, he had to do it. For the Jewish people, he had to do it. He shut his eyes tight, but could not stop the flow of tears as he shot out the salute.

He opened his eyes, panicked that his charade would now be obvious. His eyes met Rolf's. Rolf was also crying.

"I know how you feel, brother," Rolf shouted.

You'll know how I feel, Avi thought grimly. *This weekend you'll know exactly how I feel.*

18

The FBI was always inventing new and creative ways to secure communications between undercover agents and their supervisors. The latest thing was setting up obscure home pages with triple-password gateways into private, virtual conference rooms. Leverick and Walsh had planned to connect through a home page that had been registered as the Dried-Bean Collector Information Center. To the Bureau's surprise, the page was receiving 600 hits each week to the list of 165 varieties of dried beans. At the bottom of the page was a blue-lettered sentence that read: *"Add your name to list of dried bean enthusiasts."* When users typed their names and clicked Enter, they read: *"Thank you for visiting the wonderful world of dried beans."* So far, more than 1100 visitors to the site had left their names.

Walsh typed: "THE HENCHMEN 93" into the field. When the message "URL error 421" came back he typed in his second-level password: "MAAAW." Again the error code, then his social security number for the third-level password and he was in. The conference was set up to allow only Walsh,

Jacobson and Leverick access. In the almost impossible event that someone did get entry, the equivalent of a burglar alarm would immediately cut off all communication to the Dried-Bean Collectors site until the breach could be investigated.

Jacobson flipped on the television to the morning news. Walsh was waiting for Leverick to enter the virtual conference room. He looked at the clock radio on the end table next to the back-pulverizing couch. He thought about insisting that he and Jacobson take turns sleeping on the bed. He was afraid she might invite him to share the bed. He was afraid he lacked the strength of character to refuse. At least they had been busy enough and exhausted enough every night not to experience the sexual tension that had plagued them in the first few days of the assignment.

"I don't believe it." Jacobson cranked up the volume. Walsh turned to look and was himself surprised to see the image of Dalton Leverick standing on a Manhattan street next to a police car. He was speaking to a uniformed cop, a man in handcuffs standing next to them. A news reporter stepped into the foreground and described the early morning raid and the liberation of NAAC leader Edwin Moore.

"Look at that guy, Jacobson," Walsh said, studying the man in cuffs.

"The Asian kid?" Jacobson asked.

Walsh nodded. "He's the bodyguard who shot the sniper."

"Well, I'll be damned. I wonder why Dalton has him in cuffs."

The news cut away to file footage of Terrance Al-Aziz speaking at Queens College, as the news anchor speculated as to the NIS leader's involvement in the Moore case.

The telephone rang.

Walsh snatched the receiver from its cradle. "Hello?"

"Mr. Hess? It's Joe Lugo at KaratePlus. How are you today?"

"Fine. Just doing a little cruising on the Net before we open the school. I was expecting your call."

"It's been hectic. Have you seen the news today?"

"Watching it right now!" said Walsh.

"Can you believe that guy turned up alive? A friend of mine who works at *The Post* said Edwin Moore, and two of his bodyguards, were being held in a basement shelter by The New Islamic State. It's all anybody's talking about today."

"Is KaratePlus on the Net yet?" asked Walsh, moving the conversation to the communication link.

"Not yet. I'm gonna look into that soon. Matter of fact, I'll be back in my office in about two hours and plan to do a little surfing myself. Send me your order, and we'll talk about 12:15."

"Thanks, Joe. Talk to you then."

Walsh signed off from his computer and closed it. "I guess rescuing Edwin Moore is as good an excuse as any not to show up for a virtual conference."

Jacobson turned off the television. She tapped the remote against her mouth, staring at the blank screen.

"What is it?" Walsh asked.

"Now that I got a look at an old clip of Al-Aziz there's something very familiar about him."

"The guy's been on the cover of *Time,* Jacobson!"

"He wasn't bald and didn't have a goatee on the magazine covers," she snapped. "I'm talking more than 10 years ago. When I was first assigned in Washington, I used to do research for a squad that supplied reports to the State Department. We used to keep tabs on U.S. citizens traveling to hot spots like Libya, Russia and Nicaragua."

"Don't tell me ... he's Khaddafi's brother?" Walsh stood up. "I think I'll open the school a little early and get a workout."

"Laugh, but I think he's the same guy the Bureau sent a letter, warning him not to visit Sierra Leone because of intelligence reports about a possible coup."

Walsh hesitated by the door for a moment. "What happened?

"He ignored the warning. I think a cousin, or some other relative of his, wound up a big honcho in the new regime over there."

"Interesting," said Walsh. "It may be nothing, but I'd zap that information off to Dalton. You never know."

Jacobson acknowledged Walsh with a thumbs up as he left the apartment.

Walsh knocked on Dirk's door, figuring he'd ask the kid if he wanted to work out. He'd proved himself so capable during the fracas on the day the school had opened that Walsh was curious to find out just how good he was. Someone had trained him long and hard. Aside from the actual fight, it was evident in the way he carried himself. Most of these punks acted loud and tough on the outside but you could easily spot in their eyes the uncertainty, the fear. Not Michael Dirks. Someone had trained him well—physically *and* mentally.

Walsh felt in his pocket for his keys. He looked around, wondering if their young tenant might walk up those stairs any second. The FBI man gave quick thought to what he was about to do. In two days, they were going to get access to the ARCS compound and get a chance to solidify their cover. A worst-case scenario would be a punk who found his landlord snooping around his room. *"Screw you, kid. Get the hell out if you don't like it. I was just making sure that there were no drugs stashed in my house,"* thought Walsh.

It was weak, but it would have to do.

Walsh let himself in.

Except for a couple of suitcases piled next to the wall, the room was as sparse as when Dirks had first rented it. The bed was made. There was a copy of Tuesday's *Milton Sentinel* on the end table. Walsh opened the top drawer. Empty. The bottom drawer was also empty. *What, no grenades?* thought Walsh. Even the walls were bare except for a very boring print of a bouquet of flowers sitting on a wooden stool. The picture had been there when Walsh and Jacobson rented the place, and Walsh was surprised the kid hadn't at least draped a Nazi flag over it. No posters ... nothing.

Walsh next searched the dresser drawer. The first of the three drawers was meticulously packed with underwear, socks and T-shirts. More clothes in the middle and bottom drawer. *Neat little punk.* Something was protruding from the leg of a pair of jeans. A book.

"Hello. Now what reading material does a skinhead punk hide in his pants leg?" Walsh examined the volume. The small book was tethered and had three tassels sticking out of the bottom. Embossed on the cover were Hebrew characters. "What the hell?"

The sound of the entrance door opening resonated through the upper hallway. Walsh returned the book to its hiding place and was out the door in two big leaps. He pulled the door shut quickly, putting on the brakes just enough to let it latch quietly. Dirks, just getting to the top of the stairs. He looked haggard. Not only tired, but extremely troubled.

"Something wrong, Michael?" Walsh asked.

Dirks jumped back, startled. "Oh. No. I'm fine. Just a little too much partying, I think. You're not doing so well, though." The punk smirked and tilted his head. "You're going to want to see what's brewing outside your school."

Walsh had to step aside to avoid a collision as Dirks rushed past him. *What the hell's gotten into him?* Jacobson was just emerging from the apartment.

"It's about to hit the fan, dear. We've just made the local television." She pointed down the staircase. "Outside."

Walsh trotted down the steps and out to the street. There were dozens of people parading back and forth in front of the karate school, brandishing posters and shouting, "No more hate!" Some of the posters had messages that denounced The Brotherhood of Yahweh Martial Arts Academy as a house of Satan. One poster even had bright red letters stating, "EDWARD HESS IS THE ANTICHRIST."

A reporter shoved a microphone in Walsh's face, while her cameraman focused the lens of the Betacam.

"Are you Mr. Hess, Sir?"

I hope God forgives me for this. Walsh poked his finger hard into the reporter's shoulder, putting her off balance for a second. "Let me tell you something," he shouted. "This country was founded on freedom. *White* freedom. Nobody is going to tell me that I can't have a martial arts school strictly for my own people. No Jews! No niggers! No way!"

Someone threw a rock, hitting Walsh in the cheek and opening a small cut. Three policemen suddenly jumped between Walsh and the protestors. Jacobson appeared from the doorway and ran to Walsh's side.

"I'm alright," said Walsh. "Let's get back inside."

"Are you Mrs. Hess?" the reporter asked, unfazed by Walsh's injury. "Do you share your husband's racist views?"

"I stick by my husband 100%. White women have to wake up and take their rightful, God-ordained place next to their husbands. We have to be ready to fight. Guns, knives, bombs—whatever. It doesn't bother me any."

The reporter turned away as a van pulled up on the street, and six men with baseball bats jumped out and threatened the protestors. More police arrived, and within seconds, a melee broke out. One of the protestors, a young guy probably no more than 20, took a swing with his placard at one of the bat-wielders. The next moment, the protester was on the ground clutching his knee. A cop swung his club wildly, hitting protestors and bat-wielders alike.

Two of the bat-wielders were the same ARCS guys, Jimmy Price and Fred Mills, who had harassed the school on opening day. Now they were part of a wolf pack defending their fellow racists. Any doubt Walsh had about Pates swallowing their cover was squelched. The only problem now was getting out of this unhurt, and at the same time preventing the ARCS bulldogs from hurting any more citizens.

Price kicked a fallen protestor in the ribs and was poised to smash his head like a melon.

Walsh ducked under a swinging placard and wrestled the man to the ground, aiming their fall at Price's legs. As Price found himself flat on his back, Walsh snatched his bat and flung it across the sidewalk. He softly punched the protestor in the face for good measure, and then helped Price to his feet.

"Thanks for your help, pal," Walsh said.

Someone fired a shot. Several people, including Price, dropped to the ground. A tall cop with sergeant's stripes on his shirt stood on top of a cruiser. He pumped the weapon and fired into the air again.

"Let's pull back against the storefront," Walsh said to Price. Price managed to get all of the ARCS men to gather behind the increasing wall of cops. Jacobson crawled through to the other side of the fracas and was now standing next to the shotgun cop's patrol car.

More police, some from the next county, arrived on the scene a few minutes later. They now matched the protestors in numbers almost one for one. They ushered the crowd away to make a clearing as a chauffeur-driven Lincoln pulled to the curb. Milton's mayor, Alice Farrol, emerged with two lawyer types in tow. One of the men opened his briefcase and removed a pile of papers.

"I must speak with Mr. Hess, please!" Farrol said sharply.

"I'm Hess." Walsh pushed through the mini-gauntlet of cops.

"You're bleeding, Mr. Hess." Walsh thought he detected some delight in her voice.

"Are you a nurse?"

"I'm Alice Farrol." She held her hand out to the side

179

and the briefcase guy gave her the papers. Farrol shoved them into Walsh's chest.

"Did I win Publishers' Clearing House and you're personally awarding the giant prize?" Walsh glanced at the papers.

"That is an injunction barring you from opening your school, pending a formal hearing that has been scheduled for 60 days from today."

Perfect, thought Walsh. He wanted to grab the woman and give her a big kiss. Not only did Pates send his little squad to defend the racist school, assuring that Walsh and Jacobson were in ARCS's good graces, but the 60-day desist order meant that they no longer had to keep up this karate-school charade.

"You can't do this," Walsh said, dramatically waving the papers in the air. Then, just for effect, he ripped the papers in half right under Mayor Farrol's nose.

Farrol turned and walked away, taking a second to look back at Walsh. "Open your school, Mr. Hess, and you'll be arrested and the entire contents of the building confiscated." She then slipped back into the car, the briefcase boys following in line.

The shotgun sergeant was now standing with a bullhorn in his hand. "There is no reason for you to remain in the area. No arrests will be made if you immediately clear out."

The sergeant barked some orders, and the other police helped to disperse the crowd. Jacobson joined Walsh and the ARCS men by the storefront.

"I say let's open the school right now," said Jimmy Price.

"Yeah. The hell with that dike Farrol," said Mills.

"Hello, Hank," Price said to the tall cop.

"You're not really going to arrest Mr. Hess if he opens his school, are you?" said Mills.

The cop walked up to Mills and poked him in his chest. "I uphold the law, Fred."

"What happened to you, Hank? We used to be friends."

"You've gone too extreme. I prefer my own kind—don't get me wrong. But I keep to my own and I don't break the law." The big cop turned to Walsh and Jacobson. Jacobson was dabbing her partner's cut with a paper towel. "It doesn't matter that you tore up those papers, Mr. Hess. If you open the school, I'll have to arrest you. I'm ordering a watch of your school just to keep you honest. A half hour won't pass without a cruiser going by."

The sergeant dismissed the rest of the police and returned to his own cruiser. As he drove away, Mills grumbled something about allegiances and how different it was going to be once the white man took back the country.

"What now?" asked Jacobson.

"I guess we take some time off."

"We'll see you at the compound this weekend," said Price. The two agents watched the group pile back into the van.

"Exciting morning," said Jacobson. "I'm surprised our boarder didn't join the fun."

Walsh looked sharply at Jacobson.

"What? Did I say something wrong?"

"I poked around Dirks' room, right before he came home."

"And?"

"And there may be a lot more to this kid than meets the eye."

*   *   *

Matthew Pates personally oversaw the final preparations of the ambulance bomb. Fred Mills had jammed the ambulance's compartment from floor to ceiling with more than 2,000 lbs of ammonium nitrate explosive. The back and the

181

side windows were mirrored with one-way glass. Pates took a second to make sure his black beret was tilted just right. He walked around the vehicle, inspected every inch, and was impressed with their attention to detail. They had stenciled "Jerusalem Hospital" on the side, complete with a serial number. *Outstanding,* thought Pates. He was pleased. Almost pleased enough to forgive Price and Mills for being late. Pates had let himself into the warehouse almost an hour earlier where Mills stored the three tractor trailers he owned and leased out on occasion to local drivers. The warehouse was located at the edge of the Milton town line, just minutes from the ARCS compound. Mills never let customers pick up the trucks. He would always deliver them. There was nobody better at fixing up a rig than Fred Mills. There was nobody better at fixing up a bomb, either.

Mills' noisy van pulled up to the warehouse door. The door opener hummed to life, and the huge wooden door slid open. Mills and Price drove in.

"Sorry, Matthew," Price said as he jumped out from the passenger side. "A bunch of us went down to Hess' place to show a little muscle."

Mills had a duffle bag over his shoulder. "Sorry, Matthew," Mills repeated. He threw the bag to the side, the bats cracking together as the bag hit the floor. "We're ready anytime, Matthew."

Mills opened the passenger door to the ambulance. Pates hunkered outside, resting his arms on the door and roof. Mills tapped his finger on the dashboard radio. "The timing device is wired into here. No remote stuff. Too risky. There's about a gazillion radio signals flying around Manhattan, and Jimmy and me ain't gonna be sitting in this hot tamale while some yuppie dipstick with a cell phone cooks our goose."

He pointed to a digital timer on the dashboard. "This is wired to a blasting cap and a quarter stick of dynamite which I got strapped to the whole dung heap in the back." He then pointed behind the timer to a small switch. "Flip the toggle, and the timer starts counting backwards from 3:00 minutes, then ... kaboom."

Pates slapped Mills on the back. "And all the surveillance tapes will show is two suspicious-looking niggers leaving their ambulance."

"That's it. Then we go underground, catch a train to the rig and come home."

Pates turned and looked at Price. "Are you ready for this?"

"I'm ready."

"Good," said Pates. "Because I'm moving the mission up to this Sunday. They found Edwin Moore today, and he's scheduled to make an appeal for calm at a press conference Sunday morning."

Mills laughed. "I guess nobody's gonna be interested in hearing what he has to say."

19

Walsh tried again to contact Leverick via the Internet. Jacobson, wearing her purple sweats, sat on the back of the couch eating an apple.

"Didn't your mother ever tell you not to sit like that on the furniture?"

"Every damn day."

"Thought so. Dalton's not online." Walsh called up the laptop's cellular communication program. The proprietary software could send a 50-character message to any one of a dozen or so specially equipped alpha pagers, usually worn by high level supervisors. "I'll send him a quick note to his alpha pager. He's probably loaded down with this Moore thing."

"Why don't you just call him? I swept the place again this morning. It's bug-free." Jacobson threw the apple core across the room, landing it squarely in the trash bin. "Besides, Pates' men came to help us today. That places us above suspicion, don't you think?"

"Unless they were checking up on us as much as helping us."

"You know something, partner? You could make a zebra doubt he has stripes."

Walsh typed: "Some trouble today. Nothing serious. Will enter conference room at six tonight." He clicked the button on the track ball to transmit the message.

Walsh snapped the computer closed. "You always need to have a little doubt, Jacobson. It's doubt that keeps us sweeping this apartment twice a day for bugs." He got up and walked over to the couch, looking his partner in the eye. "When we go into that compound Saturday, we're only going to come out alive if we're on guard 24 hours a day. Always think they're suspicious of you. If someone puts an arm around you and invites you into a room or behind a tree to talk about this or that, you've got to think they might be planning to kill you." Walsh punched his fist into his open palm.

"Always be at your peak performance. Always be ready to change your game plan."

The telephone rang. Jacobson jumped from her perch and snatched the phone from the desk, pushing Walsh back with her palm at the same time.

"I'll get it."

"Not bad," said Walsh.

"Kimberly Hess speaking ... Fine ... How are you? ... Sure, he's right here."

Jacobson covered the mouthpiece. "It's Brian Hastings!"

Walsh took the phone. "Brian, how are you?"

"Matthew Pates is bumping up maneuvers," said Hastings. "He wants everybody to come to the compound right away. You'll get a chance to show us your stuff a little sooner than planned."

"I didn't know I was 'everybody.'"

"Listen, friend," said Hastings. "I don't like you. But for some reason Matthew does. You should be honored that he wants you to be part of this preparation time."

"Hold on a second." Walsh pressed the handset into his

186

chest and quickly brought an anxious-looking Jacobson up to speed. "Brian," Walsh then continued. "Guess what? I don't like you, either. But I'm willing to put the survival of our race before any personal feelings. If Matthew Pates wants us, we're there."

"There's a briefing at five this afternoon at the compound. They'll direct you from the gate. Bring a change of underwear." Hastings hung up.

"I hope I'll have the opportunity to hurt him," Walsh muttered.

"When do we go?" Jacobson said enthusiastically.

"Today. Damn, I'd better send another message to Dalton." Walsh left another electronic message for Leverick, informing him that he and Jacobson would be going into the compound for a couple of days, and if they didn't contact him by Monday morning, he should send in the Cavalry. He also sent some email to his home via his son Alex's America Online mailbox. He wanted to actually call them but thought this was a time to be more cautious than ever. They were about to get deep inside the ARCS organization, and between hostiles like Brian Hastings and the local media frenzy surrounding the school, there was no telling who would be breathing down their necks.

An hour later, they were packed and ready to go. Walsh put the bags by the door and walked back to the couch where Jacobson was sitting, and writing on a greeting card.

"It's a note to my parents," she volunteered. "They're not the email type." She placed the card in the envelope and sealed it. "You don't think I'm jeopardizing the operation by mailing this?"

Walsh took the envelope from his partner and slipped it into his shirt pocket. "I'll jump out at the post office on the way. I doubt anyone will rip down the outside of a federal building and sort through a bunch of mail just to guess which letter the racist karate instructor dropped in."

"Thanks. I just felt I had to ..." Jacobson punched her fist into the couch cushion. "No way." She vigorously shook her head. "Damn, I thought I had this under control."

Walsh patted his partner's leg. "It's natural to get all choked up about your family at this stage, Jacobson. Don't worry, you're not going to blow it because you're scared to death you might not see them again. If you weren't human you wouldn't feel this way. And if you weren't human you'd be no good to the mission."

"How do *you* do it? You act like you're packing for a golf weekend or something."

"I've never been much for golf."

"See! That's exactly what I mean."

"Listen, I'll admit that I've grown a little used to deep-cover, but I've never grown completely unafraid."

Jacobson made a face as if to say, 'Yeah, right.'

"The biker case against The Henchmen in California was my first, and there were times when I was so scared that I'd never see my family again I thought I was going to vomit."

Jacobson grinned.

"Really," Walsh continued. "All the major bike clubs have their nastiest members. You know, the guys that would do anything for the gang: murder, torture people, blow things up. The Henchmen called their crazies the Black Heart Squad, and I found myself in a third-story apartment, sitting on a couch with two of them who were telling me how they once caught a journalist posing as a biker to do a story on one of their parties. Just on one of their parties, mind you; not someone trying to put them away for life. They found this guy out, and about five guys held him down while one of these guys pulled the poor fool's teeth out one by one with a pliers."

Jacobson bit down on her finger. "Hurts my teeth just thinking about it."

"Imagine what they would have done to me if they found out I was FBI."

188

"Imagine what ARCS will do to us if they find out we're FBI."

"Let's make a pact right now," Walsh said, taking his partner's hand in his. He lowered his voice to a whisper. "I won't tell them who we are if you don't."

Jacobson laughed. "Deal."

"Good." Walsh released her hand. "Since this may be the last time that we get to speak to each other for a couple of days, let's go over a couple of last-minute items." Jacobson sat up tall, her fear seemingly replaced by enthusiasm.

Walsh stood up, preferring to pace a little while he spoke. "ARCS maneuvers usually include separate male and female programs. Joint programs are the rifle ranges, zip line and rappelling courses, and first aid and wilderness survival. They might separate us for hand-to-hand training, although I guess we won't be far from each other. There might be some segregated classroom sessions, and I'm certain that we'll be sleeping in separate male and female barracks."

"I don't think I can spend the night without you, honey," she teased.

"You'll have to try."

"I guess sneaking in a niner in my underwear bag is out of the question?"

"Impossible. Pates will let only a select few come and go with weapons. I doubt he'd even let you bring in a cell phone. You can also bet that when given rifles for practice it will be for limited periods and closely supervised."

Jacobson cracked her knuckles. "Up the creek without a paddle."

"No paddle? We don't even have a raft, Jacobson. Welcome to deep-cover."

A few minutes later, the agents were packed and ready. As they passed their young tenant's door, Jacobson stopped. "Maybe we should say something. Tell him we'll be gone for a couple of days."

"Maybe he'll feed the goldfish."

Jacobson tapped on Michael Dirks' door. Walsh whispered in her ear, "He's probably busy praying in Hebrew." Walsh and Jacobson agreed that Dirks probably had stolen the book and shawl from some vandalized synagogue. They planned to take a more careful look at him when the undercover assignment permitted. During many of the bias attacks on synagogues, churches and mosques, the vandals had helped themselves to valuable artifacts and books. The agents had imagined some old rabbi mourning over the loss of his most prized possession, which had been kept as some skinhead punk's souvenir. Another possible scenario, that would be more troublesome for their assignment, was that Dirks was himself an agent of the Mossad, Sons Elohim, or another radical group.

Jacobson placed her ear to the door. "I don't hear anything."

Walsh reached out and grabbed Jacobson's arm as the apartment door swung open. Dirks looked tense and had one arm behind his back. Walsh almost rushed him but held back after the skinhead relaxed a bit and folded his arms after recognizing his landlords. "Mr. Hess, Mrs. Hess." He nodded to each of them. "Is the rent due already?"

"Not yet, Michael," Jacobson answered. "We just wanted to let you know that we'll be away for a couple of days. We're not bothering you, are we?"

Dirks shook his head. "No. I'll be out for a while on Saturday myself. Is there anything that you would like me to do for you?"

"Maybe just keep an eye out for vandals," said Walsh. "Lot of hoodlums on the streets these days. Take care."

"Sure," said Dirks, slowly closing the door.

"Ready to go to Bogey Land, Mrs. Hess?"

"As ready as I'll ever be."

*   *   *

Avi took a deep breath as the door clicked shut. He watched the Hesses through the peephole as they walked down the stairs and out of sight. He was getting jumpy, and that was bad for his mission. He had to stay cool. Answering the door with a gun behind his back was foolish. The Hesses might be anti-Semitic scum, but they certainly were no immediate threat.

Avi walked to his bed, and placed the pistol back in its spot under the mattress. He had sewn a little pocket on the bottom of his bed to hold the 18-shot pistol. He would have loved to be able to take it into the compound. Eighteen shots would give him a better chance to escape. But his orders were clear. He was to take no chances with a weapon that could be detected by scanners. Avi looked up at the light fixture. A few small scrapes on the metal collar the only evidence that it had been taken down recently. Hidden inside the ceiling sat the prototype of one of Mossad's most carefully guarded secrets— The Jehu. How his father had managed to secure it was a mystery. Papa didn't volunteer the information. Avi didn't ask. Especially when execution for treason awaited anyone involved in procuring it. Avi didn't even understand completely how The Jehu functioned. Uncle Shulman had explained that the tiny pistol was 95 percent plastic and would get past all but the most expensive and sophisticated detection systems.

It held only one bullet. One bullet whose lead jacket surrounded a core of M388 plastic explosive the size of a match head. The bullet's plastic tip was designed to explode on impact. At the moment the projectile would be hitting Pates' skull, a thin, acrylic rod would puncture the lead casing and explode the M388 with a force equivalent to a quarter stick of dynamite.

The gun had no hammer. Just a condensed gas charge contained within a thin aluminum bead which exploded when the trigger was pulled, simultaneously firing the bullet and driving another pin down into the handle, which would trigger the 10-second delayed explosion of a much bigger piece of M388 in the pistol's handle, giving Avi a powerful grenade which he could toss to create a distraction as he escaped. Or tried to escape.

Avi jumped at the sound of the buzzer.

He pressed the intercom. "Yeah?"

"Mike? It's Marky. Listen, man. It's been moved up. They want everybody there like right away."

Avi's heart jumped to high speed. "Like when right away?"

"Like now right away," Marky said through the static-filled intercom. "I'll make the rounds and pick everybody up in the van. I'll swing back around for you in about a half hour. Okay?"

"Sure." Avi sank to the floor and sat there for a moment holding his head, concentrating, as if he could mentally disin-tegrate his fear. *So what's the difference? Today? Saturday? Next week? What did you expect?*

He hadn't expected to be this afraid. After all, this was what he had been preparing for all his life. From the time he was four years old, he used to fantasize about slaying the giant Philistine Goliath. His people had always managed to beat the odds and survive. Gideon beat them when he led an army of 250 to victory against ten thousand. Moshe Dyan beat them when he defended Israel against incredible odds in the Six-Day War, the tiny country surrounded on three sides by hostile nations determined to push them into the sea. These were men of courage. They were men who were no strangers to fear, either. Avi's father had told him often that courage wasn't the absence of fear, but action in the face of it. And no matter what, to always trust in God.

Avi got up and walked to the dresser, where he slowly, almost ceremoniously, opened the bottom drawer. When he pushed aside the articles of clothing to reveal the sacred prayer book, tucked under the tallis and wrapped by the leather strands of the fellaya, he thought it looked different than he'd left it, but quickly dismissed the notion.

He shrouded his head with the tallis and wrapped the strands of the fellya around his wrist and forearms. He opened the book and swayed as he read:

Tehellim
A song to the ascents.
I raise my eyes upon the mounts;
Whence will come my help?
My help is from HASEM, Maker of heaven and earth.
He will not allow your foot to falter;
Your Guardian will not slumber.
Behold, He neither slumbers nor sleeps—
The Guardian of Israel.
HASHEM is your Guardian;
HASHEM is your Shade at your right hand.
By day the sun will not harm you,
Nor the moon by night.
HASHEM will protect you from every evil;
He will guard your soul.
HASHEM will guard your departure and your arrival,
From this time and forever.

Avi prayed for almost 20 minutes, joy and confidence filling his heart with every verse of the treasured psalm. He was ready to make the supreme sacrifice, if necessary, for his people and his God. His cherished prayer articles now back in their place, Avi moved a chair under the light and unscrewed the fixture with a butter knife. He removed The Jehu from its hiding place and re-affixed the light to the ceiling.

Avi let his pants fall to his ankles. Using duct tape, Avi taped the pistol high up on his inner right thigh. He was calculating that any search for weapons would be limited to electronic scanning. *It had better be.* He pulled up his gray field trousers and buckled his belt, checking the bullet that had been soldered into the buckle's frame. When the scanner went off, he would simply remove the belt and casually hand it over.

A few toiletries and a couple of changes of underwear were all that he shoved into a small backpack. During the party in the barn loft, Marky had told Avi that they would be supplied uniforms for the three-day rally and military maneuvers.

The door buzzer sounded.

Avi felt for the concealed pistol, assuring himself that it was secured. He clutched the backpack and took a deep breath.

My God, please do not forsake me.

20

Dalton Leverick stood at the podium of the FBI's press room and apologized to the small army of reporters for keeping them waiting so long. He blinked several times and pinched the bridge of his nose while camera flashes filled the room.

"I have a brief statement," said Leverick. "This morning at approximately 10:30, Edwin Moore was found in a basement stronghold owned by Terrance Al-Aziz. Two of Edwin Moore's bodyguards were also being held at the building. Several arrests have been made, including Mr. Moore's personal physician and advisor, Dr. Carl LeGrande. The suspects are in custody and are being interviewed by agents now. Mr. Moore is currently being examined in a federal medical facility and is preparing a statement, and if ... this is a big if ... *if* the doctors give their approval, Mr. Moore will hold a press conference Sunday morning and the statement will be read by a United African-American Coalition Representative. Thank you."

Dozens of people beckoned the FBI man, calling his

name. Leverick pointed to a young reporter in the first row. "Mr. Forrest."

"Thank you, Agent Leverick. Rick Forrest, Channel Four News. Our office received a call today from someone claiming to be a member of The New Islamic State. He claimed that Mr. Al-Aziz was attempting to provide protection that the police and FBI either wouldn't or couldn't provide. Would you care to comment?"

"Regardless of intentions, it is still illegal to kidnap and detain persons against their will."

Leverick pointed to a gray-haired woman in the back of the room. "Yes, Ma'am."

"Margaret Hopkins, Connecticut Free Press. Can you now say for sure that the Jewish organization—Sons Elohim—was not responsible for shooting Edwin Moore?"

"Ms. Hopkins, we have no indication that Sons Elohim or any other Jewish group was involved. Although the suspect we have in custody still claims to be working for a clandestine Jewish group, we are in the process of gathering evidence that will uncover what group *is* responsible."

There was a quick rumble of voices and more camera flashes.

"Which group might that be, Agent Leverick?" Hopkins asked.

"I'm sorry. Until we have more information, I can't say anything else. One more question." Leverick gave a nod to Ted Jenson, the famous anchor from the local news.

"Thank you, Agent Leverick. More than 20,000 people are rumored to be poised for a heated march and demonstration on City Hall Monday morning. With Edwin Moore back in charge of the NAAC, do you think he will order this protest abandoned?'

"I believe Mr. Moore plans to call for calm and will definitely ask the NAAC not to participate in any disruptive demonstration. Thank you."

More flashes filled the room, followed by shouts of "Agent Leverick, Agent Leverick," as the senior FBI agent left the pressroom.

Leverick took the elevator to the 11th floor, where Terrance Al-Aziz was being detained in a sparsely furnished interview room.

Two agents were stationed outside the locked door. Leverick beckoned and one of the agents, a tall man in his early 30's, flipped the latch and held the door open.

"Thanks, Freddy," said Leverick. "You and Agent Weinberg take five. I'll page you when I'm done in here."

"Yes, Sir."

"Thank you, Sir," said Weinberg.

Leverick found Terrance Al-Aziz sleeping with his head on the interview table. Leverick picked up a file from a small table next to the door. Al-Aziz was handcuffed to a metal loop bolted to the top of the table.

Leverick sat down opposite the sleeping prisoner and tapped the top of the table. "Mr. Al-Aziz."

Al-Aziz jumped up, wincing as the handcuffs tugged against the clasp. For a long moment, neither man spoke. Al-Aziz stared hatefully at Leverick.

"Are you going to ask me any questions or are you just going to sit there vacuously?" The hateful look turned into a smirk. Al-Aziz was obviously pleased with himself. The seasoned Leverick was unfazed.

"You are being charged with kidnapping and unlawful imprisonment, Mr. Aziz. By the end of the day, you could probably add attempted murder to the list."

"Lies. Allah Akbar. Lies from the white devil."

"I think you can drop the religious pretense, Mr. Al-Aziz. You're no more a Muslim than the Pope." Leverick opened the folder and removed several sheets of paper, which he placed on the table in front of his prisoner. "Not more than 10 minutes after your arrest this morning, we started to receive faxes from Islamic organizations around the country. Funny thing, Mr. Al-Aziz, without exception, every one of them—even The Nation of Islam—denounces you as a phony and an opportunist with absolutely no authority to represent the Muslim people."

Al-Aziz squirmed a bit and glanced over the papers. "I don't seek the approval of others, Agent Leverick."

"What exactly do you seek, Sir?"

"I seek justice. Justice for my people. Justice that has eluded us for hundreds of years."

Leverick reached across the table, unlocking and removing the handcuffs. Al-Aziz leaned back in his chair, massaging his wrists. "Thank you," he said.

"So, Mr. Al-Aziz." Leverick glanced at the file. "Or should I say, Mr. Leonard."

"That slave name no longer has any meaning for me. All praise be to Allah."

"Sir, you don't have to keep up the charade with me. You're an opportunist hiding behind the veil of the Islamic religion and we both know it."

"Fools," Al-Aziz hissed.

"Who are the fools, Mr. Al-Aziz? Us or the people who fall for your sham?"

"You. You can prove nothing. Edwin Moore's safety was our only purpose."

"I see. We fools have a little theory. Would you like to hear it?"

Al-Aziz stroked his goatee. "That would be very entertaining."

"I'm sure. Does the name Henry Leonard ring any bells?" Al-Aziz shifted nervously in his char. "It should," Leverick continued. "He's your cousin *and* the finance minister of Sierra Leone."

"So what if he is?"

"The Fresh Water Project is what. FWP is going to cost

over 300,000,000 dollars, and your cousin is about a 100 million short.

"I don't think you were part of the conspiracy to kill Edwin Moore at first. But like any opportunist worth his salt, you saw that if Moore was dead and the Sons Elohim were blamed, you could raise enough constituent hell to sway votes in Congress for foreign aid. End result—less money for Israel, and cousin Henry gets his desalinization facility built."

"Preposterous!"

"Carl LeGrande doesn't think so. He's minus an earlobe from impromptu plastic surgery, but the offer of novocaine loosened his lips in more ways than one."

"That dog!" Al-Aziz stood up, punching the table with both fists.

"Sit down, Mr. Al-Aziz."

"I will not," said Al-Aziz, defiant.

Leverick reached across the table and grabbed Al-Aziz's wrist, twisting it until he submitted and sat down. In a few seconds, Leverick had him cuffed to the table again. Leverick left the interview room and locked the door, his prisoner spitting curses to the world.

"Get him his lawyer," Leverick ordered. The junior agent nodded.

Leverick took the staircase one flight up to his office, where Danny Park was sitting, handcuffed to the arm of a side chair.

"I'm gonna piss my pants, man. You forget about me?"

Leverick released Park. "That door." Leverick pointed to a door at the back of the office.

"Private bathroom? Not bad."

"One of the few privileges of rank. Make it quick."

Park complied, and a few minutes later, was back in the chair opposite Leverick's desk. Park lifted the handcuffs, still dangling from the chair's arm, with his finger. "Am I under arrest?"

"That depends, Danny. Should you be?"

"Listen. It wasn't my idea."

Leverick held up his hand. "By some miracle, Carl LeGrande can't be sure of more than one intruder in his apartment. He's identified Henry Perkins from photographs. He said there might have been another man with Perkins, but doesn't remember for sure."

"Where does that leave me?"

"I don't want to know anything. As far as I'm concerned, Perkins tortured LeGrande solo and told you where they were holding Edwin Moore."

Park laughed nervously. "That's the way it happened. Oh, yes. Just like that!"

"That's what I figured." Leverick walked around his desk and extended his hand to Danny Park. The FBI man yanked Park out of the chair, squeezing his hand hard. "Do not ... make a liar out of me."

"No, Sir. That's the way it happened."

Leverick let go, and Danny Park bolted out of the room. *Two more years,* thought Leverick. Two more years, and it will be good-bye to this nonsense. He must have committed half-a-dozen procedural violations today between questioning suspects without lawyers present and letting Park walk out that door. *Two more years.* Hopefully the two years would pass without another case like this. Leverick hated them. "By any means" was the phrase the agents used to describe priorities from The White House. That meant you were to get it done and push the law to its limits—and sometimes beyond. Then deny, deny, deny. Until your dying breath, deny.

Leverick turned on his computer and read the electronic-mail message from Walsh. Leverick hoped that Walsh and Jacobson would have something substantial when they came out of Pates' compound. The champagne corks wouldn't be popping for long over the rescue of Edwin Moore, and in a day or two, it would be "What have you done for me lately?"

and the validity of the ARCS operation would again come into question. Depending of course on which political group was applying the pressure on the lawmakers, the destruction of ARCS could remain an FBI priority. Then, like the Black Panthers in the 60's, it would be bring them down by any means necessary. And there wasn't anyone in the Bureau more resourceful and more willing to push the envelope than Martin Walsh.

Leverick took a deep breath and clasped his hands behind his head. There was no way he was going to get out of the Manhattan office until after midnight and he'd have to be available all weekend as well. The Bureau held leases to several apartments around New York City, using various phony corporate and individual identities. Leverick called down to the information office and checked on availability. The only apartment not in use was a studio on 83rd. Apparently, he'd been outdone by other senior agents for the apartments closest to the Federal Building. *No matter,* he thought. His private line from his Newark office was forwarded to his cell phone and he'd take a laptop back to the apartment in case Walsh tried to contact him via the Internet.

For now it was back to business. Al-Aziz would have to be interviewed at length when his lawyer arrived. It was going to be a long night.

*   *   *

Matthew Pates walked up and down the aisles of the meeting hall dressed in full SS regalia. The custom-made replica of the jet-black officers' uniform had swastika armbands on each side and SS lightning bolts embroidered on the jacket sleeves. Authentic Third Reich medals, which Pates had spent years accumulating from antique shops and personal contacts, decorated the uniform's breast. The sound of his boot heels clicking rhythmically on the hardwood floor was the only

201

sound in the empty hall. In ten minutes he would welcome the patriots. Every chair was lined up perfectly. Three rows of six, divided by two aisles, going back 30 chairs deep, and not one out of place.

He stopped at the front of the middle aisle and looked at the ARCS banner hanging behind the podium just below Adolf Hitler's picture. "A new day is dawning." Pates grabbed his jacket lapel and sniffed the old medals, savoring the smell of the musty cloth-covered brass and tin, imagining what it must have been like to be there at the right hand of the great Adolf Hitler.

"I know what you tried to do," he said to the color portrait. "I know the love you possessed for your race. You knew, didn't you? You knew that mud people and Jews would one day populate the world and threaten our race's survival. You alone had the courage to make the ultimate sacrifice."

Pates walked a few paces closer to the portrait and knelt on the floor. He folded his hands and bowed his head. "Lord, as I kneel here before You under the picture of Your great servant, I ask You to bless our cause. I know that what I am about to do is necessary. I also know that I will one day lose my life because of it. I know that in the struggle some innocent people will die. I know that I will have to accept that responsibility. I am ready."

Pates stood up, brushing some dust from his pants. He stepped onto the platform and behind the podium. He could hear voices outside the building. People were starting to arrive.

The great turning point in the history of the white race was about to begin.

21

When Jacobson and Walsh had visited the ARCS compound the previous week, a solitary soldier had stopped the car near the entrance. Tonight at least a half dozen men with automatic rifles were directing vehicles to park. The compound looked like a makeshift airport security checkpoint. Men and women were handing suitcases over for inspection, placing keys and other metal objects into trays, and walking through metal detectors.

An old school bus, painted gray with a huge Confederate flag affixed to the side, was directed to a parking spot by one of the ARCS men. A few minutes later, a dozen Klansmen spilled from the bus and took their place in the security line.

"My parents told me about hell," said Jacobson.

"Quite a sight," remarked Walsh.

"We're really deep in the middle of it, aren't we?"

Walsh nosed the car into a spot as directed and parked it. He looked sideways at his partner. "What you mean we, princess?"

She punched him hard on his arm, causing him to wince. "Screw you, Goy."

Walsh took his partner's hand and squeezed tight. "There's nobody I'd rather be partnered with. I'd trust you to watch my back anytime."

"Let's do it."

More vehicles arrived and the men and women lined up for security clearance. Once through the security checkpoint, the people were instructed to walk about a half mile to the assembly barracks which was the first of six similar buildings and had a huge letter K stenciled on its front and side walls. Walsh remembered the aerial photos of those aluminum structures, camouflaged to blend in with the forest terrain. He guessed that at least one of these buildings housed the arsenal that the Bureau suspected might include at least two stolen rocket launchers. One of ARCS' goals was to organize the local Klan and skinhead factions and send hundreds, maybe even thousands, of young men into the U.S. Army for both training and the opportunity to steal sophisticated weaponry.

They entered through the rear door of the barracks and took seats in the first row they came to. At the front of the hall was a stage with a podium, banners and a portrait of Adolf Hitler. Matthew Pates stood motionless next to the podium, with his arms behind his back, his 10-year-old son standing next to him. Both wore Nazi SS uniforms. It was hard to tell, this far back from the stage, but the child didn't look all that glad to be there. Brian Hastings and Pastor Hampton also had seats on the stage. The FBI man glanced at his partner. It couldn't be easy for her, watching these fools parading around in their Nazi uniforms, keeping hate alive for future generations.

The room was filling up quickly, the sound of dozens of different conversations gently rumbling through the assembly. Walsh looked to his right and caught a glimpse of Michael Dirks walking up the aisle to the third row and sitting in one of the few available chairs.

Before Walsh could say anything to his partner, she

snapped her head around. "Dirks? I wonder who he hooked up with to get invited here?"

"That's the million-dollar-question, isn't it?"

A heavyset man, sitting in the chair in front of Walsh, turned around and smiled. He had a wide face, covered with gray stubble. His brownish-yellow teeth—what was left of them—caused Walsh to think poster-boy-for-early-dental-intervention if there ever was one.

"John Dubois, Montgomery Lumber. You know that kid?" Dubois extended his hand and Walsh shook it.

"Edward Hess."

"Oh, I know who you are." Dubois nodded to Jacobson. "You and the missus. Saw you on the tube. We need more people like you. Not afraid to take a stand. A nigger come in my store last week. Ignored him. Son of a bitch finally got tired of waiting and left, but I was gonna tell him. Gonna tell him no service. Next time."

"Do you know Michael Dirks?" Jacobson asked.

"Yes, I do. Gave him a job as a favor to one of my buyers. Hard worker. Hasn't shown up for work for a couple days. May have to fire him."

"We rent him a room," said Walsh. "I guess we'll have to evict him if he has no job."

Dubois held up his hand. "Well, for you I'll give the kid another chance. Catch up with you later," he said as he turned around, almost in sync with the start of the music. Jacobson looked at Walsh and rolled her eyes.

Matthew Pates tapped on the microphone. "Please stand for the singing of 'Horst Wessel Lied.'"

Pates turned around and saluted the ARCS banner, his arm straight out, Nazi style, while the "Horst Wessel Lied" thundered through the auditorium. The crowd followed, Jacobson doing a good job of keeping her chin high and pretending to be a true believer in the master race. Pates prodded the young boy, who had failed to salute, by squeezing down on his shoulder.

When the music finished, Pates motioned for his wife to come onto the platform and take the teary-eyed boy away. Elizabeh Pates was dressed in green army fatigues, with what looked like a pearl-handled .45 in a holster around her waist. She was a long way from the Harriet Nelson role she had played so well a week ago.

Pates motioned for everyone to sit down. "Welcome!" He surveyed the crowd, his fists clenched and his knuckles on his hips. Someone clapped. Someone else yelled, "Hail Matthew!" More people clapped until the entire room was thundering with applause and shouting. The two agents played right along. Walsh leaned toward his partner and spoke in her ear. "I haven't seen this much excitement since my last Amway convention."

The ARCS leader called for quiet. "Thank you, White America. We stand today on the threshold of a day no less great than the founding of this nation by our forefathers. This weekend you will train for war. ARCS, Klansmen, skinheads. Housewives, mechanics, and school teachers. All working together to hone their survival skills for the inevitable conflict. These last few weeks the riots in Los Angeles, New York, Philadelphia, and other cities were just the tip of the iceberg. Our purpose is to unite the white brotherhood against those who would come into your homes and rape and murder you." Pates jabbed his finger toward the crowd. "But you will be ready.

"You will be ready to inherit Yahweh's kingdom as the true descendants of Abraham, Isaac, and Jacob. The promised land is ours and it's time to defend it!" Pates pounded the podium.

"The myth of the so-called 'holocaust' has infected the free world long enough, and it's time to break free." Pates gestured toward a group of skinheads sitting in the fourth and fifth rows to his right. "Our skinhead brothers have a slogan: 'six million more.'"

Someone shouted "Amen." There was another eruption of applause and Pates again called for quiet.

"The truth be told, a hundred thousand, maybe two hundred thousand Jews were killed in the great war. A plight that they not only brought upon themselves but, through their manipulation of the world's media and Hollywood-type special effects know-how, created. A hoax like this world had never known before. They have used this hoax to bleed the world dry of sympathy and finances. They have been working for the past fifty years to gain control of the banks and government and we are saying: NO MORE! Within five years we will have thousands of our own soldiers integrated into the armed forces. We are a force with a divine purpose and we cannot be stopped!"

The crowd was on its feet, and the agents joined in the melee of applause, salutes, and whistles. Walsh saw first hand that Pates wasn't just another boisterous Aryan trying to one-up the next group with outrageous statements about white supremacy and the occasional violent act. He was really going to attempt to build an army.

"The most insidious of all the Jewish plots," Pates continued, "is the dispatching of their nigger agents, whom they have financed to rape our women and shoot our children in the streets while depleting city treasuries with their welfare rolls.

"It all ends NOW!

"We are taking our destiny into our own hands.

"We are reclaiming our country."

Pates took his seat. The crowd continued to applaud until Brian Hastings approached the podium.

"HAIL MATTHEW!" he said.

The crowd responded in kind and chanted for several minutes before settling down to hear Hastings speak.

Hastings cleared his throat and sipped some water. "First of all I want to apologize to all of you for the extra security measures we have had to implement for this weekend's training. Since we do not personally know each of you, this is an unfortunate necessity. Hell, one of you could be a government agent." He paused to listen to the laughter, then continued. "You will be issued firearms at the appropriate times. There will be two supervised sessions for men on the firing range and one for women. Firearms will be issued for the sessions, then collected and secured by ARCS personnel.

"Now as many of you know, a dear brother of ours is in Zionist custody. This not only grieves us as a brotherhood, but has created a void in our training staff, since Raymond Hill was one of our most capable hand-to-hand instructors. Instead of being with us this weekend, he is lying in a prison ward with a bullet wound." Hastings tensed up. "I am certain that Ray has remained a soldier and has given up nothing to the enemy."

He was right about that, thought Walsh. Hill never wavered from his story that he was an agent of the Sons Elohim.

"You will be assigned a barracks tonight. Before you go, stop at the supply center just outside this building and pick up your training uniforms. I suggest you get a good night's sleep since breakfast is at oh-five-hundred sharp. Especially you, Mr. Hess." Hastings pointed at Walsh. "I'm looking forward to seeing a demonstration of your fighting skills."

Much of the crowd turned to look at the Hesses. Walsh gave Hastings a thumbs up. A few people applauded. Quietly, Walsh said, "Can't wait, Brian. I look forward to it."

Hastings sat down and Pastor Hampton walked up to the podium. Hampton wasn't decked out in the black SS uniforms like his compatriots. He wore a green, tiger-striped uniform with CLERGY stenciled above his left breast pocket. Hampton closed his eyes and raised his hands above his head. "Let us pray." Most people bowed their heads. The FBI agents followed along. "Our great and powerful Yahweh," Hampton continued. "We pray that you will bless our training this weekend and ensure our victory in the months and years to

208

come as we enter into the great tribulation. We ask you to touch the hearts and minds of each and every man and woman here today, father Yahweh, and teach us your powerful and victorious ways. Amen."

Six men in gray fatigues filtered through the auditorium, handing out little strips of yellow paper to every person. *Barracks 3* was written on Walsh's. Jacobson held hers up for her partner to see.

"Barracks 6," she said.

"Our first night apart in I-don't-know-how-long. I'll miss you."

Jacobson jabbed Walsh in the gut. "Absence makes the heart grow fonder, darling. Let's get our gear."

The agents filed out of the building with the rest of the crowd and walked to the supply center to get their uniforms. They were issued camouflage jump suits and black combat boots. Walsh escorted Jacobson as far as her barracks. "Well, Mrs. Hess. Until tomorrow." Walsh leaned over and kissed Jacobson on the cheek. "Goodnight, dear."

Jacobson smacked Walsh hard on his back. "Sleep tight."

Avi claimed the bed closest to the bathroom by tossing his bag onto the bare mattress. There were two blankets folded neatly under a pillow that looked like it was made of straw. Avi placed his boots on the floor and carried his uniform into one of the four bathroom stalls. He paused for a second as he realized there were no doors on the stalls. He looked around. The barracks was filling up quickly, and people were beginning to filter into the bathroom.

Avi looked down at his leg. His pants were wet with perspiration coming from under all that duct tape. He had to do something. Avi spied a newspaper sticking out of a garbage pail and quickly snatched it up. In an instant he had pulled down his pants, turned and sat on the bowl with the newspaper opened in front of his lap. He took a minute to catch his breath, looking up and around, making certain his deception had worked.

Someone turned on a radio, blasting some screeching guitar music through the barracks.

"What's up, Mike," said Rolf as he breezed past and into the neighboring stall.

Avi didn't answer. He swallowed hard, pretending to read the newspaper (which he worked like hell to keep steady with one hand) while he worked his other hand down his right thigh and started to peel off the duct tape. The heavy perspiration was a blessing in disguise; the tape peeled easily, but there was a lot of it and Avi had to proceed slowly, wincing as the tape pinched hairs from his skin.

"Gonna be a bitch of a weekend," Rolf yelled over. "Mike?"

"Yeah," Avi grunted.

"Oh, sorry. Having a tough dump, huh? I'm gonna apply for full ARCS membership myself. Screw that giving back the weapons stuff. ARCS members don't have to give their guns back. I figure when they see my stuff on the firing ranges, they'll be begging me to join. How about you?"

Avi peeled away enough tape to expose the handle of The Jehu. "Me too," he said a bit loud as he yanked the weapon from the tape. "Me too, Rolf." Avi tucked the gun into the folded uniform on his lap and took a deep breath, grasping the newspaper with both hands to take a moment's rest.

"That's cool," said Rolf, the sound of his toilet flushing. A few seconds later Rolf passed in front of Avi and said, "Later," not bothering to glance down.

Avi rolled the tape back around his leg. Better to try and explain a wrapped leg, than to try to dispose of all that duct tape now. The uniform pants had two large zippered pockets on either side. He quickly opened one and slipped in The Jehu. Avi then counted to himself, "One, two, three," and in a flash slipped off his sneakers and pants and practically jumped into

210

the uniform pants. They were baggy enough that only upon the closest scrutiny would the bulge of the weapon be noticed. Thank God for that. In another second he was fully dressed in his military uniform and back into the barracks.

For a moment he thought his heart itself actually stopped beating as all the eyes in the room seemed to be staring at him as he stood in the doorway, holding his shoes and clothing in his arms. He was, as far as he could tell, the only one in uniform. He looked at the bed next to his, and Rolf looked up quizzically.

"What the hell you doing in uniform so soon, bud?"

Avi puffed up his chest and said loudly, with confidence, "A soldier eats and sleeps ready, Rolf. You guys want to fumble with getting dressed at four-thirty tomorrow, go ahead!"

Rolf jumped from his bed and scrambled to get dressed. Within moments the entire group was getting into their gear, whooping and hollering and sometimes even dancing to the music. One skinhead fell to the floor when he tried to keep rhythm while jumping into his uniform.

Then, as if someone had pulled a jukebox plug from the wall, the barracks went silent. Standing in the doorway, a muscular soldier with the ARCS emblem on his chest called everyone to attention.

"Very impressive," the man barked. "Commander Pates will be pleased." He took a few steps forward and looked around the room. "When you hear the beloved 'Horst Wessel Lied' at oh-four thirty, you'll have fifteen minutes to report to mess and fifteen minutes to eat. Have a good night, men. Lights out at oh-twenty-thirty hours."

With that he about-faced and left. Someone yelled "White Power!" and the screeching music erupted again. Avi lay down on his bed and stared at the wire mesh that supported the bunk above him. He didn't bother feigning interest in the celebration. *Let them think what they wanted tonight,* thought

211

Avi. *Tomorrow they'll know I'm not one of their putrid brotherhood.*

At eight-thirty a loud horn sounded through the camp and all the play soldiers scurried into their bunks. Avi closed his eyes, one hand on his fast-beating heart, one hand on the pocket which contained The Jehu.

22

Dalton Leverick sat bleary-eyed, watching a late night news report about Sunday's upcoming press conference with Edwin Moore. The always flamboyant Reverend Hal Shelton was being interviewed by a CNN correspondent, a young woman in her twenties who looked thrilled but uncertain about her assignment on the 2:00 am re-broadcast.

Shelton sat opposite the anchor with his hands folded over his fat belly, his triple chin resting on his chest as she nervously questioned him about his connection to Dr. Carl LeGrande and the National African American Coalition.

"There are rumors, Reverend Shelton, that you have had secret negotiations with Dr. LeGrande and Terrance Al-Aziz to take control of the NAAC while Edwin Moore was missing."

"That is a lie, Ms. Fairman ..."

"Fairchild!"

"Yes, well ... I respect Mr. Moore and my constituency has always stood ready to support the NAAC. Yes, I met with Dr. LeGrande but only to pledge my support for Mr. Moore."

"Several city mayors are worried about the thousands of African Americans mobilized under your direction for protest marches on Monday morning. Would you care to comment?"

"Yes, I would, Ms. Fairfield."

"Fairchild!"

"Right. I'll say the same thing to you that I said to the mayors of New York, Philadelphia and Miami when they telephoned me this morning. Only those responsible for the planned genocidal campaign against the African American people have anything to worry about."

"So you do believe that the attempt on Mr. Moore's life was perpetrated by the Sons Elohim?"

Reverend Shelton grinned. "You said it, Ms. Fairwell, I didn't ...."

"Fairchild, please!"

"Sorry. My grandmother had a saying, Ms. Fair ... child, 'If it look like a squirrel, and it walk like a squirrel—shoot it and make stew.'"

Thank you, Reverend Shelton." Gloria Fairchild turned to face the camera, which zoomed in for a close-up. "As tension grows between the Jewish and African American communities, several incidents have been reported. Some synagogues have been defaced in Long Island and other parts of the country. In the town of Monroe, New York this morning, an African American couple claimed their car was forced off the road by Hasidic Jews when the pair accidentally wandered into their community.

"Sunday morning's press conference with Edwin Moore ..."

Leverick clicked off the set. "... will hopefully include a statement from the FBI that they have conclusive proof that the Sons Eloihim had nothing to do with it." Leverick finished the sentence with his own agenda. How sweet it would be if Walsh and Jacobson came through with something concrete on ARCS.

214

Edwin Moore's call for calm was a positive step but Leverick was afraid that even Moore himself might suspect the Sons Elohim of being responsible for the shooting.

Leverick clasped his hand behind his head and stared at the ceiling, thinking about Walsh and Jacobson in the ARCS compound. They were too deep to protect if something went wrong. The 'what ifs' intruded into Leverick's mind. *What if Jacobson wasn't ready for deep-cover? What if some low-life recognized Walsh from some chance encounter during another assignment? What if Pates was a lot smarter and more resourceful than they gave him credit for and the backgrounds they'd created for Walsh and Jacobson didn't hold up?*

The senior FBI agent leaned over and snatched the phone. He dialed the director's home number and seconds later was speaking with the none-too-pleased official.

"Jerry, I'm sorry to call you at such an ungodly hour but I think we have to mobilize in Milton."

"What happened?" Director Hazelton said sharply.

"Nothing yet." *Ouch,* thought Leverick. How the hell was he going to request a level three mobilization on a hunch, a gut feeling that Walsh and Jacobson were in too deep and something was bound to go terribly wrong?

"Have you lost your mind, Dalton?"

"Jerry, we've been so bogged down with this search for Moore that we've lost contact with the agents. I'm usually in closer communication and I don't like this."

There was a long pause and Leverick used it to his advantage, knowing that his old partner Gerald Hazelton wouldn't be able to help but think about the case that made his career. A case that Dalton Leverick, for all intents and purposes, solved himself and handed to Hazelton on a silver platter. A case that got Hazelton moved up the ladder quickly and was probably responsible for his being the director right now. It still made Leverick shudder to think about it—a group of warped, AIDS activists had compiled a hit list of government officials and were planning to shoot them with darts similar to those used to tranquilize animals. The deadly catch was that each dart was filled with AIDS-tainted plasma. Leverick had convinced the group that he was willing and able to carry out some of the hits himself. The group never even found out that Leverick was FBI.

"I got two conditions for this, Dalton."

"Name them."

"One. I'm paid in full. No, more than full. You owe me now."

"Agreed. What else?"

"If it goes wrong, you take it on the chin, not me. This isn't going to be my Waco."

"You got it. I was getting a little tired of this job anyway."

He could hear the director sigh on the other end. "We'll mobilize at Fort Reynolds in Pittsburgh. Thirty S.W.A.T., two A.V.'s, and a dozen or so ATF guys. There's no guarantee how long I can keep them there either. Goodnight, Dalton."

"Goodnight, wussbag," Leverick said to a dead line, then hung the phone up. It never ceased to amaze him how the safety of deep-cover agents took a back seat to political concerns.

Leverick closed his eyes, his mind comforted with the fact that Walsh and Jacobson would have the cavalry lying in wait. Just in case.

*   *   *

Scratchy German music blasted through the camp as promised. Walsh pressed his pillow against his face, trying to recapture the images of Amy, Alex and Anthony that had filled his dreams. His *Triple A* club, as he often referred to them. He was always grateful for dreams of his family. They always seemed to come when he needed them most. When he missed them so much that he was willing to take the chance of a home

216

visit. The Bureau frowned on it but wouldn't forbid it. If a man had to see his family, then they would find a way to make it work. Walsh thought that maybe after this weekend he would try to set something up.

An ARCS man in fatigues, carrying an M16 over his shoulder, appeared in the barracks doorway and started barking orders. Within five minutes the entire company was walking single file toward the food barracks. Nobody spoke. They weren't told it was against the rules to speak but everyone just fell silently in line behind their stoic platoon leader—the only sound besides the music—dozens of combat boots crunching against the dirt road.

That freaking music, thought Walsh. No wonder the Germans lost the war. How the hell could any fighting machine get motivated by that junk!

Jacobson was already at the food barracks when Walsh got there. She was sitting at a table with other women and looked relaxed and confident. She waved to Walsh and blew him a kiss. The other women leaned in closer and they all started to laugh.

Walsh grabbed a tray and some plastic utensils, then lined up with the rest of his crew. A heavy slap on his back almost caused him to drop the tray.

"Good morning, Hess," said Brian Hastings.

"Hastings." Walsh didn't bother to turn around. He didn't think he'd like Hastings even if membership in this warped brotherhood were Walsh's life-long ambition.

"Today we separate the men from the boys, so to speak."

"Is that what we're doing?" Walsh gripped his tray. "And I thought we were going to earn our badges for tying slipknots."

"You should have stayed in New York, Hess. Seems to me you're the kind of guy who's right at home surrounded by kikes and niggers."

Walsh turned sharply and hooked his foot behind

Hastings' leg, simultaneously pushing hard against the man's chest. Before Hastings hit the ground Walsh gripped the ARCS man's wrist and bent his arm behind his back. He dug his boot into the side of Hastings' neck.

"You could be dead in less than a second. I think you should be careful who you call a kike lover."

Someone huge and powerful grabbed Walsh from behind and pulled him off Hastings. Walsh decided to acquiesce, although he could have easily maneuvered his way out of the big man's grip. A dozen other people immediately surrounded them.

"It's alright. I'm alright," insisted Hastings. "Let him go." Walsh casually picked up his tray and utensils and got back on the food line, treating Hastings as a threat too small to be concerned with. He did manage to catch Matthew Pates out of the corner of his eye beckoning for Hastings and the other ARCS men to come to him. Jacobson was still with the group of women, only now they were all standing, stretching their necks trying to peek over the crowd.

Sitting alone in a corner was Michael Dirks. He smiled at Walsh and nodded. Walsh returned the nod. *I'm gonna keep a careful eye on you, friend,* he thought. *A very careful eye.*

Walsh picked up a jumbo pancake, grabbed a cup of black coffee, and joined Michael Dirks.

"Good morning, Michael."

*   *   *

Avi was troubled by Edward Hess. Perhaps more than any of the men in this insane compound, Hess worried him the most. It wasn't that he was any more racist than the rest of these fools. He wasn't the most physically intimidating, although Avi would never want to have to take him on hand-to-hand. He feared Hess because there was something about him he liked. Papa had warned him about that. He used to say

218

that even Hitler was probably loved by his dog. "Do not let yourself fall into the trap of thinking the enemy is any less than just that, Avi—the enemy," he had said. "If you find yourself thinking anyone of them are different—you're wrong."

Avi nodded. "Nice move, Mr. Hess."

"Thanks. Call me Ed. We're not in karate class."

Rolf joined them at the table. "Hey, Mike." Rolf wore two huge swastika armbands. Avi found himself eyeing them, and Rolf ripped one from his sleeve and held it out.

"It's yours, brother. Go on. Take it."

Avi took a deep breath and conjured up his best phony smile. "Thanks, brother." He wrapped the offensive symbol around his arm and promised himself if he made it out alive he'd take great pleasure in burning the putrid rag. After he wiped his ass with it. Rolf extended his hand across the table. "Ed," he said, gripping the martial arts instructor's hand. "I look forward to seeing your demonstration today."

"I didn't realize I was such a celebrity."

Rolf tipped his head toward where Hastings and Pates were speaking. "Brian Hastings is my uncle Jeff's brother-in-law. Mr. Hastings said ..." Rolf tapped his finger to his lips and looked up, thinking "... oh, yeah. He said, 'Someone's gonna rearrange that wiseass karate instructor's clock.'"

Avi looked at Hess for a reaction, for some look of fear in the eyes. A man's body and his words might not betray him but the eyes can't lie. Avi could always read fear in a man's eyes. Hess revealed none. He was a man either very capable, very confident, or very crazy.

*   *   *

A loud crack from the giant overhead speakers caught everyone's attention. "Three minutes." The warbling voice of Matthew Pates filled the room. "Three minutes," he repeated.

Walsh stood up.

"Gentlemen. Seeing how I only have a little over three minutes to live I think I'll kiss my wife goodbye. See you in the next life."

Walsh left the two punks and made his way over to his partner.

"Good morning, dear." He kissed her on her cheek. Some of the other women smiled their approval.

Jacobson stood up and put her arms around Walsh's neck. He kissed her hard on the lips.

"I think we should leave these two alone," said one of the women, edging away.

The agents stood there in each other's arms for a moment. Walsh smiled at her lovingly. "Whatever happens this morning, you stay in character," he whispered in her ear.

Jacobson stroked Walsh's hair. Smiling herself, she said, "What's going to happen? Why?"

"I think our buddy Hastings might have some surprises in store for me. You stay in character and proceed on your own if I get hurt."

Jacobson hugged him close, kissed him on the cheek, and whispered sharply in his ear, "What the hell are you talking about. I can't ..."

Walsh gently pushed her away and placed his finger on her lips. "You can and you will. Don't worry. It's just in case I stub a toe or something. That's all."

Jacobson turned and walked away, joining the women's group as they exited the mess hall.

*   *   *

The contingent marched through the woods for almost two miles before coming to a two-acre clearing that was as green as a professional golf course. There were three off-road vehicles parked on the opposite side to where everyone had emerged from the woods. Apparently Pates and a small com-

220

pany of ARCS men found it more beneficial to arrive here by car while everyone else trudged through the forest.

Everyone was placed in a huge circle, creating a center about eighty feet in diameter. Matthew Pates entered the grassy circle.

"Thank the Lord for a beautiful morning in which to begin our training."

"Amen," shouted Pastor Hampton.

Pates wore a black jump suit, similar to those worn by S.W.A.T., a silver-handled .45 protruding from a low-hanging holster. A black cap covered his white hair. The images of the eager crowd reflected in his mirrored sunglasses as he surveyed all the trainees.

"When the race war comes, you'll notch up your kills on your favorite rifle. Your weapon is your best friend in war. Your weapon can also, like some friends, fail you. It might be as simple as running out of ammunition. Maybe your friend will just wear out one day and break down. Maybe you didn't take the care you should have, and carbon built up on the mechanisms and it jammed. We all must be prepared to take the fight hand-to-hand."

Pates looked at Hastings. "*Mano-a-mano,* as the spics say." Pates received some generous laughs.

"Since our brother Ray Hill has been in ZOG custody, we have a void in our training staff. Ray was one of the most skilled soldiers I'd ever met. He could handle any weapon like he was born with it. Ray's mother calls me everyday to ask about him." Pates looked down at the ground. "He's still unable to walk." Pates stood silently for a moment. "We will dedicate this weekend's training to Ray Hill, a fallen brother."

A circle of armed soldiers had formed around the seated group. Pates ordered one of the men to join him inside the circle. The ARCS man stood about ten feet from Pates. Pates turned his back on him and addressed the crowd. "This is Ray's brother, Paul. He's going to help me this morning with ..."

Hill roared suddenly and lunged at Pates with a seven-inch combat-knife in a downward arc toward the back of Pates' neck. A woman screamed. A couple of the men sprang to their feet.

Pates turned his head sharply and stepped to the side, expertly blocking Hill's arm with the side of his hand and immediately grabbing onto his attacker's wrist. He twisted Hill's arm, and in an instant Hill was flipped over and on his back. In a flash Pates had the weapon to Hill's throat and, in an exaggerated gesture, showed that he could have severed Hill's carotid artery.

Realizing it was part of the training, the men who had stood sat down again. Several people applauded. Pates helped Hill to his feet and the slightly bruised soldier brushed the dirt from his fatigues.

Walsh was unimpressed. He'd seen it a thousand times at the FBI academy and in martial arts demonstrations. A standard shift, knife hand block and throw—all done with the total cooperation of the attacker. The problem in real life is that the attacker isn't going to scream out his warning like in the movies. There was also a good chance of getting cut in a real situation. Walsh instinctively touched the spot on his forearm where a similar knife was plunged deep into his flesh during a fight with the biker on his first deep-cover assignment. He thought he was in a den of psychos then, but at least the bikers looked the part—strange, dirty. These freaks looked like ordinary citizens and considered themselves the most dedicated Americans since George Washington.

Walsh was sure that Pates knew the difference between real combat and this demonstration stuff. He was probably just warming up the uninitiated.

Pates handed the weapon back to Hill.

"In a couple of minutes we'll pair off and practice that and many other unarmed defense moves. Your instructors this morning will be myself, Paul Hill, Jimmy Price ..." the powerful-looking soldier raised his hand, "... and Edward Hess. We are fortunate to have a new member of our community with exceptional," he hung on that word for a second, "martial arts skills."

Pates looked at Walsh. "You don't mind giving us a quick demonstration of *your* skills, do you, Ed?"

Walsh looked around for Hastings and found him glaring at him from the back of the seated crowd. *This is your big moment, fool,* thought Walsh. *Pay attention. You might learn something.*

Walsh stood up and brushed some dirt from his pants. Pates placed his arm around him and spoke softly. "I think it's no secret that Brian doesn't like you, Ed. Me? I got a hunch that you're the real thing, and I see you heading up our hand-to-hand training. Here's your chance to show us your stuff." Pates slapped Walsh hard on the back and stepped away from him. He had the crowd spread out into a semi-circle and introduced Jimmy Price again. The tall ARCS soldier walked up to Pates and saluted. He then handed Pates his weapon, an M16 rifle, and saluted again.

Walsh sized up his opponent. He was bigger, younger, and probably a lot stronger. Brunch time.

The FBI man stood confidently with his hands behind his back. Pates handed Price the knife which he had earlier taken from Paul Hill and whispered something in the tall man's ear.

Pates stepped away and Price took a couple of steps toward Walsh. This wasn't going to be any planned self-defense situation. Price was going to try to stab him. It actually made sense when he thought about it. Hastings thought he was a phony, and if the phony got sliced up in the next two minutes then Pates gives his lawyer a nice pat on the back for being perceptive. If he gets through it, Pates scores a qualified hand-to-hand instructor.

Walsh took a deep breath and shook out his hands to relax his muscles.

Price circled Walsh like a stalking boxer. He held the knife in his right fist, the tip of the blade pointing down, the sharp edge toward Walsh. Anyone with a little experience in the martial arts had little to fear from the slashing or poking of a knife wielder. Only serious knife fighters held it the way Price did. Which meant Price didn't fear getting in close.

Walsh turned in time with Price, matching him step for step. Price flicked a jab toward Walsh's face but kept the knife-hand steady. Walsh stepped in and parried the blow, immediately whipping a short roundhouse kick to the side of Price's knee. Price shot out his right fist, aiming the blade toward Walsh's neck. A few gasps were heard as the FBI man stepped into the blow, blocking the inside of Price's elbow and punishing the tall man with a head butt to his nose.

Walsh jumped back to assess the damage. He hoped he hadn't made a deadly mistake by not killing Price at that moment when the chance to crush his windpipe was golden.

Price was cool under pressure. Blood streamed down his nose but he ignored it and rushed Walsh, this time driving the knife in an overhead arc toward Walsh's chest. Skillfully, Price changed the direction of the strike by spinning around and targeting Walsh's neck with a sideways strike. Walsh dove to the ground, hooking his leg behind Price's, causing his attacker to fall on his back.

Walsh grabbed Price's foot and jammed his own foot under Price's right armpit. Price stabbed Walsh in the side of his calf. Murderous pain shot through Walsh's leg as he twisted Price's left ankle hard. It sounded like the branch of a tree cracking under stress. Price groaned and tried to slash Walsh's leg again, the blow weak and without focus. Walsh twisted the injured ankle again. Price tried to lift his torso and swing the blade toward Walsh's face. Walsh yelled and twisted his body sharply, sending a powerful side kick to Price's jaw. *Lights out,* thought Walsh.

224

Several people applauded. Hastings and another ARCS man rushed to help their fallen comrade.

Most everyone was on their feet now. Jacobson pushed through to get to Walsh, who lay on his back, breathing heavily.

"You okay? Dear God, he was really trying to kill you."

Walsh pulled up the trouser leg to his uniform. The blade had dug into his calf but it wasn't bleeding too badly. A few stitches and a bandage and he'd be fine.

Pates stood over Walsh and offered a hand up. Walsh gripped it and was surprised by the ease with which Pates lifted him to his feet.

"Congratulations, Ed. I think you're up for training the troops."

Walsh looked at Pates. This was one of the most important moments in a deep-cover operative's career. He was in. The target had accepted him. Most agents would embrace the target and consider themselves joined at the hip. Not Walsh.

Walsh shoved Pates hard in his chest, knocking him away. Pates drew his pistol in an instant and two more ARCS men trained their guns on Walsh.

Walsh pointed a finger in Pates' face. "Screw you!" he shouted. "What the hell was that? You try to kill me and I'm supposed to kiss and make up. Bull!" Walsh turned and took Jacobson by the arm. "Come on, Kimberly. Let's leave these toy soldiers to their war games."

Jacobson looked stunned, almost numb with surprise as Walsh practically dragged her away. People stepped away to make a clearing for the couple. Walsh stared unblinkingly ahead, fighting to ignore the pain in his leg, as he walked down the path toward the dirt road to the barracks with Jacobson in tow.

"Are you nuts?" Jacobson whispered furiously.

Walsh stopped when they reached the road. There was

lots of activity where they left the group in the clearing but nobody followed them. "Sorry, darling," Walsh said as he hugged his partner tightly. "Think, Jacobson," he whispered in her ear. He took her hand and again started to walk down the road, this time slow and relaxed. Nothing was said for a minute or two, then it was Jacobson who stopped short. Walsh took a look around to make sure they were alone.

"You look like you've just been enlightened," said Walsh.

Jacobson tugged at her hair with both fists. "Stupid. I can't believe I didn't get it."

"It could happen to anyone. You always have to re-member how the person you're playing would react in any given situation. Ed Hess was told his martial arts skills were going to be tested. He'd be ticked off after a guy tried to cut his head off. I'm actually willing to overlook it because my performance made the bad guys like me. Not to mention the fact I know my life is in danger at all times so no big surprise, right?"

"Right. What now?"

Walsh gestured for his partner to continue to walk. "Now, we go back to the barracks to get changed and then go home."

Jacobson shrugged and started walking. "You're the boss."

The distant sound of a rumbling motor broke through the calm of the forest road. Walsh grinned confidently as the rumbling became louder and Pates' jeep came up behind them.

Jacobson elbowed her partner in the ribs. "Cocky bastard."

23

Walsh and Jacobson turned around to confront Pates as he stepped down from his Jeep.

"Ed, before you leave, hear me out." Pates extended his hand, and Walsh shook it unenthusiastically.

"I'm listening," said Walsh, feigning irritation.

"You need to understand that our race is more important than any single one of us. Think about it. What if you had lied to us about your qualifications, and I had entrusted you with the training of these men and women?"

Walsh looked down at the ground and stomped down hard with his good leg. "I didn't come here expecting one of my own to try and kill me." Walsh looked over at Jacobson. "What do you think, honey?"

"Honestly? I think you would have done the same thing if you had been in Matthew's position."

Excellent, thought Walsh. *First-class work.*

"She's right, Ed. Think about it. What wouldn't you risk if the fate of the white race rested on *your* shoulders?" Pates said.

Walsh paused for a minute, then placed his hand on Pates' shoulder.

"Let's go prepare to take this country back," said Walsh.

The two agents climbed into the jeep for the ride back to the training area.

After a quick trip to the medical jeep for a bandage for his injured leg, Walsh instructed a group on disarming techniques against knife' and bat-wielding assailants, as well as several defense drills involving guns and assault rifles. Pates instructed a group, and the now-recovered Price had a group of his own. Walsh split up his group into pairs of two and ran them hard in repetitious exercises until their uniforms were drenched with sweat. Walsh glanced over to where Dirks was training with Price's group. Dirks stood with his arms behind his back, looking more toward Matthew Pates' group rather than his own instructor.

It was obvious to Walsh that this kid was honed in on Pates. Walsh thought back to the afternoon that he had discovered the Jewish prayer articles in Dirks' room. It seemed silly now to think that he was just a punk who kept a souvenir from a synagogue he had defaced. This kid was on a mission. Whether a self-motivated zealot, or an agent of the JDL or SE, Dirks was here to get Pates.

Walsh walked over to a husband-and-wife team. The man had the unloaded pistol trained on his wife's head, and she was blocking his arm incorrectly.

"Never block the arm or wrist," Walsh instructed. "Always palm the gun with a soft block, then go for the barrel like this." Walsh quickly pushed the gun away and was clear of the line of fire before the hammer clicked. In an instant he had the man's wrist bent back and now held the gun himself. "Nothing to it."

The sound of Matthew Pates' voice through a bullhorn froze all training activity. "Great work!" he said. "Our training is off to a glorious beginning. All personnel report to the food barracks immediately. We'll take 30 thirty minutes for lunch, and then all companies report to the firing range. Fall out!"

Walsh caught up with Dirks on the road to the barracks section. Dirks was nervous, almost jumping out of his uniform when Walsh tapped him on the back.

"How's it going, Michael?"

Dirks stared straight ahead. "Great."

"Quite a man, Matthew Pates. Isn't he?"

Dirks said nothing.

"Do you realize," Walsh continued, "that he could be the President of a new America in less than five years?" Dirks' eyes betrayed some surprise. "Are you looking forward to that day, Michael?"

Dirks stopped and looked at Walsh. "Aren't we all?" he said coldly.

"I would think so. I'll see you." Walsh tapped him on his shoulder and dropped back until Jacobson caught up with him.

"What's with Dirks?" Jacobson asked.

"Trouble," Walsh whispered. "Keep an eye on him."

Jacobson nodded as a group of people came within earshot of the couple. They trudged the rest of the way in silence.

*   *   *

Lunch felt even more rushed and hectic than the morning's breakfast. Pates sat in the front of the building at a table with Brian Hastings, Jimmy Price and Pastor Hampton. Jacobson sat with the same women she had breakfasted with, and Dirks sat alone on the floor next to a trash bin by the side door.

Pates motioned for Walsh to join him and his top crew.

"Gentlemen," Walsh said as he placed his tray on the table.

229

"Nice work today," said Pates.

"First-class," said Price, rubbing his jaw where Walsh had dealt the punishing blow.

"No hard feelings?" Walsh extended his hand, and Price shook it vigorously.

"None. I'm just glad you're on our side."

"Amen to that!" said Hampton.

Pates looked at Hastings. "Brian? I appreciate your skepticism about Ed, but don't you think it's time to let it go?"

Hastings sat with his arms folded tight, refusing to look at Walsh. He looked like a spoiled kid on the verge of holding his breath. Walsh found it amusing. If Pates was irritated by his attorney's behavior, he hid it well.

Pates stood up. "I'll meet up with you at the firing range at ..." he glanced quickly at his watch, "... oh thirteen ten. Jimmy, I'll leave it up to you to run the troops to the range."

Price saluted. "Yes, Sir."

The four men watched Pates walk away and out the barracks side door.

"There goes a great American," said Hampton.

A regular George Lincoln Rockwell, thought Walsh.

Hastings stood up and walked over to the coffee urn. Walsh caught Dirks out of the corner of his eye following Pates out the door. Nobody else seemed to pay any mind.

"See you at the range, gentlemen," said Walsh, quickly excusing himself.

Dirks was about six yards behind Pates and closing. Two ARCS men drove past in a camouflage jeep and waved to Pates before turning up the road toward the firing range.

"Mr. Pates!" Dirks yelled, waving.

Pates turned toward the young skinhead, his hand on the butt of his holstered weapon. Dirks had pulled a small handgun from his pocket and held it at his side, out of Pates' sight. Walsh sprinted with all the strength he could muster and quickly closed the gap.

230

As Walsh was about to disarm Dirks from behind, the young man turned and kicked Walsh in the ribs, stopping him in his tracks and forcing him to bend on one knee. Pates yanked his own pistol from its holster, but Dirks was too quick, turning and kicking the gun from Pates' hand. Dirks backed away, the gun trained on Pates, but watching Walsh out of the corner of his eye.

Walsh slowly rose to his feet.

Dirks held out his free hand. "That's far enough."

Pates had his hands behind his head. "What are you trying to prove, son? That you could get the drop on Matthew Pates?"

Dirks raised the pistol to Pates' head, still keeping a safe distance from the highly trained soldier. Walsh inched his way closer. Pates looked angry now. Walsh figured he was angry with himself for getting too comfortable with his surroundings. With all those security measures on the way into the compound, Pates probably never guessed that someone who cleared the checkpoint could actually be a threat to him.

"You are an enemy of the human race," Dirks said, his voice suddenly different—more articulate and audible—an educated adult, unlike the wild young man Walsh was used to.

"Michael. In two minutes, the rest of the compound is going to turn up that road and what the hell are you going to do with that pea-shooter?" Pates growled.

Walsh inched closer.

Dirks swung his arm around, pointing the gun at Walsh to stop his advance, then back to Pates before the ARCS leader could advance.

Walsh moved a few inches closer.

"Michael!" Walsh shouted. "Have you lost your mind?"

Dirks swung the weapon toward Walsh again. Only this time, Walsh stepped in lightning-quick and pawed Dirks' weapon hand, bending back his wrist so the gun discharged into the air before falling to the ground. Walsh fired a knee kick into Dirks' gut, doubling him over. Pates hit Dirks on the back of the neck with a thunderous karate chop, sending him hard to the dirt.

Dirks rolled out and sprang to his feet, running, Pates and Walsh right on his tail.

Then came the explosion.

Walsh felt like a horse had just kicked him in the back. The force was so great it catapulted him into Dirks. Walsh felt a sharp pain in the back of his arm and fingered his blood-soaked sleeve as he lay on the ground, dazed and staring up at the sky. He could hear the sound of people shouting and running. He slowly turned his head to see Pates on one knee, pinching the bridge of his bloodied nose. Dirks was lying, barely conscious, about three feet away from Walsh.

Pates helped Walsh to his feet and, within a few seconds, several jeeps had arrived on the scene. Two ARCS men dragged Dirks to the back of one of the jeeps and sped up the road and out of sight.

Jacobson ran up to Walsh. "What happened?"

"Dirks happened."

Pates pushed a couple of his men out of the way, assuring them he was fine and needed no assistance. He walked over to Walsh and embraced him. "Thank you," he said.

"Forget it."

"Forget it I won't." Pates motioned for Hastings. "Brian, find out who the hell this kid is and who sponsored him to come here this weekend."

"Right away, Matthew." Hastings turned to walk away, and Pates grabbed him by the arm.

"Also double-check everyone who is here, who sponsored *them,* and I want extra security at the firing range. Bring the prisoner to C building."

Hastings stood waiting, as if there might be more instructions coming.

"GO!" Pates ordered.

*   *   *

Security was tight during the firing-range exercises. Only six people were allowed to use a weapon at one time, and each of those had an armed ARCS man standing behind them during the target practice. Pates supervised from a distance, guards on either side of him watching carefully, looking for the slightest irregularity of movement or attitude. It was a tense and long afternoon.

Walsh stood with his arms folded, taking it all in and wondering what was going to become of Dirks. Jacobson was shooting an M16 at the metal silhouettes and doing a great job of demonstrating near-incompetence. Walsh almost chuckled to himself remembering how well she was classified as marksman in her profile.

A few hundred yards in the distance, Walsh spied a low, white-brick building with a heavily camouflaged roof. He'd bet dollars to donuts that that was the artillery bunker.

"I practically built that with my own two hands."

Walsh turned to see Fred Mills, the biker-type whom Jacobson had brought down that first day at the karate school.

"Fred Mills," he said. "We were never formally introduced."

"Ed Hess. Thanks for helping us out at the school. I'm sorry we got off to a bad start before that."

"My friends and me used to give each other beatings worse than that at parties," he said over the rat-a-tat-tat of gunfire.

Note to self, thought Walsh. *Do not become Fred Mills' friend.*

"You say you built that?"

"We got more fire power in there than some countries," Mills boasted. "I'm hoping after tomorrow we may get a chance to use some of it." Mills snorted and cleared his throat as if he were about to spit, but just swallowed hard instead. "When the niggers start rioting, the LA riots are gonna look like hippie love-ins. Imagine ... niggers and Jews killing each other off."

"Can't wait," Walsh said. "Why tomorrow?"

Mills looked around. "Only a few ARCS members know about this, brother." He looked around again, making sure no one was within earshot. "Tomorrow morning at eight o'clock, we flatten a Jew hospital in New York and blame it on the niggers." Mills snorted a laugh, sending a load of snot shooting to the ground. "Nobody's gonna give a rat's turd what Moore has to say tomorrow night. He'd be lucky if it was covered on TV at all."

Walsh felt as though he had just taken a bungee jump off Hoover Dam. He had to take a deep breath to keep from visibly trembling. *These crazy bastards,* he thought. He screwed up his best phony smile for Mills. Using a bullhorn, Pates called Mills over to the viewing area. Walsh looked around and found Jacobson sitting with a group of people, dismantling their weapons under the tutelage of Jimmy Price. Jacobson finished third in her group and handed the rebuilt rifle to Hastings.

Pates seemed to be arguing with Mills, frequently looking over at Walsh. Jacobson was on her feet, brushing bits of grass and dirt from her fatigues. Walsh approached her and tugged her arm, gently leading her away.

"We've got a problem," Walsh said, his lips barely moving.

Pates, Mills and two other ARCS men were rapidly walking toward them.

"It just got worse." Walsh turned to face the approaching group. Pates was shaking his head incredulously. Mills walked behind him like a dog with his tail between his legs. The two other ARCS men stood silently by, obviously positioned to prevent Walsh or Jacobson from leaving.

"We have a little situation here, Ed," Pates said. "I'm sorry Fred has such a big mouth." He turned to glare at Mills, who looked down at the dirt. "I trust you," he said to Walsh. "I think you know that."

"What do you want me to do to set your mind at ease, Matthew?" Walsh demanded. "We didn't flip a coin to decide whether to come here or to go to Club Med for the weekend. We're in it for the duration."

"What the hell are you talking about?" Jacobson demanded.

"I think we're talking about our immediate induction as lifetime members of ARCS," Walsh answered. "Fred let me in on something he wasn't supposed to." Walsh turned to Pates. "She doesn't know anything, Matthew. Whatever will set your mind at ease can be done with me alone."

"Bull!" Jacobson shouted. "I want to know what's going on."

Walsh grabbed her roughly by the shoulders. "No!" he shouted in her face.

Jacobson knocked Walsh's arms away.

"Wait a second," Pates said, stepping between Walsh and Jacobson. "We'll figure a way out of this."

Pates ordered Mills to wrap up the firing-range training and have the entire camp assembled in K building in 45 minutes. He then instructed one of the guards to bring his jeep around. He unclipped his radio from his belt and pulled out the antenna. "Brian!"

"Yes, Matthew," the static-filled voice returned.

"Have the prisoner taken over to K building. Stay put, and I'll be up right away."

Pates pushed in the antenna and returned the radio to its belt clip. The Jeep pulled up, and he gestured for Walsh and Jacobson to get inside. Walsh hesitated a moment, quickly determining that a run for it was impossible at this moment. Pates slapped Walsh on the back. "Don't worry, Ed. We're just going to sit down in private and work this whole thing out."

Walsh let Jacobson enter first and then climbed in behind her. Pates sat in the front seat next to the driver. As far as Walsh was concerned, the mission was over.

Escape was now priority one.

24

So this is how it ends, thought Avi. *Tomorrow the sun will rise on that pig Matthew Pates and I will be dead and probably buried so far and deep in the woods that the Ark of the Covenant would be found before anyone ever found me.*

The room was small, about twelve feet square. The white brick walls and concrete floor still held in the morning coolness. Avi was standing handcuffed to a single support pole bolted to the floor and ceiling. He could have maneuvered himself into a sitting position, stretching his confined arms behind him, but he refused to sit.

If these were going to be his last few hours of life, he was going to live them standing up. He was afraid. Deep inside he was afraid, yet at the same time was proud to near tears. He was going to die in service to Sons Elohim and though he may have failed in his mission to execute Matthew Pates, perhaps others would be inspired by his memory and eventually succeed.

He thought about his mother Tsila. "What a world this could be," the ever-optimistic woman used to say. She just couldn't understand that with space enough and resources enough on this planet for everyone to live their lives in peace, men like Pates were intent on spreading misery.

Avi wished he could see his beloved mother again.

Shining through the solitary window, the sun began to warm the room. Avi thought about how he used to go up to the roof of his father's building on winter evenings and watch the sunset behind the New York City skyline. That suddenly seemed like one of life's most wonderful pleasures.

The bolt on the door snapped him out of his deep thoughts. Two ARCS men entered and took positions on either side of the doorway, their Uzis strapped over their shoulders. Avi wondered if these schmucks even knew that an Israeli had invented that weapon.

Brian Hastings walked through the doorway and right up to Avi, slapping him hard across the face. Avi never flinched. He consumed the startling pain as if it were an exquisite delicacy and let it become part of his soul's fire.

"I wanted to make sure I had your attention."

Avi stared at Hastings and Hastings blinked first. *You lose.*

"You're probably wondering just as much about who I am as we are about you," said Hastings. "Let me introduce myself ..."

"You're Brian Hastings," Avi interrupted. "You're forty-one years old, married and have two children. Jonathan is nine and your daughter, Alice, is five. You graduated the University of Pennsylvania and have been Matthew Pates' personal lawyer for six years. Your past clients include the National ..."

Hastings slammed his knee into Avi's stomach. This time he did flinch but not enough to satisfy Hastings because a second later he took a punch square in the face. Avi licked the blood from his lips and swallowed hard, refusing to remove his eyes from Hastings.

"Shut your mouth! From now on you shut your mouth unless I ask you a specific question."

Avi had it in his mind to kick out this bastard's kneecaps. What the hell? They could only kill him once. Hastings must have sensed Avi's intentions because he suddenly stepped back and out of kicking range.

"You are going to stand trial for the attempted murder of American patriot Matthew Pates. *When* found guilty, you will be executed." Hastings held his hand out behind him and one of the guards dutifully placed a police baton in it. As soon as Hastings had a handle on the weapon, he took a quick step forward and swung the baton hard against Avi's leg.

Avi shut his eyes tightly. The pain was almost unbearable. He couldn't put any pressure on his left leg but he refused to fall.

"Who sent you to murder Matthew Pates?" Hastings was standing closer now, but as badly as Avi wanted to ram his knee into the Nazi bastard's groin he no longer had the strength. His femur bone must have been bruised by the blow.

Avi glared at his captor. He would never betray his family and his people, no matter how much pain he had to endure.

"Nobody sent me. I acted alone."

Hastings laughed. "I guess designing sophisticated weapons that evade metal detectors is a little something you do in your spare time."

"That's right."

Hastings lifted the baton to strike the other leg.

"No! Wait!" Avi pleaded. "No more."

"I'm listening." Hastings lowered the baton.

"Robert Hansen thinks Pates is making some serious mistakes. Too many of the smaller groups he's affiliating with are not true Aryans." Avi gambled that Hastings would immediately recognize the name of the leader of Canada's premier white-power group—The Canadian People's Militia. Sons Elohim had learned that Hansen had turned down several invitations from Matthew Pates to discuss affiliating the two groups.

Hastings looked pensive.

"What's your real name?"

Avi searched hard and remembered the name of one of the CPM members who had disappeared several months earlier. Hanson's goons had killed two Jewish activists in a street brawl and literally got away with murder, thanks to expensive lawyers who created reasonable doubt in the jurors' minds. Avi's uncle would never tell him all the details but did say that Joseph Brooks was killed as an act of revenge for the Hanson murders.

"I'm Joe Brooks," said Avi, looking down at the floor. Avi knew he had done it. He didn't have to look at that idiot's face to know he had him. They could kill him today, but he had planted a seed of discord that would have them looking under their beds every day of their worthless lives. His father would be proud of him if he only knew the blow he was able to strike for the Sons Elohim. His mission would not be a complete failure.

Hastings' phone beeped.

"Yes," Hastings answered quickly. After a couple of moments of silence he folded the small telephone and returned it to his breast pocket. He then turned to the two guards. "Take him over to the assembly barracks," he ordered. "Matthew wants the trial to begin within the hour."

One of the guards stood with his rifle trained on Avi's head while the other freed one of his wrists. Avi was ordered to step away from the pole and to leave his arms behind his back while they attached the handcuffs again. He was told that he would be shot the instant he failed to follow instructions. Avi believed it.

*   *   *

240

Walsh and Jacobson were escorted into what Pates referred to as "the bunker." It was a simple room with white brick walls and a solitary window. Brian Hastings was seated at a green metal table. Walsh sat opposite Hastings with Jacobson to his left. Pates sat to Walsh's right and ordered the two guards to wait outside.

"This is the most secure room on the entire compound," said Pates. "Simplicity. I am told that Hitler used *his* bunker when he wanted to confer with his inner circle. This ..." Pates looked around, "... this is my bunker. It was the first building constructed on the compound, even before my house. There are no hollow walls and it's completely soundproof."

"Great!" said Jacobson. "Now maybe somebody can tell me what the hell is going on."

"May I?" Walsh asked Pates. Pates gestured affirmatively with a nod of his head.

"You remember on the news the other day—the press conference with Edwin Moore? I don't think too many people are going to care about Moore's call for calm and racial peace after eight o'clock tomorrow morning."

"What happens at eight o'clock?"

"At eight o'clock ..." said Hastings. "Nobody is gonna give a hoot what that nigger has to say."

"Jerusalem Hospital is going to be bombed in retaliation for the attempts to kill Edwin Moore. NAAC extremists are going to be blamed."

Jacobson smiled. "And we all live happily ever after. Sounds like a plan. Where do Ed and I fit in?" Jacobson tapped herself on the head. "I get it. You're worried that we could screw things up."

"It's too important to take any chances," said Pates.

"What do you suggest?" asked Walsh. "That we spend the rest of our natural lives living on the compound?"

"We could be in charge of mowing the lawn," Jacobson added.

Pates smiled at Jacobson's comment. "No. I have something in mind that will commit you totally to ARCS and give me the level of confidence in my people that I must have as leader of the free America." He turned to Hastings. "Brian, you have all the information on the Korean?"

Hastings nodded. "He's living in Manhattan. We're fairly certain Danny Park will be back on the job guarding Edwin Moore Sunday morning."

"Who's Danny Park?" asked Jacobson.

Pates slapped the top of the table. "He's the slant eye who shot Raymond Hill. Ray's mom can't even visit him because she understands that he is in the enemy's custody and would never do anything to betray ARCS. But she's hurting because she may never see her son again."

"I know what's coming," said Walsh. "You want a revenge hit on Park."

"A gift to dear old mom," said Jacobson.

"We'll do it," said Walsh.

Pates nodded his head approvingly. Hastings sat with that smug look on his face that Walsh was dying to knock off.

"I appreciate your patriotism but I have a modified plan in mind," said Pates. "You'll do it, Ed. Kimberly will stay here with us and she will execute the prisoner, Michael Dirks. After he is found guilty of course."

"Of course," said Walsh. He looked at Jacobson. She was nervous. But only he could tell.

"Matthew," said Hastings. "The kid claims to be with The Canadian People's Militia."

Pates' eyes widened. "He said that?"

"I could have it checked out," Hastings offered.

"Why bother? If Roberts sent him to kill me he'd deny it to the grave."

"It makes sense," offered Walsh, suspecting that Dirks might have given Hastings disinformation. "I met one of Robert's people a year ago. Robert's vision is a united North

242

America—a merger of White Canada and America. You might just pose a threat to his vision, Matthew."

"You could send us to hit Roberts," said Jacobson. "We've been meaning to visit Canada again."

"You'll stay with us," said Pates seriously. "I don't expect this hearing to take more than a few minutes. Ed, Brian will drive you to New York." He looked at Hastings.

"That's fine with me, Matthew. I look forward to seeing if Mr. Hess has more up his sleeve than a couple of karate tricks."

"I promise you that you won't be disappointed," snapped Walsh. "But I don't like the idea of Kimberly killing Dirks. Why can't you just hold him until we get back and I'll shoot *him* too?"

"I can do it," insisted Jacobson. "What do you think, that men are the only ones who can kill in the war?"

Pates looked at Walsh with a raised eyebrow. "You have quite a woman there, Ed. She has a point. When the race war comes we are going to have to depend on our wives ..." Pates hesitated a moment, "... and even our children."

"Then it's settled," said Hastings. "Let's move out."

"I'd like to take a moment to say good-bye to Kimberly," Walsh said to Pates.

"I don't see why not," Pates turned to Hastings. "Let's give them a minute alone." The two men then walked about thirty yards ahead of the couple. Walsh hugged his partner tightly.

"I'll get back on time," Walsh promised. "I know it's hard to believe but I've been in tighter spots before." Walsh released her and looked around at the huge compound of army barracks and stone bunkers. "Well, almost as tight."

Through gritted teeth and a tight smile Jacobson said, "What am I supposed to do, shoot the kid?"

"You make the decision if the time comes." Walsh glanced over toward Pates and Hastings, who didn't seem to be paying them much attention. "Shoot the two or three ARCS men who are in the most strategic positions to do you harm. Then take Pates hostage. A gun to his head could be your ticket out."

"Sounds like a Mexican standoff in the making to me."

"Or shoot Dirks." Walsh hugged her again. "The choice is yours. I'll be back, whatever move you make."

"What if he is Sons Elohim, or a Mossad operative?"

"What if he is just another punk from a rival Nazi gang? Do you want to give up your life for his?"

"Damn, this *is* a tough spot."

"Sometimes it's not making the right decision, partner. It's making *a* decision, then making *it* the right decision."

A few minutes later they went their separate ways—Walsh with Hastings to change into street clothes and Jacobson with Pates to the kangaroo court in the assembly barracks.

About fifteen minutes later, Walsh and Hastings reached the parking lot. A solitary guard, who was patrolling the lot, saluted Hastings. Hastings didn't bother to return the salute.

"You drive." Hastings tossed the keys to Walsh and entered the passenger side of the black Chevy Blazer. Walsh got behind the wheel and secured his seat belt.

"I'm not driving this car anywhere," Walsh stated.

"What?" Hastings barked.

"You don't have your seat belt on."

The ARCS lawyer shook his head and sighed disgustedly, securing his belt with a deliberate click. "I might have been wrong about you, Hess. I thought you were just a wise ass. After you kill Danny Park I'll know that you are a patriot *and* a wise ass."

Walsh started the car and nosed the vehicle out of the parking lot.

Another ARCS guard cleared them to leave the compound and called up to the tower for the gate to be opened.

Walsh noticed that the tower and gate guard were the only two men visible. He remembered from surveillance photos that at least two vehicles, with two men in each, were constantly circling the inside perimeter.

The FBI man watched in the rearview mirror as the gate slowly closed behind him. Once they turned the corner and were out of sight of the guard tower, with a thicket of trees now between them and the gate, Walsh stopped the car.

"What the hell are you doing?"

Walsh threw the gearshift into park and surreptitiously unhitched the latch of his restraint. "I have a question. What if we drive all the way to New York City and our target isn't home?"

"He'll be there," snapped Hastings. "He's going to be guarding Moore at the press conference tomorrow. He'll be home."

Walsh clenched the steering wheel with an iron grip. *It's now or never.* He thought about Jacobson and how any minute she could find herself in the most dangerous situation she'd ever been in. She was like a soldier dropped behind enemy lines with no means of escape or communication.

He hesitated to move on Hastings because his life wasn't in imminent danger and he'd be killing more out of convenience than self-defense. The thing that disturbed Walsh the most was that the thought of it didn't really bother him at all.

Walsh felt the cold metal of the gun barrel pressed against his temple. "Stop screwing around and get going," Hastings hissed.

Walsh remained still—perfectly so. "Is this any way to treat a patriot?" Walsh said sarcastically.

"Just drive! You're not good with me yet."

"Would you really blow my brains out if I refused to drive?"

"I sure as hell would."

"Thank you," said Walsh.

"What the hell are you thanking me for?"

"For making it easy."

"For making what easy?"

Hastings never had so much as a split second to pull the trigger. Walsh flicked the barrel away from his head with the back of his right hand, simultaneously striking Hastings in the throat with a two-knuckle blow. The ARCS lawyer clutched his damaged windpipe with both hands, the gun falling harmlessly into the back seat. Walsh grabbed Hastings in a chokehold and squeezed his neck until the man collapsed dead in his arms.

Walsh opened the passenger door and was about to push Hastings' body out when he suddenly froze. The sound of a rumbling engine meant that a vehicle was on its way into the compound. He certainly couldn't turn around and head back to the gate. Without seeing who was in the approaching vehicle, there was no way to know what he'd be up against.

He quickly surveyed his options and started the car, turning off the road into the descending brush. The jeep bounced furiously down the incline before colliding with a tree. The airbag hit Walsh hard in the chest. *Damn*, he thought. *I think the tree would have hurt less.* Walsh managed to free himself and slip out of the car just as the truck rumbled by. The FBI man hit the dirt. It was Fred Mills, driving a tractor-trailer toward the compound. Walsh would lay odds that inside that rig was the ambulance which was set to go boom tomorrow morning.

When the truck was out of sight, Walsh opened the hatchback of the wrecked Blazer and rummaged through the toolbox, pocketing pliers, cat's paw and some electrical tape. He retrieved Hastings' gun from the floor of the car and tucked it into his belt. He quickly broke off several leafy branches from some of the small trees and did his best to camouflage the car.

"Your mission," he said to himself, "should you decide

246

to accept it ... is to break into the compound undetected, rescue your partner, and prevent that trailer from leaving. If you are caught or killed ..."

25

Jacobson was doing her best to look serious and dignified, pretending to be honored by the position she was given as jury foreman and chief executioner. Six chairs, set up on the left side of the stage, made the makeshift jury box—three in front, three in back. Pates sat at a desk in the middle of the stage and his son, again wearing his little SS uniform, was seated beside him. To Pates' right, Dirks stood with his hands cuffed behind his back. Two ARCS men stood on either side of the stage.

The room appeared to be even more crowded than when Pates had held the general assembly the day before. Jacobson figured that many of the guards and other ARCS men, used to patrol and organize yesterday, were now here to see the mock trial.

Pates banged the gavel on the desk.

"All rise and salute," ordered Pastor Hampton.

Everyone stood up and held out their right arms in a Nazi salute. Elizabeth Pates, standing as jury member number four, smiled when her eyes met Jacobson's. Jacobson returned the smile as well as she could fake it and saluted with the rest.

"The trial before God and the Aryan Resistance Christian Soldiers of Michael Dirks." Hampton looked over at the accused. "Or whoever."

There were a few chuckles, as well as some light applause.

"Pastor Hampton," said Pates. "Are you ready to present your case against the accused?"

"I am, your honor."

"Has the accused been assigned representation?"

Someone chuckled quietly. Jacobson wanted to laugh out loud. *What a sham,* she thought.

"The accused will represent himself, your honor."

"Very well," said Pates. "Call your first witness."

"I call you, your honor."

It was painfully obvious that this was going to make a 13th century inquisition look like a fair trial.

*   *   *

Walsh crawled the last fifty feet or so to the fence, ever watchful for the regular patrols along the inside perimeter. There were no cameras as far as he could tell but it was better to be on the right side of caution and slither the rest of the way.

"Don't you ever get tired of being right?" Walsh joked with himself as he discovered the wiring to the security alarm on the fence was laid out exactly as he had anticipated. Crude but effective: strips of wiring, the same kind used with sound system speakers, ran through the fence in fourteen-inch intervals. Each section of fence was probably zoned so a break would trigger the alarm in the guard tower and pinpoint the place of intrusion.

Walsh opened the pocketknife that he had taken from Hastings, and very carefully, stripped the plastic covering away from a section of wire near the bottom of the fence. He did the same to the next row above and then again about two feet to the left. He took from his pocket the wires that he had ripped out from under the jeep's dashboard, and created a loop connection between both pairs of exposed wire. He secured the connections with some electrical tape and took a second to wipe the sweat from his brow and take a deep breath.

"Halfway there, old boy."

*   *   *

"Please describe the events of this morning that led to the apprehension of the accused."

Pates told how he had left the food barracks early in order to inspect the firing range. He described how Dirks had tried to assassinate him and how the intervention of patriot Edward Hess probably saved his life.

Jacobson put on her best "I'm-just-beaming-with-pride look" when Pates looked her way.

"Can you point to the man who tried to kill you this morning, your honor?"

Dirks looked very calm and confident for a man who very shortly would be sentenced to death. Hampton turned toward the jury after Pates pointed his accusing finger at Dirks. "Let the record state that Matthew Pates has identified the man who we know as Michael Dirks."

"Traitor!" one of the skinheads shouted from among the rows of spectators.

"Shoot him now," a large kid with a spider web tattoo on his neck stood up.

"Sit down, Rolf," Hampton ordered. "All in due time."

"It won't be soon enough," Rolf grumbled as he plopped back down in his chair.

Hampton walked closer to the accused. "Your witness," he said.

*   *   *

Walsh methodically clipped the fence links. The fencing was thick and the pliers small, so every cut took an enormous amount of effort. By the fifth cut his hands were raw and throbbing with jolts of pain in his joints.

He cut around the electric wires, severing the links to a height of about two feet.

"Here goes nothing," he said as he cut the first wire, careful to avoid the dangling jumper connections. There was no way to be certain that the jumpers worked. If they didn't, he'd know soon enough.

On his back, Walsh pulled himself under the opening an inch at a time. When he was through, he bent the fencing back into position and wrapped some wire through the links. A casual inspection of the fence would reveal nothing out of the ordinary. Walsh dashed across the road to the wooded area and crouched behind some brush. He figured the patrol jeep would cruise by in a few minutes and that vehicle was going to be his and Jacobson's ticket out. If ever the element of surprise was a person's only hope for survival, it was now. He checked Hastings' weapon. The 10mm. pistol had a full clip—ten in the cartridge and one in the chamber. More than enough to get him to the next step of the rescue attempt. He was going to have to shoot his way out of here and there were going to be a lot of dead ARCS men in the process.

Walsh heard the low rumble of the patrol jeep in the distance. He stood up and positioned himself behind a wide elm tree. The jeep was now in sight, about sixty yards down the road. He estimated they were moving about fifteen miles an hour, probably more slowly and diligently now because of the attempt on Pates' life this morning. That was good news for Walsh because his safest approach was to run up behind them once they had passed.

Walsh readied his weapon, holding it up, elbows bent, supporting the gun arm with a tight hold around his wrist. He could see the man on the passenger side holding an assault rifle in ready position. The driver had his rifle strapped over his shoulder. It would take him a second to get to it. That's all Walsh would need.

As soon as the jeep's position was even with the tree behind which Walsh was hiding, he bolted from his cover. The man in the passenger seat turned to fire but Walsh fired first, two shots into the man's chest. Walsh jumped into the back of the jeep. The driver hit the brakes, throwing Walsh hard against the windshield. The ARCS man grabbed Walsh around the throat and pinned his gun hand against the dashboard. Walsh pried away one finger from his throat and snapped it back violently. The ARCS man howled and released Walsh's gun arm. Walsh hit him across the bridge of his nose with the gun butt and shifted his body so his back was against the side of the passenger seat. Using the seat as leverage, Walsh kicked the man out of the jeep. The ARCS man was strong and agile, and despite his injuries he was on his feet in a flash and had his weapon pointed toward Walsh. The FBI man was never more grateful for all those hours of practice at the firing range than at that moment when he neatly placed a bullet between his opponent's eyes.

Walsh threw the jeep in gear, fighting to bury the feelings and thoughts that would soon begin to erupt through the fear and excitement of mortal combat. He had to remain focused. There would be plenty of time later to deal with the fact that these young men were someone's fathers, sons, and husbands.

He swung the jeep around. The guards at the gate and tower were next.

*   *   *

Avi glared at Hampton. "I have no questions," he said firmly. "Just a statement. If I may?"

253

Hampton looked at Pates, who nodded approvingly.

"All right," said Hampton. "The court will hear your statement."

Avi wasn't sure exactly what it was going to buy him to continue this charade, but as long as he could keep them from killing him there was a chance that something extraordinary could happen. When he was a child his father would read the Passover story, and then would comment that God's deliverance never comes without some effort on the part of the delivered. Before God's power parted the Red Sea, the Israelites were in water up to their noses. "We must first do everything humanly possible and then, only then, will God intervene for us," his father would say. Avi was just about up to his chin.

"I admit that I was sent here to kill Matthew Pates."

"That's it," someone shouted. "Let's shoot him and go home."

"Order!" shouted Pates.

"Matthew Pates' mission to unite America's patriots is ill conceived and poorly executed. Robert Hanson conceived of this more than five years ago and is doing it now in Canada. Slowly. With the proper screening and organization ..."

"... Enough!" shouted Pates. "This trial is over. The jury will now render its verdict."

I got you, thought Avi, noticing for the first time a lack of confidence in Pates' voice.

*   *   *

One by one the members of the six-person jury stood up and spoke their verdict. Jacobson felt cemented to her chair, petrified that she would command her body to stand and would be unable to move—unable to stay in character any longer. Unable to play the role that would, in a short time, demand that she shoot this young man who calls himself

254

Michael Dirks. Jacobson doubted his story about The Canadians People's Militia. She suspected that it was to distract from who he really was. A standard practice in deep-cover. If your cover is blown—invent a new one. At least go down swinging.

"Guilty," said Elizabeth Pates, shooting up like she had just sat on a tack. Pates gave her an approving nod before she sat back down.

"Guilty," said juror number two.

Behind Jacobson was the third juror, Lynne Hastings. She pointed at Dirks when she stood. "Guilty."

"Absolutely guilty," said an old man who looked about eighty. People cheered, to the old man's obvious delight.

"Guilty," said the man to Jacobson's immediate right.

The second or so she delayed seemed to her like an eternity. Jacobson took a deep breath and pushed herself out of the chair. "Guilty," she said weakly. Pates called for order and pronounced sentence.

"You have been found guilty by the Aryan Resistance Christian Soldiers. You are hereby sentenced to be executed. Sentence to be carried out immediately."

Hampton walked up to the podium microphone. "Everyone proceed in an orderly manner to the firing range."

Like obedient soldiers, they left the building and headed to witness the execution.

Jacobson jumped as a heavy hand pressed on her shoulder. It was Pates. "You ride with me," he said firmly. Jacobson said nothing and waited while the rest of the people filtered out of the room. A few moments later only Pates; Pates' son; Michael Dirks; Pastor Hampton; and two other ARCS men remained in the room.

Pates instructed one of the guards to bring the jeep around while the other stood a few steps in front of Dirks, assault rifle at the ready.

"I guess your husband is well on his way by now," said Pates.

"I sure hope so," said Jacobson.

Fred Mills entered the building and walked up to Pates and Jacobson.

"We're ready to pull out. You want to talk to me and Jimmy before we go?"

The other guard returned and informed Pates that his Jeep was ready to take the prisoner to the firing range. Pates ordered him to stay inside and join the other man guarding Dirks.

"This won't take but a few minutes, Kim. Please sit here." He gestured toward a chair by the wall—about 20 feet from Dirks and the guards.

Jacobson sat. Matthew Pates and Fred Mills left the building. Hampton was speaking with Kevin Pates. Dirks stood silently, looking at the floor while the two soldiers guarded him.

Jacobson wondered if the only chance she was ever going to get was right now.

*   *   *

Walsh stopped the jeep about two hundred yards before the main gate. Using a pair of binoculars, he spied the surveillance tower and saw only one guard inside. He figured the other guard must have accompanied the truck through the parking lot and up to the center of the compound. He stopped the jeep and jumped out.

It wouldn't take long for the tower guard to spot the idle jeep. That's just the way Walsh wanted it, but he had to move fast through the wooded area and surprise the guard just as his curiosity was aroused.

Walsh approached the clearing as the tower guard was peering through his binoculars at the jeep. The FBI man darted unnoticed to the tower's staircase and scaled the steps with a speed that surprised him as well as the guard. Before the ARCS man could get hold of his rifle, he met the butt of Walsh's AK47 with his face. Although obviously dazed, his face a bloodied mess, the ARCS man still managed to grab Walsh's weapon and push him back, almost over the edge of the tower. He was a big one, and tough, too. Walsh drove his knee up into the man's groin, the momentum causing both men to flip over the railing. Walsh hooked his arm over the wooden beam. The ARCS man fell the thirty feet alone.

Walsh hauled himself up to safety and flipped the switch to open the gate. He looked down at the crumpled form of the ARCS guard who, surprisingly, was still breathing.

Walsh slid down the ladder and dragged the barely conscious guard into the wooded area. He ran to the jeep and, before turning the key, took a deep breath, and took stock of the task before him. The plan was simple—get his partner and leave right through that front gate. How to get it done without getting killed—that was going to be the tricky part.

Walsh probably hadn't prayed since he was ten years old in Sunday school but he found himself asking for God's help now because this was going to be tough going alone.

26

Jacobson made her move. No fancy diversions. Just plain, simple and vicious.

She strolled over to the guards, smiling wide as one of them turned. The fact that the thousands of times she had practiced disarming techniques in training had added up to zero in a real combat situation never entered her mind. The element of surprise was on her side. She parried the barrel of the weapon with her left hand and reached through the guard's arms with her right and ripped the rifle away from him. At the same time she fired a punishing back kick to the knee of the second guard. His rifle fell as he reached for his crushed knee. Dirks kicked the fallen man in his side, probably breaking a rib or two.

Jacobson kicked the first guard in the gut for good measure, and then jumped clear of both men so she could get a handle on Hampton's position.

He was running out the door. Kevin Pates sat wide-eyed, his lower lip quivering.

Jacobson caught Dirks, out of the corner of her eye, reaching for the fallen weapon.

"Oh no. Step back!" she ordered. Dirks jumped back. "I'm not sure I want you armed." Jacobson picked up the rifle and put it over her shoulder. She then ordered the two ARCS men to sit on the floor back to back.

Dirks held up his hands. "Could you at least take these off?"

"Maybe." Jacobson looked down at the ARCS men. "You have the key to those cuffs?"

"Screw you," answered the guard who still had both his knees in working order. The other one just sat rubbing his knee, quietly moaning.

Jacobson pressed the barrel of the rifle to the belligerent man's temple. "No, screw *you,*" she said.

Jacobson turned sharply as the small figure of Kevin Pates approached her, holding the key high in the air. "My dad gave it to me."

For an instant Jacobson thought about taking the boy with them. The idea of leaving him to Pates and this insane group grieved her heart, but logic dictated that it would be far too dangerous.

Jacobson put the key in her pocket.

"Let's go, Michael."

"What about these?" Again he held out his cuffed wrists.

"Maybe later. Let's go." She ordered the guards to lie on their stomachs.

Jacobson tilted her head toward the side door of the barracks and then took off, the handcuffed Dirks behind her. When they burst through the side door, Jacobson became convinced that there must be a God because rolling up the road in an ARCS jeep was none other than Martin Walsh.

"Get down!" Walsh shouted as he laid gunfire over their heads toward the side of the barracks, steering the jeep with one hand toward his partner. Dirks and Jacobson ducked.

Walsh skidded to a stop and Dirks and Jacobson jumped into the back of the open jeep. Jacobson fired several bursts to one side of the barracks, then the other, as she saw Pates and two other men appear.

The tractor-trailer roared past them, almost clipping the front of the jeep, as Walsh steered toward the road. More ARCS men were taking positions behind trees and on the side of the buildings.

"We have to go after that trailer," Walsh yelled. "Hold on!"

Walsh floored it. In the side view mirror he could see that Pates and several other ARCS men had hopped into another jeep and were now in pursuit. The truck was about one hundred feet ahead and nearing the open gate. The only hope was to get a shot at the back tires, but the vehicle was shaking too furiously for him to take aim.

The trailer cruised through the open gate and a black Land Rover with darkened windows suddenly appeared in front of them. Walsh swerved onto the perimeter road to avoid collision. Jacobson kept up short bursts of gunfire, then tossed the empty rifle to the floor of the jeep when it ran dry of bullets.

"They're not following us." Jacobson tapped Walsh on his back. Walsh glanced at the side view mirror and sure enough, the vehicle was still sitting by the gate where it had nearly collided with them. Walsh drove a little further until the road started to curve and the main gate was out of sight.

"Are you crazy!" Dirks protested. "At least give me a weapon if we're going to be sitting ducks." Dirks shook his head. "Who the hell are you two?"

"That's the same thing we're wondering about you," said Jacobson.

"They're going to flank us," said Walsh. He pointed toward the wooded area. "This road goes around the compound with who knows how many connecting roads through the woods. My guess is they plan to sandwich us."

"What now?"

"Hang on!" Walsh shifted into gear, and took off down the road again. Without warning he skidded to a halt and ordered everyone out of the vehicle. Walsh led them to the fence and bent open the piece that he had cut. Jacobson slid through first, followed by Dirks. When Walsh was on the other side he bent the fence back into position. Not that the ARCS men wouldn't figure it out quickly, but every minute that they could be delayed counted.

"Now what, boss?" asked Jacobson.

"Follow me." Walsh set a good pace through the woods, Dirks and Jacobson close behind him.

"We're going *toward* the mountain?" Jacobson pulled next to Walsh.

Dirks stopped. "Wait ... wait ... wait."

The two agents stopped and turned to Dirks.

"Who are you?" Dirks held up his arms. "At least take these off."

Walsh and Jacobson looked at each other, then back at Dirks. "Not yet," they said in unison. Walsh grabbed Dirks by the shoulder and pushed him forward. "Get moving."

After about forty minutes of running, the terrain became rougher and the woods more dense.

"I've got to rest," pleaded Dirks.

Walsh stopped, actually grateful for the break. Jacobson also looked fatigued.

Dirks sat on the ground, his back against a tree. Jacobson reclined on a huge rock, her hands cradling her neck as she breathed deeply. Walsh stood.

The FBI man looked up and through the dense foliage, shielding the sun from his eyes as he surveyed their upcoming climb. "Doesn't look too severe. Before we reach the summit we'll be climbing hand to foot, though."

"Can't wait," said Jacobson.

"Now all that running during basic starts to make sense, doesn't it?"

Dirks looked up at Walsh. "You're law enforcement."

"Martin Walsh, Federal Bureau of Investigation." He tilted his head toward his partner. "That's special agent Katherine Jacobson." Jacobson raised her arm and wiggled her fingers.

Walsh picked up a fat tree branch and plopped it on the ground in front of Dirks. He grunted as he eased his sore body down. "Now it's your turn."

Dirks looked down at the ground. "I cannot."

Walsh picked up a small rock. He grabbed Dirks behind his neck and pulled him forward. He rubbed the tattoo on his arm until the skin was raw, then pushed Dirks back into the tree.

"What the hell's wrong with you?" Dirks protested.

Walsh held up the rock. "Real tattoos don't rub off."

Jacobson sat next to her partner and joined the interrogation. "You had me going for a second with the Canadian Militia story, I must admit." She pulled the handcuff key from her pocket and held it in front of Dirks. "We're going to have to work together if we're going to survive."

"I saw the prayer book, Michael," said Walsh. "I wasn't sure if it was a souvenir from some synagogue you robbed or if it belonged to you. Who sent you to kill Matthew Pates?"

Dirks rested his head in his hands. "My name is Avi Pearlman."

"Are you Massod?" asked Jacobson.

Avi shook his head.

"Sons Elohim," said Walsh.

Avi said nothing. Walsh took the key from Jacobson and unlocked the cuffs. Avi massaged his wrists. "Thank you," he said.

"You could go to jail for a long time, Avi." Walsh shook his finger at the young man.

"Sons Elohim did not sanction this," said Avi. "I have acted alone."

"You'd die with that story, wouldn't you?" asked Jacobson.

Avi looked up. "I *will* die with that story."

Walsh checked the magazine of his rifle. "About 20 shots left," he said to Jacobson.

"This one is empty," she said, handing a 9mm auto-carbine to Dirks. "The Dissipator ..." she pointed to the rifle strapped over her shoulder, "... has about twenty rounds."

"What am I supposed to do with this? Throw it at them?"

"If we get pinned down, we'll give you a couple of rounds, Avi. We'd better get on the move again. It won't take long for Pates to figure we're not going to pop up on one of the roads down there."

"What exactly is the plan here?" asked Avi.

Walsh picked up a stick and drew a mountain in the dirt. He pointed to a spot near the bottom of the left side. "We're here. This whole side of the mountain is state land."

"Which means no homes with telephones and more than likely few roads," added Jacobson.

"However," Walsh continued, "about three miles down the other side is the border of Maynard County. There are some homes, roads and interstate 80 with a huge shopping mall at the base of the other side." Walsh stood and pointed his stick toward the mountain's summit. "The last two miles or so are going to be pretty rough. A lot of hand and foot climbing. We have to get to a phone before eight o'clock tomorrow morning."

"What happens then?" Avi stood up and strapped the unloaded rifle over his shoulder.

"You remember that truck that left the compound?"

Avi nodded.

"It's carrying an ambulance filled with explosives. ARCS plans to detonate it at Jerusalem Hospital in New York City at 8:00 a.m."

"Oh my God!" said Avi.

"Their plan is to blame it on the NAAC in retaliation for the Sons Elohim's attempt to kill Moore."

"Sons Elohim had nothing to do with shooting Edwin Moore!" snapped Avi.

Jacobson patted Avi on the back. "I think we believe you, sport."

"Let's go," said Walsh. "The hike of our lives is about to begin."

* * *

"Nothing, Sir," reported the young soldier. "We have six vehicles patrolling highway 165 for any sign of them trying for the county road."

"I want only the driver in each vehicle. Have the second man patrol the woods forty yards in from the road in a two mile arc toward the mountain. Go!"

The young ARCS man jumped back into his jeep and the vehicle roared away, leaving a huge cloud of dust. Pates waved a hand back and forth to keep dust from his face. He leaned back against his off-roader and took stock of his situation, looking up at the clearing in the mountain above the tree line. The radio occasionally crackled with static and then a short report from the patrols. Nothing yet. Pates had almost eighty people roaming the woods around the compound for the fugitives. Even his wife was in a group taking part in the manhunt. Pastor Hampton had volunteered to patrol the inside of the compound with three of the guards, in case the Hesses and Michael Dirks were foolish enough to try and hide somewhere inside.

Pates clenched his fist so tight his fingernails cut into the palm of his hand. There would be no trial this time. The exercise of the trial seemed to him like a childish game now. He knew that if it wasn't for that little indulgence of his ego, he wouldn't be desperately hunting for three people who could possibly ruin plans years in the making.

Pates wiped the trickles of blood on his pants. He looked up at the mountain and felt a nervous twitch deep in his gut. Hours of searching and no sign of the traitors. *Could they have ventured to go over?* he thought. He almost dismissed the notion because it seemed so ridiculous. It was at least a three-hour hike to the base of the mountain, and at least another four or five hours up to the end of the tree line. After that they would have to climb hand and foot for at least three more hours before reaching the summit. The other side was no picnic either for at least the first couple of hours.

Suddenly the ridiculous became the obvious. Of course they would go for it. They would know that ARCS would search the low ground and have every road patrolled. They would know that a person would have to be crazy to take on a hike like that without proper clothing and provisions. *And I'll bet that's exactly what those traitors did.*

Pates fit himself with the headset and spoke into the microphone. "Jimmy! Report!"

A few seconds later there was a burst of static and then Jimmy Price's voice. "Nothing yet, Matthew. We're tightening the circle and we got six to eight miles netted. They're not getting away."

"Take Henry, Luke and Bill Taylor and get over here now. We're going to take a different approach. Out."

Pates stared at the mountaintop. He'd hiked it dozens of times as a boy. Nervous energy bubbled through his stomach and chest. The hunt was on.

*   *   *

Jacobson almost collapsed, exhausted, when Walsh finally signaled for them to stop. It was hard to hear above his heavy breathing, but Walsh was sure he could make out the sound of running water. He walked slowly in a huge circle, trying to filter out the other sounds of birds chirping and insects whizzing and clicking. Then, as if blinders had just been removed from his eyes, he saw it. A small stream of water cascading over a boulder, its source probably hundreds of feet up the mountain.

They took turns drinking, then soaked their heads and necks. "Oh, that feels good," said Jacobson. "I could die happy now."

"That's still a distinct possibility, partner."

"You think we've lost our edge?" Jacobson returned to the rock for another drink.

"It'll take a while if we're lucky, but Pates will figure it out."

"Then let's get going," Avi insisted.

"What do you think he'll do?" asked Jacobson. "Try to come at us from the other side?"

Walsh shook his head. "Too risky. Don't forget, most of the other side is private property. That means houses with telephones, and roads, hopefully with the occasional state trooper. A Godsend to us but a hazard for him." Walsh started walking. The incline was getting steeper and the hike was going to get rougher.

Jacobson and Avi followed close behind him. "So you think he's going to follow us up?" asked Avi.

"The old fashioned way," said Walsh. "Probably match us step for step."

"And this doesn't worry you?"

"It worries me to death, Avi."

"Meshuga. Total Meshuga."

"You don't know the half of it," said Jacobson.

27

Everything costs money and every assignment has its budget. Lately, the bean counters in Washington had been acting like hospital administrators, under pressure from insurance companies to justify every X-Ray, blood test or prescription. Leverick was told that a ten billion dollar satellite, that could take a picture of the license plate while your car sits in your driveway, was too expensive to use for a surveillance shot of the ARCS compound. To calibrate the equipment for a series of photos in rural Pennsylvania, even for a brief period, was far too costly. Let alone the valuable intelligence that might be lost diverting the spy contraption from its normal targets in the Middle East.

"Some mullah takes a leak and we have to know about it," Leverick said as he tried to fit together the broken pieces of plastic from his telephone. "Screw it!" He dumped the thing in the trashcan and flipped open his cellular. While waiting for the series of transfers and password verifications to go through, so he could be connected to the strike force commander through a top-security phone line, he logged on to his computer in the hope that Walsh might have sent him an electronic communication.

The gruff voice of the squad leader came on the line. "C-12!"

"It's Leverick. No word from my man yet. We might be a go."

"Sorry, Sir. We've been ordered to pull back. Half my squad has already been redeployed."

"Damn it. Said who?"

"Sorry, Sir. New priorities. Order came in yesterday from D.C. It's confirmed."

Leverick calmly closed the phone and stuck it in his jacket pocket. *What the hell happened to the top priority mission,* he thought. When he had last spoken to the Director, he had been promised the full resources of the FBI, DEA and ATF if his deep-cover operators were in any danger. Well, the hell with the Director! Leverick had enough seniority that he could organize a few dozen heavily armed SWATs and take that compound before the suits even knew what hit them. Of course, win or lose, he'd be fired on the spot when it was over. No pension. No gold watch.

Screw the gold watch.

He made up his mind and set a deadline for noon to-morrow. He programmed the secured site on the Web to send him electronic mail the moment any communication came through. If Walsh failed to contact him, Dalton Leverick was going to kiss his thirty-year career with the FBI goodbye. He'd go in that compound with guns blazing if he had to lead the charge himself.

"I won't let you down," he said to mental images of Walsh and Jacobson. He set the program on his computer to beep him *and* dial his cell phone if any electronic mail was received. He checked his beeper and clipped it on his belt.

Dalton left his FBI office for the last time.

*   *   *

270

Walsh's bones cried out for relief as he boosted Jacobson over the ledge and into a clearing of mostly flat limestone. Walsh struggled over the ledge himself and was grateful for the push he received from the younger Avi. He also took some delight in the fact that Avi needed a hand over the ledge himself.

The three unwitting hikers sat with their backs against a natural stone wall. The sun was almost down, and treetops in the distance began to fade and blend with the background of the graying sky. Pates would have to stay there until first light. There was no doubt in Walsh's mind that they had an excellent start on Pates and whatever number of men who would join the chase. They would have the same problems traveling at night and would have to make camp as well. No sooner had that thought entered Walsh's mind than the tiny spark of a fire flicked down in the thicket of trees.

"There they are." Walsh pointed to the distant twinkle of light.

"About two hours behind us," Avi said.

"Seems about right," Jacobson agreed.

Walsh looked up and behind him. The remaining climb to the summit was barely visible but Walsh estimated about another hour would do it. He shifted over until he was pressing against his partner. "We're going to have to huddle close to keep warm." Avi moved over from the other side until Jacobson was sandwiched in the middle.

"Three hours sleep, Katherine. Then me."

"What about me?" asked Avi.

"You can sleep as much as you want. Agent Jacobson and I will share the watch."

"Fine with me. A lot of good this empty weapon would do me anyway."

"You could always throw it at them," said Jacobson.

Avi looked pensively at the weapon. "Incredible how we keep making better tools for killing. My mother used to say we should melt down all the guns and make farm tools."

271

"We'd still find a way to kill each other," said Walsh. He picked up a stone and held it out. "In the history of the world more people have probably been killed by rocks than guns."

"The first murder was committed with a rock," said Avi.

Jacobson laughed. "I could see the bumper stickers on the ox carts—'Rocks don't kill people, people kill people.'"

"How about 'when rocks are outlawed, only outlaws will have rocks,'" said Walsh.

"'Have rock. Will travel?'" offered Avi weakly.

"Passable," said Jacobson. Walsh nodded in agreement, and the three laughed together as the night closed in around them. Jacobson leaned her head on Walsh's shoulder as she closed her eyes for her turn at rest. Walsh took a deep breath of the cold night air to heighten his senses. He watched the twinkling fire below and thought hard about the men pursuing him. He wondered if that fire was meant to confuse the hunted. Perhaps it was part of Pates' cat-and-mouse game, designed to remind them that their pursuers were not far behind.

*   *   *

Danny Park sat in quiet meditation in his dark bedroom. He had tightly drawn the shades to prevent the light from the street lamps outside from entering. He took slow, deep breaths, letting each one out with a subtle hum that vibrated from the back of his neck to the bottom of his spine. He could hardy believe that Edwin Moore had requested that he, Lucas Green, and Max Smith be at his side at tomorrow's press conference. He had felt like a failure in protecting Moore from his enemies, but the NAAC leader apparently felt otherwise. Moore had praised the three members of his security team in spite of the disastrous behavior of Henry Perkins. Not that they were even

272

needed for tomorrow, since dozens of FBI agents and a hundred police would be all over the New York Hilton Hotel for the 11:00 am press conference.

Park journeyed deeper into relaxation and felt as if he was floating bodiless. His emotions were heightened and he felt enormously grateful to be part of such an important event. Tomorrow Edwin Moore would call for calm and introduce the NAAC's new platform of peace through mutual respect and cooperation of all peoples. Tomorrow morning Danny Park would dress in his best suit and walk out of his apartment door and head for the New York Hilton Ballroom and into a great moment in history.

Danny Park felt like a lucky man.

*   *   *

Edwin Moore looked out onto the brilliance of the cityscape at night. He had just finished a lengthy conversation, via the computer, in a virtual conference room with two prominent New York rabbis and the city's mayor. All had pledged their support and would be at his side tomorrow morning when they would assure the public that no fighting existed among the Jewish and African American groups in this country. They would stand in solidarity and call on the thousands of cultural groups in the United States to adopt one more tenet into whatever platform or political agenda was at the forefront of their mission and purpose. The tenet would read 'We recognize the right of all races and cultures to coexist on this planet in peace.' Even the controversial Reverend Shelton had agreed to call off the demonstrations if enough of a cross section of cultures was represented at the press conference. Moore feared the protests could turn into riots, so he personally telephoned Reverend Shelton and obtained his commitment to postpone any march until after the press conference.

*   *   *

Dalton Leverick hadn't spoken with his daughter in about four months. They were by no means estranged—just more and more distant since his wife divorced him ten years earlier. Jessica Leverick would be graduating this year with high honors and a degree in biochemical engineering, and the thought of traveling to California to sit next to his ex-wife during the graduation ceremony made his stomach quiver. He looked at the bedside clock—1:00 am New York time.

He called and was disappointed to get her answering machine, even though he could hardly expect a twenty-year-old woman to be home at 10:00 pm on a Saturday night.

It took a couple of seconds after the beep for him to start to speak.

"Hello, Jess. It's the old man. Just thought I'd give you a call to say hi." Leverick paused, not knowing what to say to his own daughter. "We'll ... I'll call again soon. I love you, and a man has never been more proud of a daughter than I am of you. Good-bye, Jessiecakes."

When he hung up the phone he couldn't help but feel a little foolish. He hadn't called her by that pet name since she was thirteen when, mortified in front of a couple of her girl-friends, she had demanded that her father never call her by that name again. What a wonderful young woman she turned out to be, thought Leverick. She seemed to possess all the good aspects of her parents' personalities and none of the bad. She was smart like her mother and a very persuasive orator, like Leverick fancied himself to be. She was organized just like her mom. Good thing, thought Leverick, suddenly realizing that he never so much as took the time to change his will. Ten years divorced and his will still left what meager assets he did possess to his ex-wife.

Leverick made a mental note to call his lawyer on

274

Monday. He turned out the lights and soon drifted off to sleep.

*   *   *

Jacobson was on her second watch. It was almost five am, and as soon as it was light enough to see she would wake Walsh and Avi to continue their climb. The fire below had been out for about a half hour and Jacobson figured Pates and his bunch would be on the move pretty soon. She pulled her knees into her chest and hugged them tightly, hoping to warm herself against the cold morning air.

The slightest hint of blue was starting to appear in the sky, finally separating it from the treescape. Avi sat up and stretched his arms. Walsh continued to sleep although Jacobson wondered how deeply.

Avi looked up. "Won't be long," he said.

"Twenty minutes. Half hour," said Jacobson.

"Excuse me," said Avi. "I will be right back."

"Don't go too far," Jacobson ordered.

Avi walked into the bushes and Jacobson envied the ease in which men could relieve themselves. She was dying to go too but didn't want to wake Walsh. No matter, she thought. Her bursting bladder was probably the only thing keeping her awake.

A few minutes later Avi emerged from the bushes and sat on the ground in front of Jacobson.

"You're a Jew, are you not?"

"I'm Jewish. Yes."

"Don't you think we have to strike first against men like Pates?" Avi pointed behind him, down to the assumed position of the men pursuing them.

"You think that Matthew Pates is only the enemy of the Jews?"

"He is an enemy of mankind. Like Hitler, Stalin, and Pol Pot, just to name a few. Think about how much better the

275

world would be if someone like *me* had eliminated *them* before they took power and murdered so many ..."

"Someone even worse could have taken control instead. You don't know that you could have done any good, Avi. When I was in college we used to spend hours talking about crap like 'if you could be transported back in time to kill Hitler, would you do it?' It's nonsense. Murder is murder. You work within the law and work to change the law. You don't break it."

"My grandfather obeyed the law. The Nazis killed him anyway."

"My parents lost relatives in the Holocaust too, Avi. We Jews don't hold the exclusive rights to misery, although you couldn't convince my mom of that. There is no more Nazi Germany and there will be no more Hitlers."

"Are you sure of that?" Avi asked sincerely. "Are you sure there could never be another Holocaust?"

Jacobson turned away to wake Walsh. It was time to move on.

28

It took them just under an hour to reach the mountain's summit. The view was spectacular and the morning sunshine baked away the dampness and chills from their bodies.

They didn't bask in the pleasure for long. There was a job to do and the clock was ticking. Many lives depended on their getting to a phone within the next four hours.

The terrain was rough as they began their descent, and it took a while before they were past hand and foot climbing. The going became a lot easier when they finally hit the tree line.

Walsh set a fast pace, digging his heels in the ground with every step, weaving around trees and large rocks. His clothing was drenched with sweat, and his lungs felt as if they were on fire. "Move it ... move it ... move it!" he shouted, as much for his own benefit as for Jacobson's and Avi's who trailed slightly behind.

When Walsh called for a five-minute break, Jacobson collapsed against a boulder and rested her head on it. "I'm gonna die of thirst." She patted the rock. "Where's Moses when you need him?"

Walsh held up his hand for his partner to be quiet. He studied their surroundings carefully, listening for any sounds and looking for any movement in the distance that might indicate that the enemy was near. He motioned for Jacobson to join him and whispered, "Down there. Maybe a mile or so through the trees."

Jacobson nodded. "Looks like a brick chimney."

"Let's move."

Again Walsh set a nearly impossible pace down the mountainside. Jacobson lost her footing for a second and fell face down into the dirt, scraping her forehead and nose on the sticks and small rocks strewn about. Walsh doubled back, helped her to her feet without saying a word, and continued his jaunt through the descending landscape.

"Nice partner," he heard Avi say to Jacobson. "He could have asked you if you were okay."

"I think he determined that himself," she responded. "I'm okay, Walsh. Thanks for asking!"

Walsh waved his hand in silent response.

Once the house became visible through the thicket of the trees, Walsh stopped running and ordered Jacobson and Avi to spread out and continue moving forward from tree to tree, always shielding themselves from view.

They were now about forty yards from the house. It was a simple, yet sturdy-looking structure. Cedar shingles covered the sides and the roof was made of rolled asphalt. The satellite dish on the roof next to the chimney dispelled any doubts Walsh had about the house being occupied.

Jacobson was crouched behind a tree about three feet from Walsh. "Those silver tanks are propane. My dad used to have those delivered to our country home when I was a kid."

"There's no phone or electric wires," said Walsh.

"Should we move on and try to find another house further down?"

Before Walsh could answer, a tall, wiry man with a

278

flannel shirt and a pair of blue work pants emerged from the rear door of the house brandishing a bolt-action hunting rifle.

"Who's back there spying on my house?" he yelled before firing a burst of bullets. Since he fired high up into the trees Walsh figured that he didn't really want to kill anyone. Or maybe he was just a terrible shot.

Walsh had to make a decision. A long standoff with this guy would mean a lot of dead people in a couple of hours. Walsh aimed the gun. In a second he would be an obstacle no more. His finger felt wet on the trigger.

Avi suddenly sprang into the open, waving his arms.

"Don't shoot, Mr. Hooper!"

Walsh and Jacobson looked at each other and said in incredulous unison, "Mr. Hooper?"

"It's me—Michael from Montgomery Lumber."

Hooper pointed his weapon toward the ground. "What the heck are you doing here, boy? Delivering fertilizer? Is that a gun over your shoulder?"

Avi continued to approach with his hands held high above his head. "It's not loaded, Mr. Hooper. I'm with a couple of friends and we have an emergency."

Walsh came out from behind his tree with Jacobson right after him. The FBI man also kept his hands high in the air thinking, *please, Avi, do not tell this guy that we are Federal agents. He could have 'remember Ruby Ridge' bumper stickers all over his pick-up.*

To Walsh's relief Avi introduced them as the Hesses and told Hooper that Matthew Pates was planning to bomb Jerusalem Hospital in New York City and they desperately needed to get to a phone.

"Looks like it's your lucky day," said Hooper after shaking hands with Walsh and Jacobson. "I bought one of those cellular phones two months ago."

Walsh looked at his watch and let out a sigh of relief. It was almost seven. An hour was plenty of time to mobilize a team to intercept the ambulance. He patted Hooper on the back. "You've just saved a lot of innocent people, Sir."

"I don't like to see innocent people get killed," said Hooper. "I believe whole-heartedly in segregation, mind you, Mr. Hess. We just weren't meant to live together—Black and White—Jew and Gentile. But it's a sin to murder, Sir. A sin to murder."

*   *   *

The weigh station on the Jersey Turnpike was closed just as Matthew Pates told them it would be. A few dozen trees provided them with plenty of cover from the highway to allow them to roll out the ambulance without being seen by the early morning motorists. Jimmy Price flung open the doors and pulled out the specially designed flat-rails. Fred Mills rolled out the ambulance, then helped Price retract the rails and shut the door. The entire operation took less than a minute.

Mills followed in the ambulance as Price drove the tractor-trailer into Manhattan. Both men had slept nervously in the trailer with the carefully secured ambulance. Although Mills had enormous confidence that his detonator could not go off until three minutes after he had toggled the timer, one never knew what could happen. After grabbing a couple of hours sleep they carefully applied dark brown body paint to their arms, hands, faces and necks, then concealed their hair under baseball caps. Mills wore an Emergency Service jump suit and Price a jacket with an insignia of an eagle which matched the one painted on the outside of the truck. Under the truck's insignia were the words "American Eagle Trucking—strong and swift."

Price parked the trailer on a side street near one of the City College buildings. He then walked to the end of the street and into the waiting ambulance.

"Everything is coming off without a hitch," said Price,

reaching out for a pack of cigarettes on the dashboard. They drove to the hospital and parked the ambulance near the emergency room ramp. There were two similar vehicles parked there as well, probably awaiting dispatch orders. Price flipped down the visor and studied his face. "I think my nigger color is coming off."

"Let me see," said Mills.

Price turned and pointed to a spot on his chin that he thought was fading.

"You're imagining things," said Mills. "This stuff is gonna take twenty showers with Comet to get off." Mills glanced at his watch. "T-minus sixty minutes, pal."

"It's history in the making, Fred. History in the making."

*   *   *

Walsh looked at his watch about every five seconds as he waited for Kenneth Hooper to find his cell phone.

Hooper finally emerged from the kitchen, grinning like a kid. "I forgot I stuck it in the drawer with the silverware."

Walsh snatched the phone from Hooper. He pressed the on button but got no dial tone. He shook the phone and tried again. "Mr. Hooper, when was the last time you charged the battery?"

Hooper looked embarrassed. "I never really used the phone, Mr. Hess. I only ordered the service to get cellular access for my modem."

"Modem?" Walsh bolted upright. "You have access to the Internet?"

"I sure do." Hooper walked over to a small mahogany desk and rolled up the cover, revealing an IBM laptop computer.

"Let's crank this baby up," said Jacobson.

Walsh checked his watch. Fifty minutes to go. Every second it took for the small computer to fire up seemed like an eternity. Finally the icons appeared on top of the blue skies and green field. Walsh clicked on the Internet icon and then connected to the dried beans web site. After quickly inputting the double blind passwords, he was admitted into the private conference room. He didn't expect Dalton Leverick to be there at his computer but he quickly composed a message which read: 'URGENT. Bomb in ambulance. Set to go off at 8:00 am this morning. Jerusalem Hospital. WALSH.' He fumbled for a moment with the tiny red dot in the middle of the keyboard that functioned as the mouse controller, sending the pointer up and off the screen past the send key.

Jacobson cried out, then hit the floor, as gunfire burst through the window, sending a piece of shattered glass across her cheek. Walsh tackled Hooper, bringing him down heavily to the hardwood floor. Avi managed to take cover behind a sofa as more shots burst into the tiny home.

"My house. Sweet Lord, my house!" yelled Hooper, flat on his belly with his hands over his head.

Walsh rolled out and crashed against the wall under the window. Jacobson tossed Avi half a dozen rounds of ammunition. "Now's the time, little brother." With an expertise that surprised the agents, Avi quickly loaded the weapon, rolled out to join Walsh, and both men popped up and fired through the window.

There was silence for a moment except for the sounds of heavy breathing that filled the room. Jacobson sat braced against the wall opposite her partner, ignoring the blood that poured from her face.

Walsh looked over at the computer, which was still blinking, a waiting signal for the send command to be pressed. The position of the desk placed him at risk, but it was a risk he was going to have to take. They all looked up at once.

"Someone's on the roof," Hooper said.

Then it poured out of the chimney like a choking nightmare. Smoke quickly engulfed the room, making it impossible to see or breathe.

The front door crashed open. Much of the smoke billowed out as four armed men in gas masks burst in.

It would have been suicide to even attempt to fight. A few moments later, Mr. Hooper and his three unexpected guests were kneeling in the middle of the floor with hands behind their heads.

Matthew Pates was the first to remove his gas mask.

"You lose," he said.

"Let me guess," said Walsh. "The campfire was a decoy. You came up on this side."

"Good observation. A little late but a good observation."

"Would somebody tell me what the hell is going on here?" Hooper pleaded. "I built this place because I wanted peace and quiet."

Pates helped Hooper to his feet. "Sit down over there, Ken," he said, directing him to a sofa chair in the corner. "I'm sure you meant ARCS no harm by taking them in."

"Pates! Think about what you're about to do," Walsh implored. "You don't know how many people are going to be killed by that blast. Hundreds—maybe thousands. Children, for God's sake!"

"Tell me who the hell you are!" Pates ordered. He placed the barrel of his .45 to Walsh's head.

"I'm a patriot. Just like you. Except I don't kill innocent people."

"You're an imposter." Pates clicked his fingers and one of the ARCS men came forward. "Cut the woman's throat."

The man yanked a cruel-looking hunting knife from his belt, and pulled Jacobson's hair back with his free hand.

"Wait," said Walsh. "Wait." He looked down at the floor. "I'm a Federal Agent. My name is Martin Walsh. She's my partner."

"You lying son of a dog," said Hooper. "You had no reason to lie to me."

"I'm sorry, Mr. Hooper. I couldn't take the chance. Too much was at stake."

Pates nodded his head and the ARCS man put the knife back in its sheath. "I sentence the three of you to death. Sentence to be carried out immediately."

Hooper jumped out of his seat and punched Walsh in the jaw, then grabbed him around the throat. "I'll kill you myself," he hissed.

Pates pulled Hooper off Walsh. "Easy, patriot. You'll get a piece of him." Hooper stepped back, grumbling. Pates tossed Hooper back his rifle. Walsh suddenly felt they had a fighting chance. He managed to whisper to Jacobson, "Be ready." Walsh knew by the way Hooper held his neck that he never intended to hurt him. He never so much as pressed his thumb on Walsh's throat. The whole thing was a put on.

Pates ordered the three of them to stand. "Keep your hands on your heads." The rest of the ARCS men took positions behind Pates, their weapons ready. "March outside single file. I'll shoot you in the back if you so much as flinch."

They were only outside a second when the shooting started. Three of the four ARCS men had been shot in the back by Hooper. Pates spun around and fired three rounds into Hooper's chest. As he spun around to face his prisoners again, Walsh met him with a devastating round kick to the side of his knee. The FBI man snapped Pates' wrist back, dislodging the gun from his grip. The two men rolled in the dirt, each scrambling for an advantage. Walsh heard Jacobson yell, "Don't shoot!" just as Pates managed to ram him in the side with a powerful knee kick.

Pates pressed his fingers hard into Walsh's eyes, trying to gouge them out. Walsh gripped Pates' fore and middle finger in one fist and the ring and pinky finger in the other. "Make a wish, Putz," said Walsh as he pulled Pates' hand apart. The ARCS leader jumped to his feet with a painful roar and was met with a bullet to the side of his head. Walsh rolled over to avoid Pates' falling body. As Pates hit the ground, Avi came into view, still standing with one eye looking into the rifle's sight.

"Mission accomplished," said Avi.

"Not yet," said Jacobson, leaping over two dead ARCS men and into the house, Walsh at her heels. She practically dove across the room to the computer, and sent the message.

Walsh looked at his watch, the crystal was cracked and it was frozen at 7:27. He looked up at Hooper's wall clock which read 7:33. "God help us," said Walsh.

"God help *them,*" Jacobson corrected.

*　　*　　*

Leverick was glad he didn't have a heart condition because when his beeper went off his chest almost exploded with panic.

He stopped the car in the middle of Fifth Avenue and attached the magnetized cherry light on top. He fumbled for his pocket computer and plugged it into his car's comm port.

"Martin Walsh, you magnificent bastard!" he said as he read the incoming message from his long-time friend. Then another feeling of panic, combined with dread, set in as he read the message. It was 7:45.

Leverick turned the car around and, to the outraged protest of dozens of horns, drove up Fifth Avenue against traffic until he reached Fifty-Seventh Street where he knew he would have a quick run to First Avenue. He called into Bureau headquarters and turned the whole mess over to an agent while he continued his high-speed drive through the streets of Manhattan.

*　　*　　*

"Eight more minutes," Jimmy Price commented.

"Matthew said wait until three minutes to eight before we set the timer and jet out of here." Price turned to his nervous cohort. "Don't worry, Fred. We'll be at least two blocks away before it blows."

"It's getting nerve-racking, man, that's all. My timers are the best but three minutes. Man, that's short."

They moved up a position, one of the legitimate ambulances probably responding to a radio call. They were in a very strategic spot, a wing of the hospital actually extending over the parking area outside the emergency entrance. They could almost guarantee that much of the building would collapse. An empty ambulance would be a lot more suspicious, Pates had thought, than a couple of lazy EMS workers killing time on a Sunday morning. He had been right. Nobody had so much as approached their vehicle the entire time they had been there.

Mills strummed the dashboard with his fingers.

"Seven minutes to go-time," said Price.

*   *   *

Leverick sped down Seventy-Fifth Street at almost eighty miles an hour, stopping short and turning the car sideways to prevent any traffic from passing. He ran to the edge of the hospital driveway and peeked around the building.

It wasn't hard to spot. He saw the two ARCS men getting out of the ambulance. "FBI!" he shouted, holding his credentials in one hand, his service niner in the other. They did the expected. They drew weapons. Without losing stride, Leverick dropped the tall one first with a shot to the middle of his chest. A shot to the face of the shorter man sent him crashing back to the cement.

Leverick jumped in the vehicle and started it up. It would have been all over had the idiots bothered to take the keys. He saw the timer clock on the dash—2:48—and counting down.

He sped down the street and across the avenue, throwing caution to the wind, hearing the smashing of metal behind him as cars that he forced out of his way collided. He barreled onto the FDR drive and headed North, his only hope the Third Avenue bridge and the cement factory on the other side.

The timer read 2:20.

He reached ninety-six miles an hour and almost lost control as he barreled up the ramp to the bridge.

The timer read 1:18.

He had to stop to avoid hitting a line of cars that were backed up single file because of a lane under construction. That lane was blocked by heavy equipment.

It was over. Forty seconds to go. He and every one on this bridge were going to die.

Leverick took a deep breath, cut the steering wheel sharply to the right and floored it. "Sweet Jesus," were the last words Leverick ever spoke as the ambulance roared up the curb and crashed through the guardrail, plunging one hundred sixty feet into the East River before exploding into pieces of twisted metal.

29

Martin Walsh wept unashamedly as they lowered Dalton Leverick's casket into the ground. After the full military honors, the Pastor read the usual Psalm 23 and John 14. Walsh couldn't help but wonder whether he'd ever see his friend again in another life.

He held Amy tightly in his arms and whispered, "So long, old friend," as the pastor invited friends and relatives to say their final goodbyes by tossing a red rose on top of the casket.

Walsh waited until all the people had left, including Leverick's daughter and ex-wife who needed to hurry home to receive the throngs of family and friends for coffee and sandwiches. Amy returned to their car, leaving her husband to have a last moment alone with Dalton.

A gravedigger powered up his back hoe, eager to throw dirt and get on with his day. Walsh reached up and grabbed the man's shirt. "You so much as throw a pinch of earth on that casket before I tell you to and two people will get buried here today."

"You're crazy," the man stammered, then ran off, probably to fetch some help.

Walsh sat down on the dirt, paying no mind to his best suit. "This is it, old boy." He tossed the rose on the casket. "We got 'em, Dalton. Matthew Pates is dead and ARCS is no more." Walsh snorted a laugh. "The Governor of Pennsylvania said he was going to turn the compound into a camp to help rehabilitate troubled youths. I'm thinking of getting involved as a counselor. Can you believe that?"

A cool breeze stirred up some dust and leaves. "Katherine Jacobson is very grateful for the opportunity you gave her and she couldn't have performed more courageously, Dalton. She wants to work overseas and I'm going to do everything I can to help her."

Walsh stood up and brushed some dirt from his pants. "Thanks to you, my friend, Edwin Moore made his call for unity and lots of people are excited about the idea. Who knows? Maybe our kids will inherit a better world after all."

Walsh choked back some tears, and stood at attention and saluted the friend and mentor who had meant so much to him. Walsh caught some movement out of the corner of his eye and turned, expecting to see the gravedigger and several of his buddies. It was Avi Pearlman.

"Have you been spying on this ceremony?"

"No, Mr. Walsh. I just arrived. I am very sorry about your friend."

"Thank you." Walsh pulled slightly on Avi's shirt collar. "You get all those tattoos to come off?"

"Yes. I also want to thank you. Sons Elohim appreciates your silence."

"A deal's a deal, Avi. Just remember." Walsh pointed in his face. "Any hint of anything more than intelligence gathering and I'll come after you myself."

"I didn't think guidance counselors for troubled youths could do that sort of thing," Avi replied.

"You guys are good."

"We try." Avi extended his hand and Walsh shook it. "So long, Agent Walsh. Thank you and Ms. Jacobson for saving my life."

"You're welcome, Avi."

The two men parted and Walsh walked to the road where Amy was standing in wait by their car.

"Are you okay, Martin?"

Walsh hugged her tightly. "I'm fine." He opened the passenger side door for his beloved.

"Let's go home."

291

BOOK AVAILABLE THROUGH

Milligan Books, Inc.

By Any Means Necessary $14.95

Order Form

Milligan Books, Inc.

1425 W. Manchester Ave., Suite C, Los Angeles, CA 90047

(323) 750-3592

Name_____ Date _____

Address_____

City_____ State_____ Zip Code _____

Day Telephone _____

Evening Telephone_____

Book Title_____

Number of books ordered___ Total ....$ _____

Sales Taxes (CA Add 8.25%) ....$ _____

Shipping & Handling $4.90 for one book ..$ _____

Add $1.00 for each additional book ....$ _____

Total Amount Due.....................................$ _____

☐ Check ☐ Money Order ☐ Other Cards _____

☐ Visa   ☐ MasterCard Expiration Date _____

Credit Card No. _____

Driver License No. _____

Make check payable to Milligan Books, Inc.

_____   _____

Signature   Date

www.ingramcontent.com/pod-product-compliance
Lightning Source LLC
Chambersburg PA
CBHW021507240626
47154CB00002B/538